10/09

MATTERS ARISING

MATTERS ARISING

Sarah Harrison

severn
House

This first world edition published 2009
in Great Britain and in the USA by
SEVERN HOUSE PUBLISHERS LTD of
9–15 High Street, Sutton, Surrey, England, SM1 1DF.
Trade paperback edition published
in Great Britain and the USA 2009 by
SEVERN HOUSE PUBLISHERS LTD

British Library Cataloguing in Publication Data

Harrison, Sarah, 1946–
    Matters Arising
    1. Women – Societies and clubs – Fiction
    2. Celebrities – Fiction
    I. Title
    823.9'14-dc22

ISBN-13: 978-0-7278-6737-7   (cased)
ISBN-13: 978-1-84751-147-8   (trade paper)

All Severn House titles are printed on acid-free paper.

Typeset by Palimpsest Book Production Ltd.,
Grangemouth, Stirlingshire, Scotland.
Printed and bound in Great Britain by
MPG Books Ltd., Bodmin, Cornwall.

One

Sir Anthony Chance, polymath, Tony to his many friends, held the Gentleman's Relish at eye level, the easier to scrape out the very last morsels with his knife. Unlike the Marmite jar, in whose gloomy brown depths the savoury substance seemed to lurk for ever, the Gent's Relish pot was unforgiving: small, shallow and porcelain white. You knew beyond peradventure when you had reached the end, which, even allowing for the microscopic amount needed to add flavour to toast, came, alas, always too soon.

Carefully, he applied the tiny final harvest to his wholemeal muffin, then cut the muffin in half. Before eating – Tony was a believer in deferred gratification – he laid the knife on the edge of his plate and stooped to place the empty Gent's Relish pot on the floor so that Marlon, his dog, could lick it. Marlon was a chocolate Labrador, a breed recently accorded the dubious honour, in a tabloid newspaper, of being the 'daffiest dogs in Britain'. Now Tony watched fondly as Marlon nudged the small pot frenziedly around the tiled floor with his tongue.

There was a knock and Lionel, Tony's live-in help, entered. He carried the post and two newspapers, but paused just inside the door, eyeing Marlon with disfavour.

'What on earth's he got there?'

'Just the fish paste pot. Empty, of course.'

'It'll make him terribly thirsty,' warned Lionel, putting the letters and papers down on the table.

'Then he can drink. He has water.'

'He'll drink too much and be taken short, you know what he is.'

'Don't fuss.' Tony picked up the *Daily Telegraph*. 'He's fine. Look how much he's enjoying it. How could we deny him that?'

Lionel gave the animal a look which declared unequivocally that he could very easily do so. He was fond of the dog but considered, with some justification, that he was overindulged.

Now Marlon had shunted the pot into a corner and was banging it rhythmically against the base of a kitchen unit.

'Dear oh dear,' murmured Tony from behind the newspaper. 'Sounds like people rogering in a broom cupboard.'

'I really wouldn't know,' said Lionel. 'Here – Marlon – leave! Leave it!'

Whatever his faults, Marlon was not vicious. Though he didn't actually leave the pot, he allowed it to be removed, and binned, with perfect good humour, swiping and slapping his long mauve tongue around his chops as he watched the treat disappear.

Lionel washed his hands beneath the running tap with surgical thoroughness – palms, backs, nails, thumbs, between the fingers – and then rinsed, shook, and dried them on paper kitchen towel.

Against this splashy background, Tony slowly and deliberately turned a single page, a study in calm detachment.

'I'm going to the BBC a bit later on,' he remarked, surveying a headline with raised eyebrows. 'Meeting and lunch.'

'Right you are. There's some of the tagine left if you're in this evening.'

'I can't say at the moment.'

'No worries, it won't waste.'

'There's talk of going to a show with Diana. I very well might.'

'What show would that be?' asked Lionel, a devotee of musical theatre.

'I've no idea, it's up to her. Something new and offensive, I imagine; she likes to keep up.'

'Oh well,' said Lionel, as if this couldn't be helped. 'Enjoy.' He pointed a finger at Marlon. 'I'll be back for you shortly.'

When he'd left the room, Tony put the paper down and ate the second half of his muffin. Marlon, sitting next to him, placed an imploring paw on his knee, and was ignored. When he'd finished, Marlon retreated to his bed and flopped down, on hold until the next round of excitements. Tony picked up the post. Apart from junk mail – country gentlemen's attire, Bonnings Wine and the classical music CD club – there were several bills, a clutch of begging letters of the usual kind, one invitation to dinner at the London Zoological Society and another to a private view, and a couple of speaking engagement requests. He took each one in at a glance and sorted them with practised speed

– envelopes and junk for the bin, the begging letters (no) and the invitations (yes) for his PA Clemency to deal with and the speaking requests for her assessment and advice. In principle he liked to do talks; he was a gifted speaker, he met people he might not otherwise have met, and he enjoyed the warmth of their welcome and appreciation. But Clemency's role as self-appointed curator of the Anthony Chance 'brand', as she put it, was a valuable counterbalance to his susceptibility.

Clemency Watts worked at 10 Christchurch Grove, Hampstead, three days a week. She was one of the new breed of elective middle-class single mothers; her hours were ten till three, to fit in with the school day of her six-year-old son – Tony was nothing if not a woman-friendly employer. Tradition allowed a period of fifteen minutes' settling-in time following Clemency's arrival (much of which she spent chatting in the hall to Lionel and Marlon on their way out to the Heath) before she knocked on the door of her employer's study with a cafetière of freshly ground Colombian Fair trade coffee.

This morning she was a little late. The exchange with Lionel took place hurriedly at the front door, and when she put her head into the study she was still in her rather fetching red pea jacket and black and white scarf.

'Sir Anthony – I'm so sorry!'

'No rush,' he smiled at Clemency, so pretty and flushed in her haste, and made a calming gesture with his hand. 'Catch your breath.'

She pulled off the scarf and jacket and shook her hair. 'I do hate being late!' A waft of her fresh, sweet scent reached Tony.

'You scarcely are. All well I hope?'

'Freddy's ill, nothing serious, but I had to call in the cavalry from Fulham in the shape of my mama. Anyway, she's installed now, and I'm here, so on with the comedy!' She flashed him a brilliant smile.

'I'm sorry to hear that. I do hope you were happy about leaving him.'

'Oh God, they'll be like pigs in . . . they'll be in clover. Any excuse to watch daytime TV and eat convenience food . . .' Tony smiled again. Child-free himself, these snapshots of family life were like fragments of the Dead Sea Scrolls: mysterious, foreign and freighted with strange references. Indeed he would have felt more comfortable with the Scrolls – in the case of Clemency's domestic hinterland he was both unqualified and disinclined to find out more.

Clemency shrugged off her jacket. 'I'll get the kettle on.'

'Take your time.'

She returned a few minutes later, hair sleek and glasses on, with a tray on which was his coffee, and her own mug of herbal tea.

'Sorry,' she said again. 'Right.'

Tony briefed her on the correspondence, and gave her a list of calls to make. He could have emailed the notes to her, but he liked this traditional early-morning exchange with Clemency, and felt it had a civilizing effect on the day. When he'd finished, she stared at her notebook.

'Is that all?'

'I believe so.'

'It's not much. I'll be reduced to disinfecting my keyboard or something.'

Tony spread his palms, helpless in the face of her dilemma. 'I'm going out. Do feel free to leave early and attend the sick.'

'My mother's doing that.'

'Then take advantage of her and go shopping . . . Have lunch with a friend, or something. You have my permission to play!'

'Thank you . . . I'll see.'

'Oh, I almost forgot.' Tony produced the speaking engagements. 'I'd appreciate your views on these.'

'Of course.'

'No great hurry, but the diary being what it is I suppose I'd better decide.'

'Naturally.' She glanced at the letters. 'I'll do a bit of research.'

By the time Tony left the house Clemency had dealt with the correspondence and the phone calls, and moved on to the speaking engagements. One was from the English Speaking Union to address an area meeting in Salisbury in three months' time. Clemency knew that her employer had a soft spot for the ESU, a distinguished and thoroughly worthwhile organization, but on this occasion the shortness of the notice smacked of a last-minute replacement. She pencilled 'Second choice?' at the top and set it aside for further consideration.

The other one was from something called the Marie Crompton Luncheon Club. Clemency hadn't heard of it, but she knew the genus. Unlike the ESU they were putting down a marker thirteen months in advance, for the third Friday in April next year, to be precise. It was the usual thing: the letter writer 'knew how busy' Sir Anthony must be, and also 'how many calls there must be on his time', and 'how many good causes must approach him' – but she urged Sir Anthony to treat her club as an exception. Would he, could he, consider coming down to their golden anniversary lunch next spring? It would be a guest event, so Sir Anthony would be assured of a good audience, and all proceeds were pledged to 'Bus or Bust' (Clemency had to smile), a local transport scheme for the elderly and disabled. They did so hope he would be able to say yes, and looked forward to hearing from him in due course. It was signed: 'Juanita Wade (Mrs), Speaker Finder'.

Mrs Wade was absolutely right. Sir Anthony did indeed receive a great many such requests, and weeded them out by distance and cause. Any distance that couldn't be managed comfortably there and back in a day, preferably by train, was out, as was any cause that wasn't nationally – preferably internationally – recognized. It was a question not of money, but of ergonomics. The time/effect ratio had to be worthwhile.

With these criteria in mind Clemency wrote 'Think not' on that one, and dialled her home number to check on the family.

It was absolutely seething in the Oxford Circus Topshop, and the temperature on the lower ground floor was tropical. Either that or Penny Proctor was having an early-onset senior moment. Her friend Sam, an infinitely more intrepid shopper, had disappeared in the melee, and there was a real possibility they might not find each other by lunchtime.

Penny had had enough already. She knew Topshop was all the rage, and had been prepared to go along with the idea, but now that Kate Moss was in on the act, what hope was there for a woman like her? Sam was a squeak older than Penny, but being a stone and a half lighter with an expensive haircut and a French manicure, on a good day with the light behind her she could just about fit the shop's demographic. The two of them had been at school together, and now Sam, who had divorced a year ago, lived in London and they got together a couple of times a year. Since her divorce Sam had acquired a kind of metropolitan, single-woman gloss. Penny on the other hand, a woman generally regarded as quite pretty and well-presented, in this context felt like the proverbial fat plain friend. It wasn't just that she couldn't fit into anything; she had yet to see a single item she wanted to fit into.

Just then, happily, she recalled a piece of advice recommended to mothers to pass on to their daughters: 'Never let someone else force you into doing something you're not comfortable with.' She was herself the mother of sons, but the advice struck her as eminently sensible. And though Sam hadn't exactly forced her into Topshop, she definitely wasn't comfortable. There was no law that she had to pretend to enjoy being here. She would go up and wait at the main door so she could at least breathe in the fumes of Oxford Street and do some people-watching.

Her spirits rose as she ascended on the escalator. Outside it was a fine March day and there were other retail outlets not far away that she did like and which catered for her. She didn't need Topshop's basement hell; Sam was welcome to it. She could wait.

She went past the anti-shoplifting beep-barrier and stood to one side of the doorway, leaning against the corner of the window. This was an excellent vantage point for watching the comings and goings at the entrance to Oxford Circus tube station. On the pavement at the top of the steps was a newspaper-seller; the first edition of the *Evening Standard* was on sale, its front page trumpeting the government's latest economic disaster.

A tall man stopped by the news-stand and felt in his jacket pocket for change. Amid the jeans, trainers, body warmers and leather jackets he stood out in a dove-grey three-piece tweed suit, a long navy blue scarf, loosely draped, and scuffed good quality brogues with tasselled laces. Penny noticed all these things as a matter of course. But when he turned slowly towards her, his eyes on the paper, she had to stifle a gasp. It was him – Sir Anthony Chance! The very same Sir Anthony Chance who had fluttered the hearts of the nation in the BBC's recent production of *The Winslow Boy*, who had directed the celebrated Chinese *Macbeth*, whose book *Thinking Ahead* was in the window at Waterstone's. Most importantly, the Sir Anthony Chance that the Luncheon Club had written to in the faint hope he might speak at their Golden Anniversary lunch. Penny was thrilled. It was like seeing a unicorn, or another mythical beast of whom one had only heard.

He looked up from the paper and must have caught her staring. She blushed, but of course he hadn't even noticed her. He folded the paper longitudinally and slipped it into his jacket pocket before heading off up the road in the direction of . . . the BBC, of course, that would be it. Penny had the terrible sense of an opportunity missed, but what would she have done? Gone up and introduced herself and asked if he had received their letter, and pressed him to accept? No, it was unthinkable. Rude, even, to put him on the spot when he was going about his business. Likely to do more harm than good. She peered after his retreating back, admiring the long, rangy stride, the perfect cut of the jacket, the insouciant elegance of the scarf . . .

'Hey stranger,' cried Sam. 'I was beginning to think I'd lost you!'

'I needed a breather,' said Penny. 'How've you been getting on?'

Sam raised her arms to the horizontal, with equal-sized carrier bags in either hand like Justice with her scales. 'Mission accomplished!' Getting no response, she tilted her head, and said, 'Earth to Mars. Do you copy me?'

'Sorry?' Penny focused on the bags and registered surprise and approval. 'Wow, well done.'

'I hope so – I may have got a little carried away. I shall have to apply rigorous mutton-and-lamb tests in front of the bedroom mirror . . . Penny? Are you okay?'

'You're not going to believe this, but I just saw Anthony Chance.'

'No! Him off the telly? Where?'

'There.'

Sam followed the gesture with narrowed eyes like a gunman getting a bead on target.

'Sorry – where?'

'Tall with a blue scarf . . . He's gone now.'

Sam looked teasingly suspicious. 'Are you quite sure?'

'Of course I am. He was right in front of me, buying a paper.'

'In that case, congratulations on a major sighting! Cute, or a disappointment in the flesh?'

'Certainly not a disappointment,' said Penny. 'Quite the opposite. Very distinguished looking.'

'Nice,' said Sam. 'We *like* distinguished.'

It was the following week, Thursday. The new Friday, according to some. To Murray Wade, peeling back the cardboard lid on his Moroccan chicken and piercing the polythene cover with a fork, there was still a full day's graft to go before the weekend, and it was ready-meal night.

Juanita's note lay on the kitchen table.

'At Lindy-Hop,' it said. 'Harmony at band practice. Might go for quick drink, back ten-ish xx'

He placed the container in the microwave, turned the dial to medium and pressed '2 mins'. Then he put two slices of pitta bread in the toaster, fetched a can of Brockets from the utility room, and opened it. The small pop and hiss as he tweaked the tab were music to his ears.

He didn't mind being on his own. Juanita was very involved with a lot of things in the village – in her the flame of community spirit and self-improvement burned brightly enough for two. She had many regular commitments: Tuesdays were local history, Thursday was dance night – currently Lindy-Hop but prior to that there had been jive, salsa, tango and Scottish reeling; he reckoned she must be good enough to be on the TV by now. Ever present in the background were the village hall committee (of which the internal politics made the Middle East look like a walk in the park) and the Marie Crompton Luncheon Club. The latter was centred on the local market town of Bishop's Few. Once a year there was a guest event which he always attended because the purpose of the club was to raise money for charity. Their efforts had already contributed, inter alia, towards a senior citizens' drop-in centre, a high-tech bathroom for the hospice and a well in a village in Namibia.

The toaster had popped up, and now the microwave pinged. Murray put his beer glass on the table and laid out a mat, knife, fork and napkin next to it. He went into the living room and came back with the TV supplement, which he opened to the right page and laid next to his place. Then he took out the plastic dish, peeled back the steaming hot polythene with quick, cautious movements and slid the Moroccan Chicken on to a plate with the pitta bread next to it.

Before carrying his supper to the table he turned on the radio and tuned it from Radio Four to Classic FM; something orchestral but anodyne, film music probably, filled the air. Murray sat down before his steaming plate and savoured a few well-earned sips of Brockets. In this age of designer beer a really good bitter was increasingly hard to find and though it irked him to swell the egregious Peter Brocket's already groaning coffers, he had to concede that his was a near-perfect brew.

He began to eat, nudging the food on to his fork with the toasted pitta bread. It wasn't bad, apart from that slight chemical aftertaste that was the property of all convenience food and which one ceased to notice after a couple of mouthfuls. Munching, he scanned the evening's television choices in case there was anything new on offer. His default option was to take refuge among the heritage cops, posh totty and petrol-heads of what Juanita referred to as the testosterone channel, and it looked as though that would have to be his route tonight.

Ten minutes later he'd finished – one of the down sides of eating alone was that you got through it too quickly – and stowed his plate in the dishwasher. He switched off the radio, topped up his glass, put the bottle in the appropriate bin (Juanita had finally got him trained) and went into the living room.

Surfing the channels, he came across that chap – Dance? No, that was the other one. Chance, that was it. Chance, who popped up everywhere. Juanita had written to him about being their speaker for the big do, but there had been no reply – surprise, surprise. Professor Know-All: opera, popular psychology, literature, probably dog-training and house renovation were only a power-lunch away. Murray, a keen student of other men's success, wondered what Chance got paid for pontificating on TV. He inclined towards Dire Straits' view that it was 'money for nothing'. Mind you, you'd be looking at a spring chicken a long time before you thought of Chance. Handsome fellow though. Cared about his appearance in spite of the brain-box credentials, which caused Murray to wonder if he was the marrying kind.

At the moment, Chance was talking about grants, the Arts Council, art in the market place, blah, blah . . . Murray, who couldn't have cared less either way, didn't so much listen as observe, his feelings hovering between resentment and admiration. Chance had a portfolio of elegant, airy gestures: his large hands flopped about on the end of long, bony wrists, his lanky legs were crossed and one foot wagged as if he simply couldn't sit still, as if even when he was speaking all that spare energy and brain power were being channelled into his extremities.

After a few minutes Murray switched to Planet Bloke, shaking his head as he did so; there was no way Chance would be trolling down to Bishop's Few to speak to the girls. No way.

The moment the programme ended, Gwen called Marian, the only committee member to whom she felt she could air her views.

'Did you see him?'

'Only the last couple of minutes. What did you think?'

'My opinion hasn't changed,' said Gwen, lighting a cigarette. 'But anyway we won't get him, thank God. Meretricious twat.'

'Oh, come on!' Marian laughed. 'He's lovely.'

'He certainly thinks so.'

'If I didn't know you better, Gwen, I'd suspect you of protesting too much.'

'Please! No – I really don't care either way, but it won't happen.'

'I'm not sure Juanita's prepared to countenance failure,' said Marian. 'Her heart's set on him.'

'What, no fall-back position?' Gwen tapped ash into the lid of her cigarette packet. 'That's dangerous. What about that extreme charity walker who lives in Bath?'

'We've probably left it much too late for her. No.' Marian smiled to herself. 'If it doesn't work out, *you*'ll have to step into the breach.'

'Everybody's heard me before,' huffed Gwen.

'They have, but you can't have too much of a good thing.'

'Hmm,' said Gwen, pleased as punch. 'I'm not sure everyone on the committee would agree with you.'

'Nonsense,' said Marian. 'Anyway, we're way ahead of ourselves. He might accept.'

Gwen snorted. 'Dream on.'

The village hall vibrated to the sound of Eddie Cochrane. The lindy-hoppers were hard at it. 'Summertime Blues' was guaranteed to get everyone going during those few minutes at the end of the class when they were free to put what they'd learned into practice.

Juanita and Penny were dancing up a storm. Technically they were the best couple on the floor, but technique could always be trumped by a (relatively rare) male-female combo. One such was the Figes – Della and the uxorious Brian – skipping, and twirling with isn't-this-fun faces.

'Fancy having a husband who actually likes dancing,' said Penny, eying the Figes enviously.

'Murray will dance if he has to,' said Juanita spiritedly, 'but he'd never come to a class.' She didn't need to labour the point – the implication was that there was something unmanly about Brian's attendance.

'Gosh, no,' said Penny. 'Wild horses wouldn't drag Graham on to the floor, anywhere.'

They embarked on a series of advanced manoeuvres which precluded conversation. The number ended and everyone laughed and gasped and pretended it was all too much for them. Della came over.

'Wasn't that great? And just as a bonus I reckon we're losing weight.'

Juanita smiled thinly; there was no way she was going to pick up on the cue, but Penny, predictably, obliged.

'Oh, don't say that, Della, you're so slim already! If you lose any more I shan't speak to you!'

Della laughed sportingly. 'What nonsense.' She lowered her voice. 'But it will be a jolly good thing if Brian does, so . . .' She looked at Juanita. 'You're looking super. I like the hair.'

Juanita put up her hand, flattered in spite of herself. 'Same old hair.'

'New style though.'

'I had a trim.'

'Only that, really? It looks fantastic.'

'Thank you.' Juanita found it hard to be gracious with Della, whose compliments seemed, whether intentionally or not, to be *de haut en bas*.

'Any news on Sir Anthony?'

'Not yet,' said Juanita. 'But I wouldn't have expected it for at least another couple of weeks.'

Della held out her hand to the advancing Brian. 'I suppose so, but in the meantime we're on hold. I mean how long can it take to check a diary?'

'Come on, girls,' said Brian, 'who's going to have the last dance with me? Don't all shout at once.'

'Darling, don't flatter yourself.' Della sucked her teeth and made a mock apologetic face at the others. 'You'll have to make do with me.'

'Come on then, shake a leg!'

'Bye!' Della swung away to the strains of 'In the Mood'. 'See you next week!'

Penny chuckled affectionately. 'What are they like?'

In any other company Juanita would have ventured an answer, but Penny's transparent niceness was a deterrent to bitchiness.

'How about you? Got the puff for one more?'

'Absolutely.'

'Absolutely not,' said Clemency.

Tony raised his eyebrows in a look of gentle surprise. 'You're unusually emphatic.'

'I don't mean to be unkind,' she said. 'I'm sure they're very nice women . . .'

'Oh dear.'

'No, I'm sure they are. Of *course* they are. But they're a very small outfit out in the sticks and the charity is strictly local.'

'It might make a nice day out,' mused Tony, turning the letter in his hand as if expecting to find a startling and conclusive PS on the back.

Clemency shook her head. 'The food won't be up to much, and they'll be clucking round you like mother hens. Also, your publication date's the beginning of May, there are bound to be calls on your time for that.'

'So . . .' He dropped the letter on his desk. 'It's a no.'

'That would certainly be my advice.'

'Which I did ask for,' Tony smiled indulgently, 'and which I've generally found to be sound.'

'Thank you.'

'I tell you what though; give it a couple of days.'

'As long as you like, Sir Anthony, it's entirely up to you.'

'Good heavens, I haven't the faintest,' said Lionel. 'Why ask me?'

'Call it idle curiosity.'

Lionel sighed, replaced his reading glasses and once more scanned the letter. When he looked up it was with a little frown that was both sympathetic and reproving.

'I don't think so, do you?'

'No?' asked Tony in a tone of the keenest interest. 'Why?'

'Long way, small place, obscure local cause, women only . . . Need I go on?'

'No.' Tony held out his hand and took the letter back. 'Thank you.'

'Pleasure.' Lionel replaced his glasses in their case and then in the breast pocket of his shirt. 'On we go.'

Juanita, who had been in the bathroom, rushed to pick up the telephone just as the answering machine kicked in and had to raise her voice above Murray's recorded message.

'Hello? Hello? Sorry about this – one moment – there, that's got rid of it. Hello.'

'At last,' said the voice on the other end, affably. 'May I speak to Juanita Wade?'

'Yes, speaking.' Suddenly, Juanita's heart was in her mouth. 'Who is that?'

'It's Anthony Chance here. I'm calling in response to your charming invitation.'

Two

'I confess I'm astonished,' said Gwen.

'Gobsmacked,' agreed Marian pleasantly.

Juanita bridled. 'Oh ye of little faith.'

'It all goes to show,' said Penny, 'that you never know.'

'It's a coup!' Della Figes, in whose house the meeting was taking place, pointed a chairpersonly pencil. 'I think we should minute congratulations to our clever speaker finder.'

'Definitely.' Penny scribbled assiduously. 'No sooner said than done.'

Rhada, the treasurer, cleared her throat. 'I hate to inject a note of alarm, but have we broached the question of his fee?'

'I never mentioned a fee,' said Juanita.

'But did he?'

'No . . . I did tell him we were a charity fund-raising organization.'

'Of course you did,' said Penny. 'You've done brilliantly.'

Rhada's gaze had not left Juanita. 'So the question of a fee hasn't been discussed.'

'Well . . .' Juanita looked round for support. 'No.'

'Oops,' said Gwen. 'While it is, mind if I pop out for a fag?'

'Come on, Gwennie,' Della chided pleasantly, 'we're here to talk about these things. There'll be no point in getting umpty later on if you weren't here.'

'OK, OK.' Gwen, who had already taken her cigarettes from her bag, turned the closed packet round and round, tapping it on the table. 'I knew it was too good to be true.'

'I'm sure it will be fine,' said Rhada. 'But we do at least need to ask. Or offer. There must be a clear arrangement.'

'I think that's right,' said Della. 'We'll have to write anyway to confirm what was said on the phone, and when we do we can ask what he would usually charge for a charity event.'

'Very well,' said Juanita. 'On your heads be it.'

'On our heads be what?' asked Rhada.

'Well, we could be giving him ideas.'

Gwen snorted. 'Please! No-one needs to do that. Chance didn't get where he is today without developing a sound appreciation of his own market value.'

'Don't be such a cynic!' cried Penny. 'He's a perfect gentleman, you can tell. I've actually seen him, remember?'

'Oh yes, I'd forgotten you're his new best friend.'

'I only meant that you can tell just by looking at him.'

'I must say.' Juanita shook her head as she brushed something invisible off her lap. 'I thought everyone would be pleased.'

All except Gwen chorused that they were, they were, and Della added soothingly: 'Even if he does charge us something, his pulling power will more than make up for it. Juanita – tremendous. Can we leave it with you?'

Rhada performed her bedtime beauty rituals with the sense of a job well done. This was how she liked to end each day – boxes ticked, goals attained, order maintained and skin cleansed, toned and moisturized.

Her bathroom was white, with one mirrored wall. The basin was a large glass bowl with a harebell-shaped mixer tap. All her products were kept out of sight in the cupboard beneath the washstand. In here, as in the rest of her flat, elegant minimalism was the keynote.

Wrapped, fresh and fragrant, in her spotless waffle-cotton robe, she went into the bedroom. On her bedside table lay the Orange-shortlisted novel of the moment, the silk tassel of Rhada's embroidered bookmark marking her place. She propped the pillows against the rattan headboard, tweaked back the white, self-striped duvet, sat on the ice-smooth fitted sheet and swung in her feet. The duvet settled back over her legs with a soft exhalation of goose-down.

She didn't pick up the book, but sat with her hands resting quietly in front of her, reflecting on the evening's meeting. She slightly regretted that her responsibilities as treasurer had obliged her to appear a killjoy, but one couldn't always be courting popularity, and better to have a moment's perturbation now than an unpleasant surprise later on. All that aside, Juanita had done well; Sir Anthony Chance would be a big draw. They might even have to consider a bigger venue, though of course that would incur more cost, so . . . Numbers floated gently, soothingly, around in Rhada's head like images on a screen saver. Figures were her element, where she felt most at home and in command. They were beautiful to her; she had always instinctively understood the affinity between music and mathematics – the complexity, the harmony, the layering and accretion of signs and symbols to create a perfect, truthful whole.

She picked up the book, but didn't open it. She had been truthful. Yes. Rhada liked to be truthful, but she was not always transparent. That was why she'd chosen to keep quiet rather than declare, in front of the committee, that she shared Gwen's unfavourable opinion of Anthony Chance. Perhaps not for the same reasons – she didn't, for instance, regard him as a 'tosser' – but what she had seen, she didn't care for. For all his numerous talents and enterprises, he struck her as lazy; as someone who was coasting, doing many different things in order to present a moving target. But he was clearly clever, and enormously successful, and that, for the purposes of the Luncheon Club, was more than enough.

Rhada picked up her book and removed the bookmark.

Brian handed Della a glass of Sauvignon and sat down on the opposite wing of their rectangular sofa in the den.

'So, how were the ladies?'

'All very happy. We've netted Sir Anthony Chance to speak at the golden anniversary lunch.'

'Really?' Brian was impressed. 'Well done indeed. You must be well chuffed.'

'We are.' Della sipped. 'Mostly.'

'Don't tell me, I think I can guess.'

'Gwen doesn't care for him.'

'Of course she doesn't. But then she doesn't have to. Nobody has to like him; they just have to exploit him to the full.' He lifted his whisky. 'Cheers! Many congratulations.'

'Thanks, but actually Juanita's the one who deserves those.'

'I'll tell her the next time I see her.'

Della frowned. 'What you just said – that's not quite true. The audience has to like him, too.'

'They will – he's on telly! They'll worship and adore, and want to touch the hem of his robe . . . And whatever else he may or may not be he's a seasoned performer. You can bet he's not going to come all this way and fail to impress. This is his fan base we're talking about.'

'That's true,' agreed Della.

'What's he asking? If it's not too crude a question.'

'How do you mean?'

'What's the going rate for a top speaker of Chance's calibre?'

'Oh God, don't.' Della sighed and pinched the bridge of her nose. 'We still have to sort that out.'

'You don't know?'

She sighed. 'We are hoping he'll come for expenses only.'

'And pigs might break the sound barrier.' Brian laughed jovially. 'Worth a try though.'

'Juanita's going to get back to him.'

'Is she now? Wouldn't you just love to eavesdrop on that conversation?'

'No,' said Della, 'I wouldn't.'

Clemency, eyes still on the screen and the mouse hovering in her right hand, picked up the phone.

'Four five eight?'

'Oh – hello!' The woman on the other end sounded slightly startled, as if she hadn't expected an answer. 'Is that . . .? I'm just . . . Do I have the right number for Sir Anthony Chance?'

'Yes, you do. May I help you?'

'I wondered if I could speak to Sir Anthony.'

'Who is that please?'

'I'm so sorry, this is Juanita Wade from the Marie Crompton Luncheon Club – Sir Anthony has kindly agreed to speak at our Golden Anniversary next year.'

'Mrs Wade, he's rather tied up at the moment,' said Clemency, on autopilot. 'Could I ask what it's about?'

'Well . . .' The woman laughed nervously. 'We are all absolutely thrilled that Sir Anthony's coming, but I foolishly forgot to enquire about his fee.'

'I see. Let me take your number.'

'Actually he has it, he's already—'

'Let me take it anyway,' said Clemency with a hint of steel, 'just in case. Mm. Mmm.' She took her hand off the mouse and wrote the number on a Post-it pad.

'Shall I give you my address as well?' Juanita Wade asked, adding, 'Just in case?'

Clemency wondered whether she was being mocked, and decided not. 'Please.' She took down that as well. 'I have it. I'll pass on your message and Sir Anthony will be in touch.'

'Thank you. Oh –' Juanita intuited, correctly, that Clemency was about to hang up, and intercepted her. 'I wonder, would it be possible for you to, perhaps, give me some idea – so we know what we're working towards?'

'I'm sorry,' said Clemency firmly. 'I'm afraid not.'

'I mean, is there for instance a scale of charges?'

'Not really. Sir Anthony is not a plumber.'

'No! Good lord, that's not what I meant at all.'

'He'll get back to you, Mrs Wade.'

'Thank you.'

'Goodbye.'

'Bye-bye, thank you so—'

Clemency replaced the phone. She rebuked herself, only mildly, for being sharp with the woman, but she was already annoyed with Sir Anthony for eliciting her advice and then doing the exact opposite. She had warned him before about getting mired in these unbusinesslike arrangements with provincial outfits; he had only himself to blame.

Her concentration broken, she left her desk and went through to the kitchen. Lionel was cleaning silver to the accompaniment of Woman's Hour. She glanced around as she filled the kettle.

'Where's Marlon?'

'With himself.'

'In the study?'

'Where else?' Lionel gave the base of a Georgian candlestick a quick final buff. 'I do everything for that animal but his heart is elsewhere.'

'You love him really.'

'Yes.' Lionel admired his handiwork. 'It's the dog I have problems with.'

'Funny.'

They kept a reflective silence as the kettle's crackling purr rose to a crescendo. When it boiled, Clemency asked, 'Would you like anything?'

'Some of the Arabica would be nice.'

'I'm talking instant.'

Lionel pulled a face. 'No, thank *you*.'

'You are *such* a big old coffee snob,' said Clemency, pouring.

'I have refined tastes, if that's what you mean.'

She took her cup to the table and sat down, running a finger over the gleaming curves of a claret jug. 'Doesn't he have some lovely things?'

'He does.'

'Would you mind if I smoked?'

'You know I would. And so would his nibs.'

Clemency moaned. 'It's the one time I really crave a ciggie – with a glass of wine or a coffee.'

'I can imagine.' Lionel tilted the silver polish against the cloth and began applying it, meticulously, to another candlestick while Clemency sipped. Without looking at her he said, 'I suppose you could always distract yourself with some work.'

'I was on my way to have a word with him, actually.'

'Sorry to detain you.'

'All right,' said Clemency, getting up. 'I can take a hint.'

Tony told himself he was devoted to Clemency, and she to him, but there were occasions when he suspected this mutual devotion was a mere fantasy in which the two of them colluded.

This morning he detected an air of censure the moment she entered the room, and he prepared to overwhelm it with benevolence.

'My dear!'

'I'm sorry to disturb you, Sir Anthony.'

'You're not. I was dreaming.' He indicated the chair on the other side of the desk. 'Please.'

She perched. 'I've just had a call from a Mrs Wade, from the Marie Crompton Luncheon Club.'

'Oh, yes.'

'The one you accepted – for next spring? Down in the west country?'

'Yes indeed.'

'She's extremely exercised because she forgot to ask you about your fee.'

'Poor woman, I hope you told her there was no need to worry.'

Clemency bridled. 'I told her I'd have a word and get back to her.'

'Don't worry, I will. Do we have her number?'

'I could simply email – or write?'

'No, no, that's all right, I'd like to set her mind at rest.'

'So I'll leave it with you?'

'Absolutely.'

Clemency got up. Anthony's smile was that of a man without a care in the world, and that annoyed her slightly, as he intended it should.

'Will you be charging a fee, Sir Anthony?'

'I very much doubt it, they're a charity . . .'

'As a matter of fact, they're not.'

'*De nada* – they're raising money for a good cause.'

Clemency went to the door. 'So you'll call her.'

'I think we've established that.' His eyes drifted to his computer screen.

'Right.'

'Oh – Clemency.'

'Yes, Sir Anthony?'

'Number?'

'Don't these people eat dinner?' Brian Figes' reaction was automatic rather than acrimonious as his wife got up to answer the phone.

'They do, but at a different time . . . Hello? Juanita, hi!'

Della flapped a hand and carried the handset out of the farmhouse kitchen/diner, closing the door behind her. In the drawing room her voice rose and fell as Brian replenished his Semillon and gazed patiently at their half-finished plates of Thai crab cakes.

After only a couple of minutes she came back in and sat down, looking bright and pleased.

'Sorry about that.'

'All well?'

'I'll say. Sir Anthony isn't going to charge us a thing.'

'I'm delighted to be proved wrong. But hang on . . .' Brian pointed a finger at her. 'What about expenses?'

Della shook her head. 'Not even those.'

'What on earth did Juanita do to wrest these concessions from the great man, turn up on his doorstep in a trench coat and suspenders?'

'Brian! Please!' Della chuckled and raised her glass. 'No, apparently he said he was going to look on us as a nice day out!'

Three

At the night shelter in town, Gwen was de facto troubleshooter. Not only did she walk and talk tough, but she was a woman, attractive in a rangy, raw-boned way, and so able to exercise authority with less likelihood of starting, or being the centre of a full-on ruck. Among the night shelter's clientele there lingered the residue of a curiously old-fashioned code of honour regarding the weaker sex. The fact that most of them, worn down by drink, drugs and living rough, could have been felled by a sharp slap from Gwen was beside the point.

Gwen's involvement with the shelter was chief among her credentials as the Marie Crompton's resident radical. The rest amounted to little more than an acerbic manner, a much-vaunted independence, and an address in an area of town known as The Horn. Most of the committee members lived out in the attractive satellite villages, and Rhada's apartment was in a smart new canal-side development. The Horn was something of a no-go area and Gwen's living there was regarded with a mystified respect by the others.

The shelter was in a converted Methodist chapel a quarter of a mile from her terraced house in Savernake Road. She worked there one night a week throughout the year, and more often over the Christmas period when charity chimed nicely with expediency in enabling her to avoid the tedium of the festive season with her sister's family. In the grimly titled 'run-up' to Christmas her commitment to the shelter also provided her with a wonderful excuse not to go to social events or, if she did, to go dressed down and primed for an early departure.

A case in point was the Figes' festive drinks party. Gwen was prepared to concede that it was good of its kind: the champagne (not her favourite, but still) would flow, the food (prepared by Della herself) would be delicious and abundant, the surroundings transformed into nothing short of a winter wonderland, and the company – well, that was the problem. Marie Crompton committee excepted, Gwen didn't care for her fellow guests.

Though there was a perverse pleasure in being the odd one out and feeling faintly superior, she preferred to have a reason to leave when she felt like it. And a reason with such utter, blanket credibility, too – in this area, many were called to do charity work, but few actually got their hands dirty.

This year, Della's theme was Nature. The well-proportioned rooms of Brook House were rosy with wooden apples, acorns and berries, verdant with pine, holly and ivy and fragrant with scented dried twigs. The giant tree in the hall was tastefully decked with fruits and flowers and tiny high-tech lights which gave a soft, golden glow. Logs burned in the hearth and flickering clusters of church candles and tea lights adorned polished surfaces and niches. Della herself was every inch the chatelaine and founder of the feast, in apricot velvet and pearls, and Brian (a licensed character) amusingly seasonal in orange and green tartan trews with a matching bow tie.

Having to leave early did not mean that Gwen was among the first to arrive. Far from it. The invitation had said seven-thirty and it was a little after eight when she made her entrance, her ensemble of combat trousers, Converse boots and black roll-neck proclaiming the urgency of other, weightier calls on her time.

Brian was first to greet her.

'Gwen!' he cried, taking her by the shoulders. 'God, look at you, our very own Lara Croft.'

Gwen ignored this, though she was unable to avoid her host's boisterous kiss, which had something of the *droit de seigneur* about it. 'I'm a bird of passage, I'm afraid.' she said. 'So no taffeta cock-tail frock this time.'

'Thank goodness,' chimed in Della. 'How would we have recognized you?'

Furnished with a long buck's fizz, Gwen worked the room. In spite or perhaps because of her professed disdain for parties of this kind, she had perfected the art of putting herself about. The first Marie Crompton-ite she came across was Juanita Wade, who had been there some time.

'So where is it tonight then?' she enquired gaily. 'The writers or the down-and-outs?'

'The night shelter,' replied Gwen. 'We could easily have fifty in tonight.'

'Fifty?' trilled Juanita. 'That's nothing – look around you!'

'I already have,' murmured Gwen dryly. 'Which reminds me, I mustn't be long.'

'Now tell me.' Juanita laid a hand on her shoulder. 'How are things with you and Paddy?'

This was a question no-one, least of all Juanita, would have dreamed of asking unless in their cups. Gwen's brow darkened.

'What do you mean?'

'You know . . .'

'What "things"?'

'Your relationship. We don't seem to have heard anything about Paddy for yonks.'

'That's because I don't choose to talk about it.'

At this point a sober person would have read the warning signs and stepped back from the brink. But Juanita was not sober; for someone who drank only rarely and then in moderation, the disinhibiting effects of three glasses of Moët were particularly marked.

'Time you did,' she said, wagging a finger. 'Come on, it's Christmas!'

Gwen grasped the finger and lowered it before leaning forward confidingly. 'Give it a rest, Juanita.'

'I'm sorry?'

'Mind your own business, hm?'

Gwen left the startled Juanita and made her way to the far side of the room, where a lively discussion was taking place between Murray, Penny and a couple of others about the administrative load of schoolteachers.

'It's like doctors,' said Murray. 'Hi, Gwen! They've lost the personal touch. It's all targets and league tables. That said, the drama teacher's a gem, Harmony's in *Grease* and I can't wait.'

'Neither can my Jamie,' said Penny. 'I think he fancies your daughter. But he's only on props, so what hope does he have with a cheerleader?'

There was a great deal of guffawing and the discussion continued, which gave Gwen time to compose herself.

Paddy was a sore subject. He had joined the writers' collective as that rare thing, a published writer, and as such a kindred spirit. However, it hadn't take her long to discover that his novel dated from some years ago, had not been successful at the time, and was long out of print. So he was a has-been, but an alluringly damaged one whom she had taken upon herself to rehabilitate. This process had involved, as well as personal tutoring, intensive one-on-one counselling conducted in Gwen's abrasive style, which always culminated in vigorous therapeutic sex. Several people had commented on the spring in Gwen's step and the sparkle in her eye and she had made the mistake (which she bitterly regretted and now reminded herself never to repeat) of mentioning his name. Only six weeks ago he had sent his apologies to the collective, explaining that he had moved away from the area. Not 'was going to' – 'had'. The other writers, expressing their disappointment, had looked to her for elucidation, but it was the first she'd heard of it. Her ignorance heaped humiliation upon humiliation. It appeared she had been well and truly used, and by an expert. The bruises were still fresh.

'Gwen, you're very quiet?'

This was Penny, eliciting her views on the teachers' predicament.

'I've been listening. Weighing up the arguments.'

'I can't believe,' said Murray, 'that you of all people don't already have an opinion.'

'Opinions can change.'

'Well said!' Penny squeezed her arm. 'I wish there were more open minds about.'

'If you'll excuse me I'm going to take mine for a walk,' said Gwen. 'Watch this space.'

She felt them watching her, and went through into the Figes' huge conservatory, beyond which in the darkened garden winked a constellation of tiny white lights.

'Gwen!' It was Marian, glass in one hand, skewer of beef satay in the other, leaning forward for a kiss.

'Hi there.' Gwen allowed her cheek to be bumped. 'Phew, there's a bit more air out here.'

'Lovely, isn't it? They do know how to throw a party.'

'Well, it's lavish all right,' said Gwen. 'I just wish they could resist the temptation to invite everyone they know.'

'Just so long as we don't get crossed off the list!' In the absence of an endorsement, Marian went on, 'What are you doing for Christmas?'

'I'll be IC gravy at the shelter.'

'God, Gwennie, you're a saint.'

'As a matter of fact, there's nowhere I'd rather be.'

'I rest my case.'

'What about you?' asked Gwen.

'With Mum and Dad and my brother and his family. Then I do Boxing Day.'

'Now who's the saint?'

'It's only once a year. We believe in the family Christmas, God help us.'

'Sounds like an endurance test to me.'

'It is.' Marian flexed a bicep. 'I'm in training already.'

'How's Ros?'

'Fine, and Lucy-Anne's adorable. I'm going over in the summer.'

Della appeared between them. 'I'm glad I've caught you two fraternizing. This may not be the ideal moment, but remember there's a meeting on the Thursday after New Year. I'm sure the usual reminder will go out, but what with Christmas in between it might be rather last minute.'

'I'm not sure I'll be able to make that,' said Gwen.

'Can't be helped. Can you do that date, Marian, as far as you know?'

'I should think so.'

'Good. Only I want to firm up a few details for the Golden Anniversary, and make sure the February lunch doesn't get neglected in all the excitement.'

'Remind me who's speaking?' asked Marian.

'That woman from local radio, the one who does the consumer phone-in, what *is* her name . . .?' Della snapped her fingers abstractedly.

'Daisy Martin,' supplied Gwen.

'Daisy, that's right – she comes across as charming on air,' said Della. 'And I'm sure she'll have some amusing stories. I must circulate – happy Christmas, girls!'

'Thanks for the lovely party if I don't see you,' said Gwen, adding sotto voce, as Della moved away, 'I wish she wouldn't call us girls.'

'She's being ironic.'

'If you say so.'

'What's eating you?'

'Nothing.'

Marian was slightly flushed. 'Why do you keep on with the Marie Crompton if it gets on your wick?'

This was a good question, to which the honest answer was: vanity. Two years ago in the wake of her well-received novel *Green Shoots*, Gwen had gone down a storm as a speaker, and in the euphoric post-luncheon glow had been flattered into joining. Since then a kind of perversity had kept her on side and in post.

'Money for good causes,' she said now, brusquely, glancing at her watch. 'Speaking of which, I must be off.'

'Okay. And we won't see you in January?'

Gwen shook her head. 'I'm sure you'll all be relieved.'

Marian decided not to go there. 'Have a good one.'

'And you.'

Brian was in the hall, seeing off Penny and Graham who, unlike Gwen, had been early arrivals.

'Not you too!' he cried.

'I'm afraid so.' She collected her flying jacket from the coat rack and shrugged it on. 'Duty calls.'

'Well,' said Brian, manoeuvring her under the mistletoe and kissing her on her lips. 'Mmm . . . me too. I have a date with the hardcore partygoers and a proper drink.'

'Don't let me keep you,' said Gwen. 'Nice party, thank you.'

Brian closed the door and turned to see Rhada, looking especially fetching this evening in a turquoise salwar kameez. 'Ah, the Bollywood babe herself!'

Gwen arrived at the shelter to find a noisy altercation in progress between Rose, a diehard regular, and a skinny, sad-looking youth who believed (almost certainly correctly) that Rose had insulted him – a scenario designed to bring out the best in Gwen. She stepped in, calmed the youth, affectionately chastised Rose, offered roll-ups and got the kettle on.

Home at last.

Tony Chance was at the ballet with Diana Lyttelton. In making tonight's choice Diana had gone resolutely unseasonal and off piste and had chosen an American touring dance company presenting a mixed programme of three short items: 'Epiphany',

an impressionistic piece with the girls and boys all in flesh-coloured
bodysuits and bare feet; 'Happy Hour', a fun interpretation of
waiters and barmen, equally androgynous but at least set to
infectious piano rags; and finally (now just ending), 'Advent', a
two-hander with a nod to Christmas in the title if not elsewhere.
Here the boy and the girl were distinguishable which was just as
well because physical passion was the keynote – to such an extent
that Tony, watching the rapturous contortions of their climax,
wondered whether ballet dancers were forever destined to mate
only with their own kind.

'Wonderful . . . quite wonderful!' declared Diana, rising to her
feet during the second of many curtain calls. When they eventually began to make their way out, she smiled teasingly at him,
and asked: 'So, Tony, how was it for you?'

'I particularly liked the middle section.'

'The crowd-pleasing waiters, yes, weren't they sweet?'

'Diana . . .' They reached the aisle and he helped her with her
coat. 'You know I find modern dance difficult.'

'Yes, but it's very good for you.'

'Mention my "comfort zone" and I shan't take you to dinner.'

Diana gave her warm, honeyed chuckle. 'I wouldn't dream of it.'

In Orvito's they were greeted like the second coming (especially Diana who was the sort of woman at whose feet Italian
restaurateurs instinctively fell) and asked where they would like
to sit. Diana chose the window, and they ordered: liver *fiorentina*
for him, fettucini with fresh pesto for her and mixed leaves with
walnut oil to share.

Diana and he were such old friends that Tony was sometimes
in danger of forgetting how beautiful she was. Beautiful, charming,
and accomplished, in the old-fashioned sense of being widely read
and travelled, well-informed, a good dancer and competent musician (she played the piano). There had never been a hint of anything
sexual in their relationship, but he was well aware – and was sure
she was – that they made a striking couple. From time to time
they were pictured together in the pages of high-end gossip magazines, just enough to keep general speculation simmering.

Tonight, Tony was conscious of the admiring glances and
adjusted his body language accordingly. This was instinctive; he
was a natural exhibitionist who responded reflexively to an

audience. He leaned a little towards his companion, smiled confidingly, looked into her eyes, and touched her lightly on the back of her hand.

'What are you up to?' asked Diana.

'Up to?'

'The charm offensive – not, I hasten to add, that I have any objection.'

'It's quite simply that I'm aware of being the most envied man in the room.'

Diana cocked an eyebrow. 'You're famous, silly.'

'No, no . . . I'm your fortunate escort.'

'Well.' She watched indulgently as he tasted the wine, and gave the waiter a sweetly grateful glance for pouring hers. 'Gallantly said.'

They clinked glasses.

'Here's to us.'

'Us!'

Neither of them had ever married, though they agreed that they had nothing against it in principle. Particularly in Diana's case; at sixty, she was of the generation that had still – Woodstock and the pill notwithstanding – expected to marry eventually. Her singleness was a question not of missed opportunities nor of a life blighted by false expectation, but of a choice, made thoughtfully over the years. Diana was sociable but solitary; she liked her own company and space – most of all, her own bed. Her few romantic relationships had been kept strictly private (would never, for instance, have been the subject of press tittle tattle) and conducted by her rules. She was discreet. She liked peace.

Tony, generally speaking, was a gossip (or at least gossipy; he never gave away anything of importance), a show-off, a man who liked the buzz and dazzle of company. He was protean, a playful shape-shifter who could be subtly different for effect whenever he chose. It was a tribute to Diana that with her he approached, occasionally, something like his real self.

They didn't discuss Christmas; it was understood that Diana would stay with her merrily widowed cousin in Bath, and Anthony would attend a sophisticated adult Christmas dinner with neighbours, arrangements that suited both of them perfectly. The new year and its resolutions were another matter.

Diana announced her intention of spending more time out of town, at her riverside cottage in Henley.

'Why on earth would you want to do that?' asked Tony. 'You mustn't cut yourself off.'

'I shan't be cutting myself off from anything; I shall be extending my repertoire.'

'Don't go,' he implored. 'I shall miss you.'

'Nonsense, it's only three quarters of an hour from London, we can meet whenever we want.'

'In theory,' said Tony. 'In reality, that won't be very often.'

'You're being ridiculously negative. Uncharacteristically, if I may say so.' Diana tilted her head to catch his eye. 'Anyway, I haven't gone yet, so it's Kensington and business as usual for the time being.'

'Good. You were making me nervous.'

'Tony, please! It would take a lot more than that to unsettle you.'

'I'm a creature of habit.'

'Break the habit. It's good for us as we get older, or we'll become hidebound. What about you – what does the year hold?'

'Let's see,' mused Tony cheerfully, always happy to talk about himself. 'I'm practically retired, you know. A few days in the States, book coming out, the usual round of talks . . .'

'You see?' said Diana. 'What a wonderful life you have. We are very fortunate people, you and I.'

'That's true,' he conceded.

'Especially in each other.'

They clinked glasses again, and the fellow diners who'd been keeping an eye on them smiled tenderly at one another.

Once he'd seen Diana into a taxi, Tony decided to walk at least some of the way home, partly to burn off the rather good dinner and its accompanying alcohol, and partly because to do so late in the evening accorded with his image of himself as a true Londoner, at ease in his surroundings.

His route took him past the Nelson's Eye, a riot of coloured lights and festive appurtenances, including a reindeer with a flashing red member. About a dozen smokers were outside on the pavement. As Tony had half expected, Lionel was among them

— not himself a smoker but accompanying a sweet-faced young man in a scarlet baseball cap trimmed with white fur.

'Hello,' said Tony. 'Banished by the weed?'

'Hi there,' said Lionel, who was just this side of drunk. 'This is my friend Alex. Al, this is Sir Anthony Chance, who I told you about.'

'How do you do,' said Tony.

'How you doing?'

'Can I buy you a drink?' asked Lionel.

'No, thank you very much; I've just come from a very nice dinner. That's why I'm walking home.'

'Good grief, you're not are you?'

'Not all the way.'

'Home's in Hampstead,' Lionel explained to Alex.

'Nice one.'

Alex didn't sound in the least interested, but Tony was aware that several other men were looking their way, some with that familiar look of recognition.

'Right,' he said, 'onwards. Enjoy the rest of the evening.'

'Don't overdo it,' said Lionel.

'Never fear, the taxi fare's right here.' Tony slapped his pocket. As he walked away several men wished him a happy Christmas and he raised a hand in a relaxed, reciprocal kind of way.

One of Lionel's acquaintances came over. 'Your boss?'

'My employer, yes.'

'You kept quiet about that silver fox. Very nice.'

'It's a living,' said Lionel and turned to Alex. 'If you've finished that disgusting thing can we go back in?'

Sulkily, Alex dropped his cigarette end and swivelled his foot on it. The other man put a hand on his shoulder.

'I'd give less of the attitude if I were you. You've got competition.'

Peculiarly buoyed up by the encounter with Lionel, Tony walked almost the whole way, only hailing a taxi on Haverstock Hill, and replying to the cabbie's stock enquiry: 'Delightful, thank you. A perfect evening.'

Four

The evening before Christmas Eve, Penny was baking three dozen mince pies, two for the carol service and one for family consumption. What with one thing and another this was her third batch since the beginning of December, and she was still keeping a contingency boxful in the freezer just in case. Because of the baking, the family were having a simple spag bol for supper, with plenty of crusty bread and grated cheddar – with three growing boys you couldn't have too many carbs, and they weren't keen on parmesan.

Already her middle son, fifteen-year-old Jamie, was beginning to wander in and out and hover with an air that managed to be both accusing and wheedling – the food look.

'Won't be long,' said Penny. 'Spaghetti's on. You can tell the others five minutes.'

'Where's Dad?'

'He's late back.'

'I can see that. Where is he?'

These glancing shafts of rudeness – of *scorn* – hurt Penny more than her sons knew, because she never let on. Agitating the spaghetti with a wooden spoon, she said cheerfully: 'In London. At his office do. But from tomorrow he'll be home for nine days!' Just saying it made her wonder how they'd manage – how she'd cope with Graham's ill-disguised restlessness.

Jamie stared at the stove. 'What's for afters?'

'There's ice cream.'

'Can we have some of those?'

Penny thought, *Please, no, because I'll wind up having to make more!* but said, 'Why not? I've got more in the freezer.'

Jamie made no further comment, but left the kitchen. She heard him speak perfunctorily to his younger brother Dom who was watching television, and then yell up the stairs to Nathan who was in his room.

'Nathe! NATHE!'

Penny winced and before she could stop herself said, 'Not so *loud*, Jamie!'

'His door's shut, for Christ's sake.'

'Then go and knock on it.'

Grumbling and puffing Jamie went up the stairs three at a time, hauling on the banister in the way that had made them wobbly in the first place, and hammered on his brother's door.

'NATHE! TEA!'

This provoked a sharp monosyllabic response. Jamie did not immediately come back down, but Dom appeared from the living room. Her baby. Penny smiled at him.

'Hi, big boy – did you switch it off?'

Dom sighed heavily, returned to the living room, switched off, and returned.

'What is it?'

'Spags.'

'Yay.'

That one word made the sun come out for Penny. She would have kissed Dom if she hadn't known how much he'd hate it.

Marian's ex-husband Dennis had called round, and they'd got in a takeaway. She had never realized (or had long forgotten) what pleasant company Dennis was until they'd dispensed with their marriage. Neither had remarried and these occasional evenings together were one of the great pleasures of the new dispensation. There was no sex – that was another thing they'd left behind with some relief. They drank, talked, ate and laughed, but never for a moment wondered if they'd done the right thing – these evenings were proof that they had jettisoned the marriage to salvage the friendship.

Dennis had recently been in the States and had visited their married daughter near Atlanta. He had digital photographs of their granddaughter, Lucy-Anne, now one and a half, whom Marian hadn't seen since for some months. They were young grandparents – neither of them yet fifty – and still couldn't quite believe it.

'Isn't her hair glorious!' exclaimed Marian. 'She doesn't get those curls from our side of the family . . .'

'Perhaps Jay's is curly when he lets it grow.'

Marian smiled ruefully in contemplation of their son-in-law's shaven head. 'We shall never know. How's Ros?'

'Good. Well, you speak to her often.'

'It's not the same.'

'I appreciate that. She misses you.'

'I want to go out for a month in the summer.'

'She'd love it. They all would. And you need to catch up with Lucy-Anne.'

'I so do.' Marian glanced at Dennis. 'How does she look? Ros, I mean?'

'Umm . . .' Dennis considered this. 'Tanned, well-presented, in control—'

'Stressed.' It wasn't a question.

'Not in any obvious way.'

'But in a way we'd recognize.'

'Okay. Yes. A little, perhaps.'

'God!' Marian took off her glasses and massaged her eyes. 'I wish I was closer.'

'You want to get a video link.'

'Yes – yes, I must.'

'It's the way to go for the geographically challenged grandparent. Jay'll set it up.'

Marian replaced her glasses. 'Yes, and what *about* Jay? Any improvement?'

'You make him sound like a chronic condition.'

'You wonder why?'

'He's not that bad,' Dennis protested, laughing. 'In fact he's a nice bloke. Just a bit reserved.'

'Come on, Den, he redefines the term! He shows the way! He has personally and single-handedly raised the bar on non-communication.'

'He hasn't a mean bone in his body.'

'That's true, I grant you.' She was laughing too now. 'Especially no backbone.'

'You can't hold that against him . . .'

'No . . .'

'Oh, *stop!*'

'What?'

★   ★   ★

Laughing – really laughing, uncontrollably – *was* good for you, reflected Marian later, in bed. Perhaps not quite the best medicine (that was sex, which resembled uncontrolled laughter in many ways), but it was certainly therapeutic. But with Dennis gone and the mood of childish hilarity with him, she started worrying again about Ros. She didn't doubt that Jay adored Ros – how could he not? – but as for the other way round, well . . . frankly, only love could explain it. But that didn't alter the fact that from what Marian could see her daughter was carrying the whole shebang. It was Ros's competence, her head for figures, her good sense and perfectionism that kept the show on the road, while Jay (admittedly talented, though underachieving on the computer games magazine where he worked) meandered along as though it all happened by magic. Christmas done by Ros would be the full fairy-tale monty and of course the ante would have to be upped every year in perpetuity because Jay and Lucy-Anne would take it for granted.

Just as well, perhaps, that she didn't live closer, thought Marian. The temptation to get too involved might be overwhelming. In the meantime there was tomorrow to think about. On the drive to Beaconsfield, she would mutate from concerned grandmother to rebellious younger child. And then mutate back to competent daughter overnight in order to poach a whole salmon on Boxing Day.

Brian Figes was asleep, along with the Figes' five house guests. Della on the other hand was in overdrive and unable to close her eyes. She loved Christmas, the preparing for it, the doing of it, the presentation and the presents, it was a feast exactly suited to her talents. The only trouble was the adrenalin high – great while it lasted but which would result in her being felled by exhaustion when they'd all gone. And then there was only a brief, dyspeptic lull before the Hogmanay Hop when she was committed to providing cranachan for sixty and Brian was on the bar.

She got up, pulled on her dressing gown and went into the big, rustic kitchen-diner. Breakfast for seven was already laid up, using the advent china with its holly and mistletoe pattern, and green napkins. On the day itself, in the elegant dining room, they would use her grandmother's gold-edged Coalport and the white

damask table linen. A simple table centre of fresh evergreen with
a frosting of gold . . . ivory place cards, elegantly handwritten.
Everyone's bedroom had a Christmas arrangement, spice-scented
tealights, new matching towels and face-flannels, a selection of
up-to-date paperbacks and magazines and a basket of Jo Malone
toiletries in the en suite bath- and shower-rooms. As a hostess
Della went to a great deal of trouble, because it made her
happy; she loved to see her guests' faces lit up with delight and
appreciation. Standing looking out of the patio doors into the
pewter-tinted night garden Della wondered how she'd have
managed a family Christmas – that is to say, one with children. She and Brian had never wanted a family, but she was
aware that a lot of people thought that Christmas was 'for the
kids', so where did that leave people like them? She loved their
grown-up Christmases – midnight mass, brunch with buck's fizz
and presents, a walk, a bath and a rest, a sparkling, formal, candlelit
dinner – and could scarcely imagine the mess, muddle and make-
do that characterized a child-centred occasion, all packaging and
tantrums and not wanting to sit at the table. Let others do that.
The people she invited were like themselves child-free, with occasional refugees from family-land who for one reason and another
had been left high and dry. Plus the odd wild card, because in
Della's experience the presence of someone new or different made
everyone else behave better and more entertainingly. On this
occasion she had invited Rhada Vashkar for Christmas dinner and
she had accepted, which was lovely.

She drifted happily into the drawing room. The tree was dark
and mysterious, the presents heaped around its base like some
curious shiny rock formation. The Proustian scent of pine needles
hung in the air. The hearth still glowed an ashy red from the
night before: polished wood and favourite pieces of glass and
porcelain gleamed in its soft light. There was a mirror over the
hearth, beneath which, on the mantelpiece, stood a phalanx of
invitations, testimony to the Figes' popularity. In the mirror was
reflected the portrait of Della's mother, belle of her season, in her
white lace coming-out dress.

Della stood quietly, feeling the warmth of the embers on her
bare ankles and drinking in the tranquil comfort of her home.
She loved it; it was her kingdom. How could people who were

forced to live in squalor and ugliness bear it? At this very moment, for instance, Gwen was at the night shelter cutting the toenails of the indigent (the least of the services she performed for them if Gwen was to be believed). Della shuddered, full of appalled admiration. She could not in a million years have done anything like that; she liked her charity work to be fun and elegant. The Marie Crompton was perfect, and she was steering it, as she was steering her house party, towards a triumph.

She lifted her hair off her neck and held it on the crown of her head, in an imitation of her mother's debutante chignon. These days she often considered having her hair cut from its thick, swinging shoulder length, but what always stopped her was that if she went in for a sharp modern bob she would not be able to put her hair up, which she liked to do on occasions. She let it drop again, reassured by the soft, heavy swish against her neck. Andre's cut and colour was second to none; she wasn't too old yet. The big chop could wait.

She yawned. In spite of the dying fire her feet and hands were beginning to feel cold. Back in bed Brian would be waiting, large, warm, embraceable and, happily, unconscious, so a little self-interested snuggling-up would not light the blue touch paper.

Nonetheless he grunted as she slipped in beside him. 'Mm . . . Where've you . . .?'

'Nowhere. Ssh.'

'Happy Christmas . . .'

The words faded into a wheezy snore. He was ahead of himself, bless him, but Della didn't correct him. Tomorrow was Christmas Eve, her favourite day of the year.

Rhada's parents had come over with the influx of Asians from Kenya in the sixties. The family were Hindu, but since her parents had died Rhada had largely let that go, and her older sister Mina, who was more of a traditionalist and keen on ethnic and religious roots, had married an Indian and gone back to live near the sisters' uncle and aunty in Chennai, so there was no-one to nag or censure her. She liked to be her own woman, it was important to her. Sure, she wanted to get married to the man of her choice, but she didn't need to. All in good time, and due to her own hard work, at thirty-two she was both time- and cash-rich.

She derived enormous pleasure and satisfaction from her chic,
well cared for flat, her job with the town's most respected firm
of accountants and her social and charitable activities; she didn't
for one second take anything for granted. She had broken the
Vashkar family mould and was proud of having done so. A man
would have to be something remarkable to ruffle Rhada's
enchanted self-sufficiency.

On Christmas Day she woke early as usual, made herself a
light and delicious breakfast of fruit and wholewheat cereal and
went back to bed with a tray. When she'd eaten she read for an
hour before running herself a deep bath and luxuriating in it
while listening to classical music – she had splashed out on speakers
in every room, so Pachelbel could seep dreamily into the steamy
air along with the scent from her exotic oils. After some more
coffee she put on velvet jeans, Ugg boots and her white fur-
trimmed parka and went for a long walk through the deserted
streets. Her step and her heart were light, unfettered by giant
greasy turkeys, unwanted presents or hordes of bickering rela-
tives. She had sent cash orders to her nephews and nieces in
Pakistan, and had bought an embroidered silk scarf for her hostess
tonight – that was the extent of her Christmas shopping. Except,
of course, that she herself would be gift-wrapped for the Figes'
festive dinner; she had made a trip to Southall in November and
treated herself to a pink and silver sari and silver beaded slippers.
When it came to the big occasion, nothing the high street had
to offer could hold a candle to traditional dress.

At two o'clock she had some more fruit, and watched a film
– a bitter-sweet romantic comedy that she had purchased expressly
for today – and then had a rest with her book and some more
music. The invitation had stipulated six-thirty, so at five she began
the process of getting ready – the transformation that would make
Della, and especially Brian, glad they had decided to ask her
along.

At Marian's parents' house it was all over by six, but there was
no relief because no-one was going anywhere. In order to escape
the liverish, fractious torpor of the sitting room Marian slipped
away into the kitchen, tuned in to Classic FM, and began dismant-
ling the turkey carcass. There was something obscene about the

scale of the damn thing, like dinosaur remains, the white meat desiccated and the legs still pinkish, a pool of cooling fat forming underneath and stuffing spilling out untidily from every orifice.

It would have been too much to expect her mother not to notice her absence, and it wasn't long before she came in from the living room wearing a reproving expression.

'Now what are you doing out here?'

Marian turned Prokofiev down a notch. 'I thought I'd get the meat off before I go, and then you can throw the bones away, or whatever you do with them.'

'Your father likes his soup.'

'Then he shall have it,' said Marian briskly. 'I'll put them on to simmer.'

Her mother sighed. 'You don't have to do that right now. It's Christmas evening.'

QED, thought Marian, but said, 'I'm happy, Mum – I don't want to watch TV, and I have to hit the road before I'm much older.'

'We're going to play Pictionary.'

'Then you go and play. Really, I mean it.'

Her mother turned away, and then back again. 'I can't relax knowing you're out here slaving away.'

'I'm not slaving. And that's blackmail.'

'The children would like you to play.'

'Mum!' Marian gave her mother a sidelong look. 'Please. Cajole if you must, but don't lie.'

'Will you come and join us when you've finished?'

'Sure. For half an hour or so.'

'Promise? Don't go finding something else to do.'

'Promise. I may not play, but I will come and watch.'

'All right, but . . .' Leaving a doubtful note to drift in the air, her mother went back to the family. Marian walked softly to the door, closed it and turned the music back up, resuming her assault on the tepid turkey with a sense of blessed relief.

She was not agin the family Christmas – quite the opposite; she would like to have been engaging in one of her own. She had spoken to Ros already today and would do so again last thing, when they would just have finished their lunch. Earlier Lucy-Anne, strategically positioned and encouraged, had gurgled sweetly down the line. Jay had mumbled affably.

It was the disparity in their domestic situations which distanced Marian from her older brother Michael. She'd married and had her child young; he had done so relatively late, with the result that she was already a grandmother while his two were still at primary school. In spite of her greater experience he insisted on behaving as though his was the correct – even the definitive – parenting model. Plus, his wife Olwyn was a likeable community nurse whose obvious qualifications provided Michael with further ammunition on the child-rearing front. Even now, through two closed doors, Marian could hear her sister-in-law's boisterous laughter; she genuinely enjoyed the company of six- and eight-year-olds while Michael, the paterfamilias, would be looking on benignly, imagining himself to be the pivotal figure in all this seasonal fun . . .

'What's going on out here?'

No sooner the thought than the man himself. Marian wiped her hands on a piece of kitchen towel and smiled brightly.

'A spot of rationalization.'

'From choice?'

Michael knitted his brows slightly to indicate that he was speaking over the music, and Marian lowered the volume.

'Of course – do you honestly imagine Mum asked me to do this? She's already been out here once trying to coax me away.' She forced a laugh to take the edge off her words.

Michael leaned on the work surface and picked a piece of meat off the turkey, popping it in his mouth. 'Nearly done?'

'Nearly, yes.'

'They're all having a riot in there.'

'I can hear. That's great.'

She began parcelling up the meat for the fridge, dark and white separately. Michael watched.

'Mind if I ask you something?'

'No,' she said. 'I don't mind you asking.' She placed the emphasis on the last word, not guaranteeing an answer.

'How's the love life?'

Marian had anticipated something of the sort, but anticipation did nothing to stifle the flare of pure rage that made her face burn and her hands shake. There was a long simmering pause while she rinsed her hands and then stared out of the window, clutching the edge of the sink.

'Did I put my foot in it?'

She knew he didn't mean it, that his questions were prompted by the best of intentions, but she could still have smacked his face. The first question was crass and intrusive, and the second implied, however unintentionally, that she was being touchy. She took a deep breath and said evenly:

'No, you didn't. And everything's fine.'

'Jolly good.'

She closed her eyes for a moment. 'Jolly good' in Michael-speak meant 'Have it your own way'.

'Seen anything of Dennis?'

'From time to time.'

'How is the old reprobate?'

It was no good; he was simply incapable of finding the right tone.

'Good, last time I looked.'

'What about him, has he hooked up with anyone yet?'

'I don't know. I haven't asked him.'

'No, well, sorry, of course . . .' Michael assumed a sympathetic expression. 'Why would you?'

'Michael.' Marian, who had remained at the sink, pretending to wash her hands, turned to face him.

'What is it?'

Oh God, he thought she was about to unburden herself of a confidence, one that he had wrung from her.

'Michael,' she said, fixing him with a steady gaze. 'Please.'

'What?' He grinned encouragingly.

'Please – just shut up and bugger off!'

Five

Marie Crompton's February lunch went well. Daisy Martin of Radio Wold, who sounded so sweetly spontaneous and jolly hockey-sticks over the air waves, turned out to be a seasoned professional and luncheon-club veteran whom long experience had taught exactly what was required. She arrived punctually, dressed in an expensive, understated suit, drank slimline tonic, worked the room without the need for hand-holding and commented favourably on the food, of which she ate only a little. Her talk ran to time and contained two well-judged compliments, a generous reference to the day's charity and half a dozen droll anecdotes saucy enough to flatter her audience's broad-mindedness without causing offence.

When she'd gone, some members of the committee convened informally in the hotel lobby over a tray of tea. Rhada had returned to work and Juanita had gone to visit her mother. There was a general sense of satisfaction, of a box ticked and energies now free to focus on the Main Event.

'Actually,' said Della, 'I was favourably impressed. I was sure she'd be professional, but she was a lot better than that, she was excellent.'

'I suspect,' said Gwen, 'that she's so used to this sort of thing she does it on autopilot.'

'Well if she does, she disguises it well.' Marian took a biscuit. 'She gives good spontaneity.'

They laughed. Penny said, 'She didn't look like her voice. I expected someone more, sort of, mumsy.'

'That's their cunning,' observed Gwen. 'We shouldn't confuse the on-air persona with the real thing.'

'Well, on that basis we didn't see the real thing here, either,' Marian pointed out. 'This was just as much a performance as her programme.'

'Good point. She's probably gone straight from here to the nearest crack kitchen.'

Della smiled anxiously. Gwen had a tendency to push the envelope a little too far. 'Anyway . . . Now it's onwards and upwards for Sir Anthony. I wonder what *he'll* be like?'

'Charming, I bet,' said Penny.

'So he should be,' harrumphed Gwen. 'Just as long as he doesn't call us "ladies".'

'What else would he call us?' Della exclaimed. 'We are ladies!'

Gwen took out her cigarettes and stood up. 'Speak for yourself.'

There was a micro-pause when she'd gone, which Marian broke.

'"Dear ladies" would be worse.'

Lionel had only just let Marlon off the lead when the Cavalier King Charles came round the bend in the path. The Labrador took off – too late to do anything, but he could at least be seen to be trying.

'Marlon!' he shouted, breaking into an awkward run. 'Marlon, wait! I said wait!'

It was futile. The spaniel's owner appeared, a woman in a cape and an Indiana Jones hat. She probably had a bull-whip too; she looked the type.

'Marlon! Bad dog!'

He was indeed a bad dog, bounding up to the spaniel and mounting it at the wrong end, thrusting vigorously at its head while its back end struggled to get free.

Lionel and the caped woman confronted each other over this disobliging congress.

'I'm so sorry,' said Lionel, clipping on Marlon's lead and dragging him off his victim. 'I don't know what's got into him.'

'You shouldn't let him off at all, you know.' The woman was steely, patient, patronizing. 'Not if he gets up to that kind of thing.'

'He doesn't,' Lionel lied, staggering to control the panting Marlon. 'I've never known him do it before. I think he was just overcome by enthusiasm.'

'I dare say.' The woman brushed this aside. 'All the same, take my tip and keep him on the lead. Safest thing.'

As they went their separate ways Lionel didn't know which

he hated more, that bitch or the dog. Her, probably. At least Marlon had the excuse of being a dumb animal, prey to instinct and impulse. Whereas she . . .! He pursed his lips. Bitch!

He told Clemency about it in the kitchen when he got home.

'I must say I think she's right.'

'Traitor!'

'It's not as if you didn't know Marlon's horrible habits.'

'But *she* didn't know I knew! As far as she was concerned, it was a random incident.'

Clemency shrugged. 'It's between you and your conscience, Lionel.'

Lionel considered this as he sorted Sir Anthony's laundry and dry-cleaning (two silk ties, half a dozen pure cotton shirts, three cashmere sweaters, a bespoke suit and a Boateng blazer). His conscience was agreeably easy to live with because as a moral compass it had no magnetic north; it was a faculty that swung according to mood and circumstance. This was a useful facility he had in common with his employer; their mild sparring concealed a profound mutual understanding, an appreciation that guilt was the great enemy and not to be entertained. Lionel rolled the shirts and put them in the laundry service's zip-up bag. Beautiful shirts. All Sir Anthony's things were of the highest quality, unshowy and classic, beyond the range of competition.

He examined the suit jacket for any particular marks that would need attention. None. He turned his attention to the blazer. When he had first come to work here ten years ago he had often specu-lated about a certain sexual ambiguity on the part of his employer, but had since reached the conclusion that the ambiguity was deliberate, and the truth rather more surprising: that Sir Anthony was that rare thing, a genuinely non-sexual being. What in another man might be taken for broad-mindedness, an openness to new and different experiences, was in Sir Anthony no more than a sincere lack of interest. The truth was, thought Lionel, his lips pursing in an introspective smile as he scrutinized the suit trousers, the only stirring in Sir Anthony's heart or loins was occasioned by what he saw every morning in the mirror.

Penny was counting her loyalty points from the supermarket, accrued since before Christmas, when Sam rang.

'How's it going?'

'Fine.'

'Coming into London again any time soon?' Sam always spoke as though Penny had a myriad reasons for popping into town.

'I hadn't planned to, particularly.'

'You sound a bit down, if I may say so. A girlie day out would do you good.'

Sitting there with her paperwork spread over the kitchen table Penny had never felt less 'girlie', but then Sam couldn't see her – for all Sam knew she might be sitting perched on the sofa in silk pyjamas painting her toenails vermilion.

'. . . new Motown musical,' Sam was saying. 'Do you fancy giving it a go?'

'It sounds lovely, can I think about it?'

'Sure. Have a think, give me a few dates and I'll book.'

'Wonderful.'

'Okay,' said Sam, 'well I can tell you're up to your eyes, so I'll let you get on with it . . .'

'Sam, I'm sorry . . .'

'Don't be. Look after yourself. And give me a buzz soon, right?'

'I will,' said Penny, 'I promise.'

She was glad to return to the tokens. Seventy-five pounds worth, a lot better than a poke in the eye with a sharp stick. But she deserved it, the amount of custom she brought to the place. A massive, tottering trolley-load every week and even, during school holidays, the odd top-up in between. Looking at the tokens she considered, as she always did, whether it would be best to hang on for a bit longer before spending them; to wait till the autumn's batch (a fat one after the school holidays) and put the accumulated sum towards this year's Christmas stock-up. Some people she knew got all their festive booze with loyalty points. Experience showed that she'd probably wind up spending them on her next outing, but it was pleasing to have, for the time being, this sense of choice.

She fetched an envelope out of the drawer and began putting the tokens into it. As she did so she came across the other sort – the ones that promised extra points on specified items up to a certain date. It was impressive, if a little creepy, how the computer had tracked and analysed her shopping habits so that it could now offer inducements on cornflakes, own-brand butter, sausages, men's toiletries, chocolate biscuits . . . She paused and took a second glance, her brows drawn together. Men's toiletries? The selected brands were Aramis and Paco, which she supposed she had vaguely registered on the more rarefied and expensive shelves. Aramis, according to the picture, had sleek black packaging with a silver handwritten logo. Paco was stubby and metallic, like ammunition.

She sat for a moment with the tokens in her hand, then put them down on the table and went upstairs and into the bathroom. They only had the one, reasonably large, but there was a separate toilet, fortunately, and another one downstairs – one was never enough in a house full of men.

Various products stood on the side of the bath, the basin, and on top of the medicine cabinet: two-in-one shampoo and conditioner, bubble bath, soap, toothpaste, mouthwash, all the usual stuff. The boys' shock-headed toothbrushes – due to be replaced, she reminded herself – stood in a wooden rack like malefactors in the stocks. A jumbo moisturizing shower gel hung from the hook in the shower, depositing, drip by drip, a viscous blue puddle on the tiles; Penny snapped the lid shut. The inside of the medicine cabinet revealed only the usual jumble of dusty bottles of cough mixture and out-of-date analgesics and antibiotics.

In the master bedroom she hesitated for only a second before opening the drawer in Graham's bedside cabinet. She was only curious, she told herself, and anyway there was nothing there.

On the landing she paused for longer – she didn't like going into the boys' rooms without telling them, partly out of respect for their privacy, and partly out of trepidation; you never knew what you'd find. Now that they were growing up she preferred to give them a chance to hide anything disobliging before she got there. Not that (at the moment) she had any worries about drugs or, God help us, knives – no, it was just that the hormones were kicking in with the usual consequences.

She drew a deep breath and entered Nathan's room. It was dark – the curtains were still drawn over the closed window – and musty. She opened the curtains, and the window, and looked about. Nothing too awful. The walls over his desk were plastered with huge posters of the fierce, androgynous young actress he admired, pale-eyed, wild-haired and worked-out. There were a lot of discarded clothes, which might have been dirty or clean, and one or two scummy mugs and plates. These she retrieved and put by the door. No smell of smoke, she noted with relief. She moved cautiously round the room, peering as she went. No sign of fancy toiletries, either, though he was appearance-conscious these days.

Penny picked up the dirty crockery and closed the door behind her. A mystery. Or maybe just a promotion. Downstairs she tore off the toiletries token and dropped it in the bin before putting the rest in her wallet.

Rhada was being honest, not arrogant, in her assessment that the men she met weren't intelligent enough for her. She also knew that by the standards of most other women, and certainly those of self-help reality TV, she was too quick to judge. It was okay to be choosy, but not everyone had it in them to dazzle at a first meeting, and those that did might, by virtue of that fact, be dodgy.

Had she been desperate (which she was so not, though the vibrations from the subcontinent suggested that her family were), she might have considered the workplace. That was what they said, wasn't it − the workplace or the ready-meals aisle in the supermarket? But most of her colleagues were partnered, and of the two that weren't one was so shy that his true colours were a matter of the purest conjecture and the other was a card-carrying Lothario of the kind she most disliked.

Rhada was not a romantic; she was far too risk-averse. She neither expected nor hoped for a *coup de foudre*. She recognized in herself a revisionist gene which might (whisper it low) have been well suited to an arranged marriage. What she sought was a harmonious partnership that ticked the necessary boxes: stimulating companionship, equality of intellect and ambition, a degree of freedom and respect, and sex, of course, which should be mutually satisfying. Separate bedrooms would be a must − she would always need that private, personal space. There might even be an argument for maintaining separate accommodation . . . However, all this was detail. Her observation at present was that there was no-one out there in whom she could be remotely interested, because there was no-one sufficiently *interesting*. So she was quite content to wait.

More than quite – perfectly content. Content with her flat,
her job, her income, her few carefully chosen friends . . . Only
an exceptional person would be able to improve upon this enviable
situation.

Colin Goodyear, whom she was meeting this evening, was not
exceptional, though he was nice, and had lovely, gentlemanly
manners that reminded Rhada of her father. She had known
Colin for two years, since his landscaping company, Goodyear
Gardens, became her client. Their friendship (she did not, though
he may have done, think of it as a 'relationship') had progressed
at a circumspect pace to a certain point, and remained there,
which suited Rhada. For all she knew Colin may have regarded
it as stalled, and was politely concealing a riot of unspoken passion.
In any event, they continued to see one another every ten days
or so; tonight it was film club followed by dinner at the Jade
Garden.

The film was *Volver*, part of the club's Almodovar season. They
discussed it over peanut chicken and Thai vegetables. Rhada, while
allowing that she had liked his other films, declared this one just
too whimsical for her.

'I know what you mean,' agreed Colin. 'But it had great charm.'

'You mean Penélope Cruz.'

'No.' He lifted his head in a little silent laugh. 'She is very
pretty – but no, I meant the piece as a whole.'

Rhada shook her head. 'Not for me.'

'Playful might be a better word.'

'Mm, possibly . . . But then I don't like to be played with.' She
caught a glimpse of something on Colin's face, and added, 'I don't
like to *feel* that I'm being played with.'

'Right.' She heard the relief in his voice. 'I understand. Perhaps
it was a little manipulative.'

'That's what I think.'

There was a pause while they selected and helped themselves
to more food.

'This is absolutely delicious,' said Rhada. 'A good choice.'

'I thought you'd like it. Rhada . . .'

She glanced at him over a forkful. 'Mm?'

'I wanted to ask you something.'

'Then do.'

'I wondered . . . I was planning a weekend break some time soon, a dose of sunshine, a change of scene. I wondered if you'd care to join me?'

Ah, thought Rhada. *This is the problem with formality and friendship. It means that if one person wants to move things on they have to do things by means of a step change; force the issue.* Instead of matters evolving, she had deliberately held them in stasis. Now she was going to have to make a decision.

'Where were you thinking of going?'

'I thought perhaps Madeira, Minorca, somewhere of that kind – warm, scenic and undemanding.'

'It sounds delightful.'

'I'd love you to come.'

'I just don't know. May I think about it?'

'Of course! You don't have to make your mind up now, there's time in hand.'

She put down her fork and held the stem of her glass. 'Colin.'

'What?'

'If I were to come, what would that mean – to you?'

'A very great deal.'

That wasn't quite what she had meant, but he had given her the answer anyway.

'I really don't think I can.'

'Sleep on it, at least.'

'No.' She sighed and shook her head. 'I'm snowed under at the moment. Weekends mean work.'

'Oh dear. I think you work much too hard. A little holiday would be a good investment.'

He was trying to appeal to her practical nature. She would have to be more direct.

'I'm sorry, Colin.'

'Okay.' He held up his hand. 'I understand. Never mind.'

She found herself rather taken back by his ready acceptance.

'I just thought I'd ask,' he said, smiling. 'Nothing ventured, nothing gained.'

'No.'

'Do you have plans to go away somewhere yourself, in the summer?'

'No,' she said carefully. 'Not yet.'

'You surprise me. I had you down as one of those people whose year was mapped out well in advance.'

'There you are then – I'm more of a creature of impulse than you took me for.'

'Obviously.' He gave her a gentle, serious look. 'Good.'

Rhada thought about this exchange as she drove home. In spite of her unequivocal refusal of Colin's invitation, she couldn't help feeling that he had remained, as it were, in the driving seat. It was he who had taken the initiative by asking her away, and somehow, she wasn't sure how, he had retained it. She was ruffled, and annoyed that she'd let herself be ruffled. Even the sanctuary of her flat had temporarily lost its power to soothe. She pottered about restlessly, too wired to go to bed, or relax with music, but unable to focus, even on mindless television. This was a situation, she realized, when it would have been useful to offload on a sympathetic friend. It was not that she did not have friends, but that her pride would not allow her to use even the closest of them as an emotional diuretic. She could not bear to lose face, nor to be too well understood. In fact – she plumped down on the sofa and gazed out of the uncurtained window at the lights of the industrial estate on the other side of the canal – that was what was irritating her now. Colin, quite probably unintentionally, had given the impression of knowing what made her tick and (worse) what was good for her. Understanding gave people power, it eroded one's control over one's own life.

Damn.

Hugging a cushion she switched on the television, surfed the airwaves and stared furiously at *Worst Celebrity Style Moments*.

One way or another she suspected that the days of her association with Colin were numbered.

Six

'Bus or Bust!' shouted Della. 'Sign here!'

Her voice cracked dangerously.

At the beginning of her Saturday morning stint outside the superstore Della's approach had been subtler. It was one of those April days that teases with a taste of summer. The sun shone, undisturbed by the odd lamblike cloud. Elegant and unthreatening in her Hobbs new season print dress, she had targeted susceptible looking individuals – over forty, respectable, well-heeled – and taken time to explain the excellence of the cause, before inviting them, charmingly, to put their names on the petition. She had actually seen Graham Proctor, a prime target, sitting in his car, but he had been deep in conversation on his mobile for ages, and she didn't want to interrupt. Now it was eleven-thirty and restraint had been cast to the winds. She and her co-volunteer Gary were yelling like a couple of fairground barkers and grabbing signatures indiscriminately wherever they could. Motivation, understanding and commitment were taken as read – only monikers mattered.

The petition was something new for Della. She had rattled tins for innumerable charities in her time, and you got used to being ignored; that went with the territory. It was the people who wanted to discuss the issues that really drove you mad. Or the ones who so didn't want to be thought mean that they bent your ear about all the other charity commitments which precluded them supporting yours, while scores of potential donors swarmed past. And then there were the people with nothing better to do than spend valuable minutes pointing out that you would be better employed on behalf of innumerable other, more deserving causes than this one, to which, by the way, they had no intention of lending their support.

Today she'd found out that not actually asking for money was no protection against what Brian would have called 'arseholes'. Some people seemed to put the scribbling of a signature right

up there with organ donation – they considered it gave them
the right to comment and criticize and (as often as not) to go
away again, no doubt invigorated by the exchange and feeling
even more self-righteous than when they'd started.

So now it was no more Mr Nice Guy. She had cast embarrassment and delicacy to the winds. She shouted. Anyone would
do. Even when some *uber*-arsehole cracked a joke about bussing
(ha ha), and busts (tee-hee), she had smiled sweetly and suggested
she help him make his 'X'.

Gary was a sprightly pensioner kitted out (Della recognized)
in Mohawk, the supermarket's own smart-casual line. They were
taking it in turns to stay at the table with the petition while the
other circulated in the forecourt area distributing B or B leaflets.
Now Gary returned, leaflet-free and carrying two cardboard mugs
of coffee.

'Thought we deserved this, Della. I took you for a skinny latte
lady, was I right?'

'Lovely, how kind,' said Della, trying not to think of full-fat
cappuccino with three sugars and liberally sprinkled chocolate.
'I'm getting a bit hoarse here.'

Gary glanced at his watch. 'Nearly midday. Cavalry'll be here
soon.'

'You did well to get rid of all those leaflets.'

'Wouldn't take no for an answer. I shall be one of the bene-
ficiaries, after all.' Gary sent her a slightly roguish look that invited
admiring disbelief, but Della played it with a straight bat.

'Good for you.'

'You were doing pretty well yourself – I could hear you from
down by the trolley bay.'

'I cast caution to the winds, I'm afraid.'

'Only way to go,' said Gary, adding, 'You know, I think we
missed a trick.'

'Oh?' Della was instantly on the alert. She liked to be ahead
of the game. 'What's that?'

'We should have got Sir Anthony on here somewhere.'

'You think?' Della considered the small stand with its leaflets
and forms. 'Where?'

Gary shrugged. 'He's a well-known face; we should have
advertised your luncheon thing, had his photo displayed. I'm

not mad about him myself, but it would have given us some credibility.'

Suspecting he was right, Della bristled slightly. 'Surely,' she said, 'we already have credibility.'

'You know what I mean.'

'I do, actually. The lunch is sold out.'

'Yes, well,' said Gary, as if we all knew why *that* was. 'I'll look forward to hearing about it.'

Two weeks before the luncheon, on belt-and-braces principles, Juanita sent off final details to Sir Anthony via email and letter. She had mentioned the email in her letter and vice versa, just in case he thought she was being forgetful. She had also politely asked if he could acknowledge receipt of these communications. Once that happened her duties would be over, and she could sit back and enjoy.

A job well done, though she said it herself.

Clemency wondered what on earth these people imagined went on here – that Sir Anthony had no PA? That he needed arrangements to be repeated, loudly and clearly as if he were old and deaf?

She clicked reply.

Thank you. Sir Anthony will see you on the 26th.

She supposed she would have to show him the letter and send a longer reply on his behalf, but this would all help make her point – that they were dealing with an internationally renowned speaker who could tell the time, eat without getting soup on his tie and who could afford (she bridled involuntarily) the best administrative help available.

'Now, now,' said Lionel when she unburdened herself over a Prêt à Manger brie and grape sandwich at lunchtime. 'Calm down. They're only trying to be businesslike.'

'Can't they see it's the opposite?'

'They know they've hooked a big fish. They don't want anything to go wrong.'

Clemency sucked on her mango smoothie, swallowed and sighed. 'I still don't know why he's going.'

'You're too harsh.'

'You agreed with me to begin with!'

'That was then. What does it matter?'

'You're right. I've taken against them.'

'Know what I think?'

Clemency gave him a look. 'Usually I do, but on this occasion I can tell you're going to surprise me.'

'Maybe.' Lionel tapped her wrist as she was about to throw a crust to the waiting Marlon. 'I think you don't like the idea of all those lusty country wives getting their mitts on our Tony.'

'You what?' cried Clemency, banging down the smoothie so that it splashed everywhere. 'I don't like . . .? Please!'

Smiling, Lionel pointed out the smoothie drops on the floor to Marlon. 'QED.'

Rhada was considering wearing salwar kameez for the Marie Crompton anniversary. She'd recently been on her annual trip to Southall and had a beautiful new one made up for her in kingfisher blue silk with a filigree pattern in silver. It depended what persona she wished to project – the elegant business woman in a pared-down dark suit or the Indian beauty, lustrous and feminine. Colin, whom she had not seen for some weeks, would have recommended the latter; he liked to see her in traditional dress, and in his wallet carried a photo of her in her sari.

In the end she plumped for a compromise – a tailored black suit over one of her most vibrant embroidered silk camisoles: a professional exterior with a provocative flash of the exotic. She hated to admit it, but Colin's tactical withdrawal (she wasn't quite ready to call it a departure) had stung her. It had also put her on her mettle. Let Anthony Chance beware. As treasurer there was always a certain frisson when she was introduced, especially with male guests. 'Ah, the lady with the cheque book!' She was not in the least interested in Sir Anthony, beyond visiting his website for research purposes, but she wished to make an impression, to stand out in his memory of the day.

Having hung the black suit and the cerise cami on the back of the door, she placed on the floor beneath them a pair of exiguous black and gold strappy sandals. She was not, she told herself, the sort of woman that got dumped.

*   *   *

Penny gave a great deal of thought about how to frame the question she wanted to ask Graham. After all, he was perfectly entitled to buy high-end toiletries if he wanted to; male grooming was on the up if the TV makeover tsars were to be believed and there was no reason why he should be an exception. And the only reason he'd been using their card was because he would quite often go to the superstore for her, which was more than some men. He claimed he actually liked it, that it made a change. Graham was a good husband, good with the boys, handy about the house and garden and appreciative of what she did. Everywhere. He had a little phrase he used after they'd had sex: 'You're a good woman, Pen,' he'd say, and give her bottom a pat. It was a nice thing to say, even if it did make her feel a bit like a brood mare. Looked at objectively, and ticking the boxes, she and Graham had a good marriage.

But still, wasn't part of a good marriage openness, not letting secrets develop? She would have to be direct, but light-hearted.

After supper that evening as he leaned over to put his plate in the dishwasher she sniffed his head and neck with a blissful expression, like a Bisto kid.

'What are you doing, woman?' He frowned and sniffed at his shirtsleeve. 'Do I smell?'

She said coquettishly, 'It's enough to drive women wild!'

'What do you mean?'

'Must be all those fancy products you've been buying.'

'Oh!' he smiled, getting it. 'Yes, I decided it was time I became a new man. You don't mind, do you?'

'Mind?' Penny kissed his cheek, which was comfortingly evening-rough. 'Why should I mind?'

'A bit of an extravagance.'

'You carry on.' She put a tablet in the dishwasher, closed the door and pressed Start. 'As long as you get me some from time to time.'

'Sure.' Graham asked without looking at her, as he filled the kettle, 'How did you know about my habit? '

'Oh.' She chuckled. 'The loyalty vouchers arrived.'

'I see.' His hand hovered over the mug tree. 'Brew?'

Cleaning her teeth in the bathroom later on, Penny found herself conflicted. Graham had been natural, cheerful, had not acted in the least like a man with something to hide. But standing as she was facing the bathroom shelf and windowsill she had to ask herself: Where *were* all the cans, bottles and jars that made her husband smell so sweet?

Marian was on the Internet. What other people called surfing she thought of as doodling – idly typing in this and that, looking up trivia, wondering at the incomprehensible massiveness of it all. It was like trying to get your head around space, the galaxies, and the universe . . . Or time! God, yes, time! She shook her head: impossible. But once you got over that, it was a wonderful play-ground. Her finger hovered over the possibilities of a pampering weekend in the Lake District . . . The other phrase you heard was 'information highway', which meant you could get to where you wanted to go quickly, but also that while doing so you were in a dangerous, unprotected place where facts, options, ideas and opinions rushed at you from all sides and at breakneck speed . . . She exited the pampering site and gazed reflectively into space for a moment before typing in 'Timetravel.com'.

Dennis's history tours company was doing well. Activity and special interest holidays suited the mood of the times, and Time Travel offered exactly the right mix of leisure and learning. The website had been recently redesigned with more illustrations and photographs, and to be more user-friendly. Dennis had learned about that from talking to her, a borderline technophobe. The potential customer had to be able to slip seamlessly from page to tempting page, scarcely realizing that they were doing so until they reached the point where it would seem almost churlish not to give that little tap of the finger on 'Book Now'.

The ten days' Recollections of the Raj looked nice, not that she could afford it. Dennis's trips were good value because the price included everything – travel, accommodation, and an expert guide – but that still didn't get round the fact that you had to find fifteen hundred pounds up front. This year Marian's scrupulously saved holiday money was earmarked for her visit to Ros in the States.

She was about to exit when a name caught her eyes. Under *'As usual, Time Travel will bring you the most brilliant and entertaining experts in their field, including . . .'* was none other than Sir Anthony Chance! What a coincidence. She clicked on 'Massachusetts and the Road to Revolution' and yes, there he was, an inducement for June. She wondered if the photo was one he'd provided or whether Dennis had had it specially taken. It showed Sir Anthony out of doors, casual and preppy in chinos and loafers, a pair of sunglasses tucked in the open neck of his shirt, one hand in his pocket and the other on a gatepost. The gate stood invitingly open. Step this way for what the text described as 'an enriching and enthralling experience' with 'one of our most celebrated and engaging lecturers, guaranteed to bring an extraordinary period vividly to life . . .'

Chuckling, and with the picture still on her screen, Marian picked up the phone and dialled Dennis's number. As it rang, she glanced at her watch: eight-thirty. A drink might even be in order . . .

'Hello?'

The woman's voice was throaty and humorous; charming. There were other voices in the background.

'Oh, hello. May I – is that Dennis Langham's number?'

'It absolutely is. Who's that?'

Marian's heart stumbled. 'Could I have a word with him, please?'

'You could, but I'm afraid he's not here. I can give him a message.'

'Oh . . .' Marian dithered, her face was hot. 'No, don't worry.'

'I shan't, but at least let me tell him who called.'

'It's Marian.'

'Marian . . .' The woman was writing it down. 'Shall I put a surname with that?'

'No, it's all right. He'll know.'

'Excellent!' There was a burst of laughter in the background and Marian could hear a smile in the woman's voice as her attention wandered back to her friends. 'I'll make sure he gets back to you.'

'Thank you.'

'My pleasure. Bye, Marian.'

'Goodbye.'

When she'd rung off, the room was peculiarly silent. The furniture seemed to be watching her attentively. She herself sat very still but panic flapped and buffeted around in her chest like a moth inside a light shade.

Though she never, except in company, drank after dinner, she went into the kitchen and poured herself a glass of white wine. There had been something shocking about hearing her name spoken by the strange woman; spoken, and then repeated, in Dennis's flat. It was as if her name had been stolen from her, and in that instant *she* had become the stranger. Her teeth clinked the edge of the glass and her eyes stung. She told herself that she was overreacting and, far more importantly, that it was no longer any concern of hers, so her feelings were irrelevant. But this desolating reminder of how much she didn't know and was excluded from was too much to bear and she cried like a child, wiping her nose and eyes with her hand and slopping her wine on to her lap.

After a while she was exhausted. Bed, that was the thing. Perhaps not even with a good book but with the kindly and intelligent voices of Radio Four to distract and occupy her. She left her glass in the kitchen and went to turn off the computer. In doing so she absent-mindedly pressed the wrong button so that for an instant there was Sir Anthony Chance again, urbane in his quasi-country togs, smiling away by the open gate.

'Oh, please,' said Marian, out loud. 'Get over yourself.'

Hearing her own voice sounding so strong and sarcastic cheered her up, and she took considerable pleasure in switching him off.

In the managed mess of her own home, Gwen was perfectly able to acknowledge her demons. 'Issues' would have been her preferred term, but it came to the same thing. To say she confronted them would have been to overstate the case, but she was sufficiently self-aware to know they were there, and what form they took.

Then again, awareness was no guarantee of correction. With her feet up on the sofa, with a roll-up of home-grown weed between her fingers and a herbal tea at her elbow, she could admit pretty cheerfully that she was prickly and prone to jealousy. Her increasing irritation over the anniversary luncheon was largely a form of jealousy. All this fussing and fretting and excitement over the media smart-alec, it was enough to make you barf! The trouble was she remembered only too well when she herself had been the subject of (almost) the same fuss and admiration and it had been a heady experience. She'd lapped it up, and it was galling to see all that enthusiasm diverted elsewhere. Her own fault; she should have left them all to it long ago instead of being flattered into staying. After this wretched event she'd hand in her resignation. That would shake them – she hoped. With a bit of luck when she finished her current book she'd regain sufficient kudos to be invited back as a speaker.

For various reasons the writing was a bit constipated at present. Gwen had many calls on her time and energies and she had allowed the work in progress to get squeezed out. She had received a moderate advance for the book – a novel about a woman who was an inspired friend but a rubbish wife and mother – but that was now spent and she had taken on some freelance work to make ends meet. The trouble was that the freelance work had to be assiduously sought, then written and delivered, which in turn ate into her novel-writing schedule, and so it went on . . . One or two members of the Writers' Collective were coming up on the inside, and there was a serious danger she would be overtaken if she didn't pull her finger out. With people's thirst for novelty, whoever got published next would be flavour of the month and Gwen had no appetite for the role of old warhorse.

She stubbed out her smoke and laced her fingers over her abs (nice and taut; she worked out). Her feet in baseball boots rested on the arm of the sofa, ankles crossed. There was a cushion behind her neck. She closed her eyes. She must get her act together . . . Soon.

'I'm going to stay a couple of nights with my god-daughter,' said Sir Anthony. 'I've just realized how close she lives.'

'Let me check the diary,' said Clemency, 'before you finalize things.'

'There's nothing that I know of,' he said pleasantly. 'And if there is, maybe you could use your wiles to clear it.'

'Very well.'

'She's always asking me to visit,' he went on, 'so it's the perfect opportunity.'

'Of course.'

'She was a charming girl last time I looked.' Sir Anthony smiled his most wicked, conspiratorial smile. 'But she married landed gentry and I haven't seen her for years, so we are both running a dreadful risk.'

'Bloody hell,' complained Edmund Kingshott. 'He's an ocean-going intellectual, what on earth are we going to say to each other?'

'He's always been a very sweet godfather,' said Madeleine, 'so I can't possibly say no. And it's not for very long. We'll all have to shape up for a couple of days.'

Edmund looked glum. 'I hope he likes a malt. I'm going to need it.'

Seven

Tony wondered why he didn't use the train more often; the ride down to Wiltshire was a delight. He didn't dislike driving, and anyway for long journeys he used a limo company these days, so he'd almost forgotten the charm of this mode of transport. He'd had a hot breakfast of smoked haddock and poached egg – a combination that he regarded as a culinary litmus test, and which the rail company had passed with flying colours – and read his usual newspaper, plus a tabloid, from cover to cover. The scenery moving smoothly past the window was so quintessentially English that he found himself humming an accompaniment of Elgar under his breath. Also, there was the charm of bunking off. His work involved a great deal of travel, much of it international and long-haul, but work was what it was. This unstressful little adventure, with a mere hour's performance of the sort he could deliver on autopilot, to a captive audience, plus a reunion with Maddie whom he had last seen some years ago, filled him with a hum of happy anticipation.

At one point the train stopped in the middle of nowhere. In the silence that preceded the passing of the eastbound express he could hear birds singing.

Adelstrop, he thought.

Madeleine parked the Range Rover in the only remaining space, which was the awkward one next to the pay-machine. This meant the car's backside stuck out, but that couldn't be helped. God willing she wouldn't be more than half an hour and she'd had to pay £1 for the privilege. She'd come direct from the vet's, from where she'd collected her border terrier, Finlay. Still comatose from the anaesthetic, and now consigned to eternal puppyhood, Finlay had lifted his upper lip grumpily as she tapped on the rear window. She realized that she didn't know what Uncle Tony thought of dogs. Most of theirs were gun dogs who lived outside, but Finlay and the Jack Russell, Cosmo, had the run of the house and a consequent sense of entitlement.

She went down on to the platform. The village station was on a commuter line, but only the slower trains stopped here. The ticket office was manned during peak hours morning and evening, and there was no-one about. The banks on either side of the line were covered in slouching early weeds – thistles, bindweed, and the like – and a scattering of non-biodegradable rubbish. Irritably, Madeleine leaned one knee on the low wall and reached to retrieve the nearest Carling can, which she tossed in the bin. Her irritation was compounded by the suspicion that her own teenage sons were quite likely to have chucked the cans there in the first place. At home, William and Jack were almost sullenly teetotal but she knew (the evidence was all-too apparent) that when out and about they were fully paid-up subscribers to Britain's binge-drinking culture. They were home this weekend, too. Never mind the dogs, she thought, what would Uncle Tony make of the boys?

She glanced at her watch: eleven forty-five. Five minutes to go.

The cloud of anxiety which had been no bigger than a man's hand was increasing by the second to nuclear proportions. Dogs, boys – and then there was Edmund. Ed and Uncle Tony hadn't met since the wedding, when both had been pleasantly pissed and disposed to overlook their manifest differences in the interests of the occasion and (she hoped) their fond feelings for her. Since then Anthony Chance had become a household name on both sides of the Atlantic, and Ed had made a fortune out of intensive farming and rapacious land and property development. Plus, he was to culture what Vinny Jones was to needlepoint.

She heard the two-note whistle of the train closing on the station, and she blew heavily, puffing out her cheeks and settling her shoulders in preparation for the fray.

She could only pray that Uncle Tony still liked a drink.

Now they were slowing down, between banks of wild flowers. Good God, it actually *was* Adelstrop! Tony took his case down from the rack and went along the carriage to the door. He wondered if he would recognize Maddy . . .

Only two people got off, and one of them was a stout girl wearing a peasant smock over leggings. Madeleine waved energetically at the other one.

'Uncle Tony!'

'Dear girl, can it be . . .?'

He put down his case and held out his arms. Madeleine, feeling self-conscious, walked into his embrace. He smelled nice and his shirt was smooth and fresh. She had forgotten how handsome he was. People one saw on TV were often a disappointment, but her godfather, even allowing for his advanced years, was better looking than his on-camera self.

He pushed her gently back and held her at arms' length; everything he did was slightly theatrical.

'You look quite lovely,' he said.

'Really?' She glanced down at herself. 'If you say so!'

'I do. More beautiful even than before. Motherhood suits you.'

She pulled a wry face. 'Maybe. They're not sweet tousle-headed imps any more, you know.'

'I realize that.' He followed her along the platform to the steps. 'Shall I meet them?'

'It may be unavoidable'

'Now, now.' He laughed agreeably. 'Don't say that! I'm looking forward to it.'

Madeleine had been dreading it, but she had reckoned without her godfather's famous ease of manner and legendary charm. Drinks and supper passed without incident, in fact went with a swing. Tony admired everything, from the Stubbs painting to the Delia stew, and confessed ignorance and an eagerness to learn on the subject of land management and development. If the interest was feigned, it was impossible to tell. Edmund waxed expansive, it was all really rather nice. The boys had put in a brief appearance after supper, Jack from the upper reaches, William from the Slug and Lettuce in town. Tony leapt to his feet and greeted them like heroes, asked one or two unclichéd questions, paid close attention to their replies and laughed uproariously where appropriate. He made no mention whatever of their clothes and hairstyles. When they'd gone, he said 'What delightful boys' with every appearance of sincerity. He had not, in short, put a foot wrong.

Even Edmund, coming into the bedroom after the lengthy business of locking up, winding clocks and seeing to dogs, conceded that Chance was not a bad bloke.

'I told you,' she said.

'You implied it was going to be a nightmare.'

'But I said he was a sweetie, surely.'

'I must have forgotten,' said Edmund, unlacing his shoes and discarding them. 'Anyway, if you'd said that I'd have known it was going to be hell.'

'But it wasn't.'

'No. No – in fact there's a strong possibility we'll get through the weekend unscathed. Just as long as he doesn't start quizzing me about contemporary novels or whatnot.'

'He won't quiz you about anything; you can tell he has perfect manners.'

'Oh, silky smooth.' Edmund sloughed off his trousers and strode naked to the bathroom.

Madeleine, detecting mockery, said, 'It does make life easier.'

'I agree, I agree,' he mumbled, through toothpaste, and then, more distinctly, 'Single, yup?'

'Yes.'

'Always?'

'As far as I know.'

'And do we also know,' said Edmund, bouncing into bed next to her with much vigorous adjustment of the pillows and duvet, 'whether he ever would?'

'Probably not, but I don't think we should infer anything from that. There's never been a whisper. And anyway these days why would anyone stay in the closet? He'd be out and proud, like Sir Ian McKellen.'

'Or,' said Edmund, 'he might just prefer to keep us all guessing. Mind if I tune into TMS?'

Tony had turned his bedside light off, but drawn his curtains back. He lay on his side gazing out at the soft, grey country night. It was peaceful, but not quiet. He supposed he'd got so used to the sounds of London that he no longer noticed the distant yelp of police cars, the soft grumble of distant traffic, the occasional (mercifully rare) shrill cries of partygoers in the road at the front. Sometimes he heard Lionel return after an evening out and go about his kitchen routine, but the moment he'd registered it he would always go straight back to sleep; it was part of the pattern. Tonight, he could hear a dog barking, faint music (if you could call it that) from another part of the house, doors opening and closing, and the clunk and hiss of alien plumbing. There was some sort of animal noise outside, or it might have been a bird – a screech, anyway, that reminded him he was in the back of beyond.

As he became more attuned to the household and the household itself began to settle he picked up muffled voices – Maddie and Edmund (he didn't feel ready for 'Ed') in their room. Talking about him, probably. He reflected that Maddie was the only female here; even the two small hyperactive dogs were male. More or less. Tony winced. 'Hey,' Edmund had said, 'Finlay, you poor little bugger, has she scuppered your sex life?'

Tony had been taken by the boys. Fifteen-year-old Jack, dark-browed and sardonic, not giving an inch, was particularly impressive in a spiky, scowling way. William, like his royal namesake, was more obviously personable, with the sort of looks that are designated 'handsome' but which amount to no more than a kind of inoffensive regularity of feature. He'd been slightly the worse – or it might have been the better, who knows? – for drink, trying to be funny, not getting it quite right, while his sibling stayed poker-faced, opaque brown eyes unblinking beneath a heavy fringe. In this most traditional of English settings, both were dressed like surf bums. Tony could scarcely believe that Maddie, in his eyes still a slip of a girl, was the mother of these strapping young men.

It was a truth acknowledged by Tony that a single man in possession of a good fortune would be much in demand as a godfather, and Tony had five godchildren, though two of them were nephew and niece, which he regarded as cheating. Madeleine's mother, Corinna, had been a close friend at Cambridge. Her elegant, cultivated beauty had shone out among the tousled manes and rumpled clothing of her fellow students like a good deed in a naughty world. She had also been athletic, a key member of the women's eight, which he had found rather provocative in a Betjeman-esque way. At the May Ball it was piquant to reflect that the smooth white shoulders emerging from her strapless ball gown were the same that had pumped rhythmically, gleaming with sweat, during training that afternoon. He had always wanted Corinna to find a husband worthy of her, and though she hadn't quite done that (it was perhaps impossible), she had married Alasdair, an amusingly raffish and hugely rich something in the world of racing, who collected horse paintings. To his credit he had an eye for paintings as well as horseflesh; that was how he and Corinna had met, apparently – at Sotheby's where she worked as a researcher and valuer. Tony had liked Alasdair while recognizing that the horse-racing world and those connected with it were notoriously dodgy. At least Corinna, more than most women, was able to look after herself.

Madeleine had been born six months after the wedding, so Alasdair had taken his admiration of the sculpted shoulders further and faster than Tony had ever done. There had been a posh but pleasant christening, and Tony and the godmothers had made their responses while each holding a lighted candle – the first time he'd come across the practice, which was later to become commonplace. Six-week-old Madeleine was seraphic in antique lace, the guests had passed her around jovially during the champagne, after which a calm, competent maternity nurse swept her away so that they could lunch in peace. Tony had given her a pair of seed-pearl tudor rose earrings and a meaningful cheque to launch her savings. She had worn the earrings on her wedding day, eighteen years later. The cheque – well, you only had to look around. She was a girl both lovely and fortunate. The good fairies had seen to it that she inherited her mother's beauty and athleticism, her father's quicksilver charm and way with horseflesh though not, as far as Tony could see, either parent's appreciation of art: the inherited Stubbs was badly hung and ill-lit. You couldn't have everything.

Over dinner she'd told him that she had not had time to work while the boys were growing up, with such a huge house and the horses and so on (she still rode competitively to quite a high standard, Edmund pointed out with some pride, which Tony liked him for), but that she was now going to throw herself into Riding for the Disabled, and the local hospital improvement scheme. Edmund said that in his view she was too young for good works. Tony applauded her and asked whether she'd heard of 'Bus or Bust'.

'How could I not have heard? They were all over Tesco's car park the other day. But anyway I am coming to the lunch.'

'Really?' He was surprised and touched. 'How sweet – you didn't have to.'

'It's not a last-minute thing,' said Edmund. 'She booked her ticket ages ago. You won't see me, I'm afraid.'

'Please – I wouldn't have expected to.'

'No, it is mixed,' said Madeleine pointedly. 'The big ones always are, so there'll be a smattering of men, but you're going up to town, Ed, aren't you?'

'Yup, swapping places with you,' said Edmund to Tony. 'I'm going to a meeting at Chatts Price Chandler in Daunt Street. Where is that, do you know?'

'I do. Portland Place is your closest tube.'

'We're going to buy some land with fishing rights,' explained Madeleine.

'That sounds interesting,' said Tony. 'Near here?'

'Bang next door!' Edmund pointed past his left shoulder. 'With a following wind, this time next year rock royalty will be all over us!'

Rather to his surprise, Tony was genuinely glad Maddie would be there tomorrow. Usually he preferred not to have people he knew in the audience – there was a distinct possibility that they would see the join and infect others with their mild scepticism – but in this case he rather liked the idea of covering his god-daughter in reflected glory, especially as he considered that this evening had gone well; they had become friends. On the other hand he was relieved that Edmund was out of the frame, nice chap though he'd turned out to be.

A rural stillness had descended, at last. Still gazing out of the window at the point where the opaque black shoulder of hill gave way to the luminous dark of the sky, he began to drift into sleep. But as his eyelids grew heavy so his heart, curiously, became light.

Eight

The Marie Crompton lunches were usually held at the George in town – a large former coaching inn with a sympathetic manager and a modern dining room that could accommodate their numbers comfortably. But for the Golden Anniversary the committee had settled, after intensive consideration and debate, on the Tithe Barn at Polsworth House. A few people had been to events there over the years, and Della, Rhada and Juanita had done a recce, meeting the hospitality and catering directors for lunch in the Buttery. They were looking for a place with the wow factor, and the barn delivered it in spades: a wonderful vaulted roof with beams, long windows and a huge double door on to the park and the lake, along with ample parking and cloakrooms, which made a crucial difference.

'Sir Anthony alone would justify the ticket price, but this really makes it something special,' said Della, wandering down the centre of the barn. Even Rhada, who had the unenviable task of making sure that all investment increased the profit margin, had been won over by the barn's mellow magnificence, and it had more than paid off: they'd sold 120 tickets and there was a waiting list for returns and cancellations

On the big day, doors were to open at eleven forty-five, and the committee had agreed to be there by eleven to make sure everything was in place. When Della arrived the catering manager was addressing his troops by the kitchen door and there were a couple of waiters flitting around the tables adjusting forks and wiping glasses with a soft cloth, a sight that gladdened her heart. She and Penny had brought in the pale yellow and white table centres the previous afternoon, and now they were all in place and their scent filled the air – jonquils, narcissi, and lily of the valley, all set in moss. Simple, charming and fragrant was the note Della wished to strike. Something told her that Sir Anthony would respond to that. She wanted him to think (as she herself did), 'Oh, how absolutely lovely!' as he walked in, to feel that this day and this place, no matter how provincial it might at first have sounded, was something special and uniquely memorable. In all humility she knew that this creation of a mood and an atmosphere was something she could do and do well – it was a gift, on which she had learned to capitalize. But Della's greatest gift was one that she herself scarcely recognized: that of measuring her success by the pleasure of others.

Penny was struggling. She was not a whinger, she didn't want anyone to notice – and so far no-one had; they were all far too busy and excited to see that she was in bits. She still couldn't quite believe she had turned up. What was she doing here, when her life had just imploded? She could very probably have cried off, to use a horribly apt phrase, but something – programming? habit? shame? – had propelled her out of the front door in her green linen Boden suit and matching ballet flats, and here she was. She had certainly not been safe to drive; she had shivered and wept all the way, and had to go straight to the Ladies to put on a new, braver face.

Graham had rung – rung! – from Nottingham at seven a.m. She had known right away something was wrong because his voice was unusually warm and affectionate. He was always quite affectionate but this, her sensitive antennae told her, was qualitatively different.

'Pen?'

'Oh – hello!'

'Did I wake you?'

'No, I'm in the kitchen.'

'Ah yes, that early cuppa you're so fond of . . .'

She could see now that he was already processing her, turning her into a memory.

'What's up?' she'd asked, spooning sugar instead of adding the usual sweeteners. Upstairs one of the boys thumped across the landing to the loo.

'Why should there be anything up?'

'It's awfully early.'

'I wanted to talk to you.'

He'd made it sound almost romantic, as if he'd rung simply to hear her voice. *I just called to say I love you . . .*

'Right, well,' she said guardedly. 'Here I am.'

'I mean, not if it isn't a good moment . . .'

'No, this is fine.' The loo flushed and the footsteps thumped back. School holidays. 'I've got my tea.'

'Good.'

She sat down at the kitchen table. 'I'm listening.'

'We need to think about the future. I mean, really think. Don't you agree?'

She felt deathly cold. 'I don't know.'

'I'm sure you do, Pen. Really. Things aren't right, are they? We're neither of us stupid, quite the opposite. I mean, back before Christmas – the stuff on that list – you had some idea.'

Now she was not only cold, but breathless. She lifted her tea to her lips but the mug rattled against her teeth.

'Pen?'

She lowered the mug, with two hands, to the table. 'You never said. You explained.'

'Yes, but you knew . . .' She could almost hear him shaking his head in admiration. He sounded positively appreciative; he was giving her a compliment! Now he was going on, 'You gave me the opportunity but at that moment I was too cowardly to take it.'

What did he want, a medal?

'You still haven't told me why you're calling, Graham.'

'We both have some serious thinking to do.'

'Do we?'

'I think so.'

'I see.' She didn't, she was just making sounds so that she could draw the shock into herself and not disintegrate – yet.

'I hope you don't mind me broaching this on the phone; it was an impulse. I thought if I got the ball rolling we could talk when I get back.'

'Got the ball rolling?' She closed her eyes but not before she saw Jamie come into the kitchen, ready to go out on his paper round. 'I'm afraid I've got to go.'

'Of course. Pen—'

'I'm going.'

'Penny, I hope—'

'Bye.'

She clicked the ring-off button and opened her eyes. The click helped, actually. It was as if she was switching her mum-self back on.

'Morning, love,' she said to Jamie. And thought, almost immediately, to music, *Bye-bye love, bye-bye happiness.*

Five minutes later, horrified at herself, she dialled 1471 and discovered that the call had been from London. So he was hardly even trying any more.

And now here she was in the Tithe Barn at Polsworth House, setting out the menu and programme cards, on autopilot. Perhaps she did know why she was here. It was a comfort. She had a role, a focus, and friends around her, even if they didn't know what had happened. She reached the last table and once she'd positioned the menu just so in the centre she stood there, very straight, staring fixedly into the corner of the room with her back to the rest of it, struggling.

He hoped she didn't mind him broaching this on the phone. 'Broaching' wasn't a Graham word, not one she'd ever heard him use. Like the grooming products. A flash of something different. And of course she minded, because everyone knew that delivering bad news down the line was low, and cowardly, and she could not bear to call her husband, the man she loved, those things. She caught herself thinking: *He let himself down.* But it was her he'd let down. Till the very last, which this probably was, she was trying to save him from himself. Was that being a doormat? Or was it being a good wife? She didn't know. Nowhere in her head, in her idea of herself, could she find any strength, any certainty, any normality, to cling on to. She was all at sea, and drowning.

'Penny?'

It was Juanita, flamboyant in hot pink.

'Yes?'

'You were miles away!' Juanita laughed. 'Everything okay?'

The rhetorical enquiry made Penny suddenly swell with tears, and she couldn't trust herself to speak.

'Penny?' said Juanita again, this time with a more concerned inflection, touching Penny's shoulder and inclining her own head sideways to look into her face. 'What is it?'

The dam burst. Penny tried to contain the outburst as much as possible to avoid embarrassment and attention. Juanita put an arm around her shoulders, she could feel her hand flapping as she motioned others to stay away; Juanita was dealing with it, with her.

'Poor you, go on, that's right, you let it all out.'

Penny stopped crying as suddenly as she'd started.

'Now then,' said Juanita, 'what would you like to do?'

'Go to the Ladies.' Penny blew her nose. 'I'd better get straightened up; they'll be arriving any minute.'

'You're not staying!'

'Definitely,' said Penny. 'I don't want to miss it and anyway I'm better off here.'

Juanita nodded her head slowly. 'Trouble at home?'

'Sort of.'

'All right, I shan't ask, it's none of my business,' said Juanita virtuously. 'But you know where I am.'

'Thanks Nita.'

'My pleasure. Here . . .' Juanita opened her arms and enfolded Penny in a hug. *Bust to bust* thought Penny, as they were so often at Lindy Hop.

'Thanks,' she said again and then, extricating herself clumsily, 'Right.'

As she crossed the barn in the direction of the Ladies, the others were all busy in their various ways, asking each other unnecessary questions, admiring shoes and bags, but their emotional-crisis antennae were waving. While she was out of the room Juanita, in the nicest possible way and from the best of motives, would play her supportive-and-discreet card, and when she got back there would be lots of affection and no questions. No intrusion, just the 'we're-here-if-you-need-us' vibe. There was no-one else in the Ladies, and as she splashed her face and repaired her hair and mascara in front of the mirror she realized that it would be good to talk to someone, someone who wouldn't take sides, and either demonize Graham or remonstrate with her for being spineless. She had no idea who that person might be. Plus, before that happened it appeared she and Graham 'had to talk'. That was what he'd said. He seemed already to have done a lot of talking to himself (she hoped it was to himself), and to have argued to his own satisfaction that the matter for discussion had been inevitable, something they'd both been able to see coming, which had at last happened and now had only to be managed.

Was he right?

A young woman in a chic white trouser suit entered the cloakroom and went into a cubicle. The ticket-holders had begun to arrive.

Penny pushed at her hair with her fingers. She looked so much more all right than she felt. The prospect of going back in, though, was not too terrible. After all, for the next three hours or so, she would be safe.

Some habit of perversity prompted Gwen to agree when the night shelter people asked her if she could stay over the night before the lunch. Doing so fulfilled a dual function: it flattered her image of herself as a socially committed person with serious calls on her time, and it served to keep the Marie Crompton in its place. If need be she could, as so often, legitimately claim to have hurried over there with no time to change.

She had spent nights at the shelter before, so she knew the drill. The front door was locked at ten, lights went out at eleven. At this time of year, in the spring, a proportion of the ever-changing homeless population was on the move, and the place wasn't always full. She didn't expect to be especially busy, and had agreed to stay and serve breakfasts too. In the event she had very little sleep because she and the others were up most of the night dealing with a troublemaker. The man claimed to have a knife and to be ready to use it. Exhaustive checks were carried out on the service users when entering, and nothing had been found, but there was always the possibility that he was right, and a knife had been missed, so they had no alternative but to take him seriously. A tall, ramshackle man, like a great ragged pine whose roots were giving way, he bore a grudge against pretty much everyone, but his specific beef on this occasion was that he had heard others talking about him insultingly. In this he was almost certainly correct. Insults and thieving were part of the shelter's social weave, along with micro-friendships of tremendous passion and brevity, and equally volcanic fallings-out. The accusations in themselves were of no great consequence, but a

semblance of investigation had to be gone through, and a reso-
lution reached. Truth and reconciliation, Gwen reflected, were
surely more achievable goals in post-apartheid South Africa than
in the Bishop's Few night shelter.

For several hours the whole place seethed with activity and
excitement. Everyone enjoyed a good bust-up, provided they
weren't in the firing line. Claims and counter-claims abounded
and subsidiary confrontations broke out like small fires around
the main conflagration. These tended to burn out quickly and
could be safely ignored; the important thing was to gain control
at the centre. In extreme cases they could always call the police,
but that was very much a last resort; if the shelter came to be
regarded by locals as a fomenter of trouble, there was a danger
of it being closed down.

By three a.m. the offended party had been mollified, the falsely
accused vindicated and everyone else sent back to bed, with only
a few minor bruises and breakages. A stertorous peace descended,
and the helpers congregated in the kitchen for a brew. Like the
service users, they were tired but elated. Gwen in particular, with
her mix of firmness and tough humour, was recognized to have
done well.

Sean, one of the regular wardens, spoke for everyone. 'We ought
to get you off the bench more often.'

'For God's sake,' said Gwen, who had rarely felt happier, 'it was
nothing.'

'No, you're a real asset.'

'Glad to be of use.'

Boyd, a relative newcomer, said, 'My turn to write the report,
I'll mention you in dispatches.'

'There's no need for that,' said Gwen, and was met by a heart-
warming wave of disagreement.

She helped serve breakfast in the mildly euphoric state that
accompanied lack of sleep, but no hangover. The service users ate
well, mumbled their appreciation and left quietly. The architect
of last night's ructions appeared chastened.

After they'd washed up, Gwen participated in the usual sweep
of the shelter, which revealed, among other things, a dinner knife
amongst the big man's rumpled bedding. Sean appeared in the
corridor, holding it on the flat of his hand like a poisonous spider.

'Not sharp,' he said, 'but given enough wellie it could have done real damage.'

Boyd shook his head. 'How did we miss that?'

'Because it's from here?'

Gwen picked up the knife. 'That's not like the ones downstairs.'

'Whatever,' said Sean. 'We screwed up. But it could have been a whole lot worse.'

The near-miss, the sense of a brush with death narrowly averted, sobered them all up. They had another round of strong instant coffee, and Gwen left at ten thirty feeling a little bilious as well as exhilarated. Back at her house the postman had left a package propped against her front door, with an irritable scrawl across the front: 'TOO BIG FOR LETTERBOX'. She'd already picked it up before it occurred to her that on any other day and in any other place such a thing would have screamed 'letter bomb'. This increased her sense of well-being as, without a qualm, she picked it up and took it inside with her. There were a couple of other, less interesting letters on the floor. Bills. These she moved aside with her foot.

She dropped the package on the sofa – no explosion – and went into the kitchen, where she opened both the window and the back door. Her neighbours' cat, Huggy, ran in with an expectant air, tail aloft. The neighbours were a yuppyish cohabiting couple in their early thirties. Huggy, a cat-flap pet, was a rangy black opportunist, who pretty much lived with Gwen during the day when his owners were at work. Now, in response to his lustful writhings, she got the milk carton out of the fridge and replenished the blue saucer by the door.

Gwen was not normally someone who counted her blessings – she regarded those who did so as insufferably smug – but as she watched Huggy lapping away, tail trembling and eyes half-closed, she found herself thinking how nice it was to be home. She was lucky; she had one. She was not homeless.

She went out into her small back yard, where post-Christmas enthusiasm had long since given way to spring's *laissez faire*. Maybe this summer she would spend a bit more time out here, do a bit of clearing, perhaps introduce a couple of pots . . . Huggy's owners would be pleased. They had decking and a pergola – quite a little bower going on. But if Gwen had felt put to shame by that, which she didn't, she only had to peep over the fence on the other side where her other neighbours, students, had done no more than introduce a blackened barbecue and an old sink full of marijuana plants (she couldn't complain about that, having some herself) into the jungle of weeds.

It was that time in the morning when her yard caught the pale April sunlight. She fetched the package from indoors and sat down on the rickety wooden chair to open it. It was a book, she could tell that much (the only other possibility was a box of chocolates, which was supremely unlikely), but the address was written in capitals so there was no clue as to the sender.

The book was a novel in proof form. 'No Doubt', by P J Moynihan. For a moment she was baffled and then it came to her.

Paddy!

She turned the book over in her hands. Cautiously, because now it *did* feel like a bomb.

Inside the cover was a letter from Devon and Green, publishers – or at least from someone called Millie Postgate, Editor – the gist of which was that they were delighted to be publishing this, P. J. Moynihan's brilliant debut novel, and hoped that Gwen would be as wildly enthusiastic as they were. So they were palming him off as a newcomer, courtesy of the cryptic 'P. J.'.

This was accompanied by a postcard from Paddy. The picture was a sepia print of a tattooed lady. On the back, he'd written a short note.

> *Case of if you can't say anything nice, don't bother . . . But be great if you could. How's yours going? Time we compared notes. I.O.U. x P*

So it was '*x P*' was it? Gwen slipped the card back into the folded letter and turned, with trepidation, to the dedication page.

For everyone who helped – you know who you are.

Was that intended as a message? Should she read something into it? Gwen couldn't reconcile the cryptic, almost offhand tone of the dedication and the postcard with the long, torrid evenings of artistic angst and fervent mentoring they had shared. She was shocked to discover that her body was reacting all on its own – her arms in the sunshine had broken out in goose-pimples and the page shook slightly in her fingers. She studied the back cover, which listed the novel's impressive pre-publication credentials: an American deal, a book club edition, film interest (well, maybe . . .) and a four-figure promotional budget. More than Gwen had ever had; she experienced a prickle of jealousy. This being a proof copy there was no author photograph, which was perhaps just as well. But on a second sheet of paper accompanying Millie Postgate's breathless letter there was an author biography, which made inter-esting reading.

> *PJ Moynihan has lived and worked in six countries, from mixing cocktails in Chicago to teaching maths in Swaziland* [he had?] *but his great dream has always been to write, and this is triumphantly realized in this stunning first novel, already short-listed for the Betty Trask Award* [it was?]*, he reached a turning point when he realized that he was becoming one of those people who could spend their whole life talking about writing and not actually doing it. 'The day I moved out of my comfort zone was the day I started seriously to write,' he says. 'The group I was part of were great people but I had to leave the nest to learn if I would fall or fly.'*

Gwen had thought that the manner of Paddy's leaving was the most painful thing she'd ever experienced. Now she realized that had been nothing. This was far, far worse. This put her in her place – sidelined, and parked. She was nauseous with humilia-tion. In a couple of lines he had dismissed those intense, hot evenings as part of his 'comfort zone' and herself as one of the 'great people' – by which he meant not great at all. 'Nice' was what he meant; he was damning with faint praise.

All the exhilaration, the positivity that had buoyed her up on her return from the shelter were gone. She felt only a leaden, miserable anger. The same yard that had so lifted her spirits a few moments ago was back to being a depressing shambles, as always. Huggy, legs braced and tail kinked, was crapping in the corner.

'Fuck off!'

She threw Paddy's book at him, and missed, but the cat yowled and disappeared over the end wall in two scrabbling leaps. Jealousy was an undignified emotion and she despised herself for feeling it. She pressed her hands to her face and tried to gather herself. After about a minute she got up and retrieved the book, using a handful of grass to wipe the suspect stain off the cover. She supposed, since her opinion had been invited, she would have to read it. On the other hand, what had he said? *Case of if you can't say anything nice, don't bother.* Well that was plain enough. If she hated it, or couldn't bring herself to read it, her silence would speak for her. But it wasn't as easy as that. In the unlikely event that she was overwhelmed with admiration, wouldn't that be even more difficult? The words of praise would stick in her throat and choke her, the awful jealousy would paralyse her fingers and she would be unable to write.

On the other hand, curiosity was creeping through her veins like a strong drug, gradually transcending every other emotion.

She turned to the first page and began to read.

Marian had been given the job of table-monitor (the school expression was her own; it seemed right). After Della, to whom, as chairman, it naturally fell to be greeter-in-chief at the main door, she was the one with the best interpersonal skills. Marian may not have had Juanita's vivacity or Della's elegant charm, but she was sensible and calm, and could be relied upon to smooth things over when a late-arriving group of five found that they could not sit together. Twelve years as a legal secretary, the first line of defence in dealing with her employers' agitated clients, had taught her that there was no advantage in pointing out the bleeding obvious – in this case that when seats weren't allocated such a situation was likely to arise – and everything to be gained by a quietly sympathetic 'Oh-dear-right-let's-see-what-we-can-do' approach. Today, because of the unusually large numbers at the lunch, her diplomatic and managerial skills had already been stretched to the full, and Anthony Chance had not even arrived yet. Earlier, before the doors opened, Juanita had swung by with a directive concerning Penny, who apparently was 'very fragile, in a dreadful state', which prompted the (unasked) question, why was Penny here at all? Marian had seen her come into the barn with Della at her side, arms linked, Della wearing the warm, bright look of the designated comforter.

That was a role Marian was relieved not to have to undertake today. She could just about fake sympathy for the vexed late arrivals, but providing a shoulder for Penny's tears would have been beyond her.

The woman who had answered the phone in Dennis's flat was called Ruth. Dennis told Marian that when they met for a curry a couple of weeks later.

'I gather you spoke to Ruth.'

'Sorry?' She smiled in pretend puzzlement. 'Ruth who?'

'When you rang the other day. Ruth Martin, she's a new guide on some of our literary walking tours.'

'Ah.'

Marian had asked questions of a non-personal nature. She wasn't interested in the answers, but straightforward information kept things on solid ground.

'So what is she mainly, a walker, or a lecturer?'

'Her background is academic, but she's always been quite a serious hiker.'

'Good combination.'

'Yes, I was lucky to get her, she's perfect for us.'

'Where—' She was about to ask where Ruth did the guided tours, but Dennis cut her off.

'We're getting married.'

He picked up his glass as he said this, and looked at her over the top of it as he took a swig.

'Good heavens.' She raised hers. 'Congratulations.'

'Thanks.'

She smiled crookedly. 'I thought she sounded very at home in your flat.'

'She doesn't live there,' said Dennis. 'She's got a place of her own in Oxford.'

'But presumably . . .'

'We mix and match at the moment. We may even continue to do so for a bit till we decide on the best base.'

'Good idea.'

Her voice was steady, but he knew her too well; she saw her

feelings reflected on his face. He put his glass down and reached
for her hand, which she moved away by pretending to adjust her
napkin; she didn't want to hurt his feelings.

'I hope,' he said, 'we can still go on getting together like this.'

'Do you?'

'It's important to me. And Ruth's all for it.'

'Really?'

She couldn't keep the sad, misplaced sarcasm out of her voice,
but he ignored it. It was easy for him; he was the happy one.

'Yes. She knows what you mean to me.'

That's big of her, she wanted to say, but managed not to. 'Fine.
Well, we'll see. When's the big day?'

'Next month. And it won't be that big a day; we're too long
in the tooth for any fussation. Just a civil ceremony and lunch
for a few people at her college.'

'Very nice.' Everything she said, however simple, was coming
out with a small stain of bitterness.

'Has—?'

'Marian—'

She'd been going to ask if Ruth had been married before, if
there were children, but they both spoke at once, and said, 'Sorry.'

She flicked a hand. 'You go.'

'Oh, I don't know . . .' He rubbed his face, beginning with the
lower part, chin and mouth, then moving his hand up to massage
his eyes and nose, knead his temples, then over the back of his
head, fingers spread through his hair, ending with a tight squeeze
on the back of his neck. He was giving himself time to think,
time to put on a different face.

'Try,' she said. 'You'll feel better if you do.'

'It's so hard to say anything that you might want to hear.'

'You don't have to. Why would you need to do that?'

'All right, that I might want to express. I suppose it's something like, things change, life moves on, but the changes don't
wipe out what's gone before. History and memory and shared
experience and whatnot, they're all part of the present. *You* are
part of it, and always will be.'

'Good. Yes, thank you, I hope so.'

He tilted his head. 'And vice versa, naturally.'

'Yes, of course.'

'After all, we have Ros, and Lucy-Anne, our family.'

Something practical and relevant occurred to her. 'Do they know?'

'I told Ros about Ruth, but she doesn't know we're getting married. I wanted you to be the first to know. I'll call her later on or tomorrow.'

'Thank you,' said Marian. 'So when did you talk to her about Ruth, then?'

'Over the past few weeks. She asks sometimes.'

'Asks?'

'Whether I'm seeing anyone. So obviously, the last time she asked, I said that I was.'

Marian nodded. 'Right.'

Ros hadn't quite asked her that question, but she had asked, 'So, you and Dad still seeing each other?' Marian had always believed that was an enquiry expecting, and hoping for, the answer 'Yes'. In the light of Dennis's revelation it looked like the opposite. 'Still seeing Dad?' *Same old same old.*

'Did she seem pleased?'

'Let's see . . .' Dennis closed his eyes for an instant, trying to get it right. 'She sounded positive. Not as much as pleased but a bit more than just accepting.'

'She didn't mention it to me.'

'It wasn't her business to.'

'Did you tell her not to?'

'No. I didn't have to. We're very lucky in our daughter. She loves us and she's protective of us. She knows we care about each other, and we'll do the right thing.'

'Yes.' Marian knew it was true, and it was a nice thing for him to have said. But it was all too much – too much niceness, too much reasonableness and modernity. More grown-up than she could currently manage.

'She's a complete star, actually,' added Dennis, and for the first time he was unable to keep the adoration in check; she heard it in his voice. As a result her own voice came out thin and dry, devoid of any feeling at all.

'I'm sure she is, but Dennis – please tell her soon, tonight if you can, when you get in. And say we've had this conversation.'

'Of course I will.'

'I want to be in the loop.'

'You always have been. Anyway, what loop? There is no loop.' He waved a hand dismissively, and then laughed. 'Now then, remind me when you go to the States?'

After that, conversation had reverted to normal, superficially anyway, but on the drive home she subjected the evening to intensive mental scrutiny, and found herself lacking. This had been her opportunity to show that she had moved on, to display the maturity and generosity of spirit on which other people, seeing how things were with her and Dennis, complimented them. She had done neither. So far from being mature, she'd behaved like a touchy teenager, and as for moving on, well – Dennis certainly had, but her own reaction had been that of a woman with one foot firmly planted in the past.

At home she went straight to bed and lay in the dark with her arms folded, staring at the ceiling, fretting. Of course you could say that it was easy for Dennis to be grown-up and magnanimous – he'd found someone else, his eyes were on a new and different horizon. Whatever he said about continuing as they were (and Ruth's gracious endorsement of the plan), she herself was now part of the furniture of his past. But for God's sake – she rolled on to her side with a flounce – was she honestly saying that she needed a man to complete her, to affirm her own identity, to enable her to get on with her life? How sad was that?

She remained awake for a long time, unable to drop off and feeling alternately furious and melancholy. The phrase 'letting go' was usually applied to children, but it appeared she had difficulty letting go of her ex. She had wilfully mistaken their continuing friendship as a kind of immunization against other relationships, when of course it had been nothing of the sort: Ruth's arrival proved that. She'd seen in Dennis's face, and heard in his voice, the brilliant flashes of light and heat he'd been unable to conceal and which put her so utterly in her place.

Chewing away on the bone of misery she went back and back . . . Had Dennis looked and sounded like that, to other people, when they were first together? Had she? What had she actually felt for him, and he for her? They'd been terribly young and green, unthinkingly conventional. They'd thought to get wed, and then get on with their lives. Marriage had not, she realized, been treated as an adventure, or a challenge, but a box to be ticked. And ticked it had been – wedding, flat, house, progress, baby, second house (and car), a period of dinner parties and carefully chosen holidays . . . And then there had come that stage of gradual subsidence from contentment to complacency, to anxious boredom (is this it then?), to a gradual acceptance that they no longer had the right stuff, if they'd ever had it at all, and trepidation, always unspoken, about the future. It became a case, as she recalled, of who would blink first – who would do the unthinkable and say what they both knew had to be said.

And – no excuses – it had been her! Marian grimaced and shook her head in the dark. She it was who had found the courage to spit it out.

'We can't carry on like this,' she said when they were clearing up after her parents had been to Sunday lunch. It was a statement open to several interpretations, but Dennis had understood at once.

'No,' he said, 'you're quite right, we can't.'

His answer came quick as a flash, in a hot rush, an orgasm of relief. Shocked, her bluff called, she'd crashed on as if more needed to be said, as if she had to explain, whereas she was scrabbling wildly to regain a foothold on the slippery slope.

'This isn't how it's meant to be.'

'I agree.'

He was wiping the table mats, she was putting plates in the machine, but at this point they stopped and stared at each other

'So what are we going to do?' she asked.

'First of all . . .' He held his hand out. 'We're going to take a deep breath and sit down.'

She'd put her hand in his like a trusting child and he led her through to the living room with its Sunday papers and dishes of crisp crumbs. There was still chamber music trickling from the radio, and Dennis turned it off. That in itself was weird, like undoing a safety belt.

They sat down on the big three-seater sofa, she at one end, Dennis in the middle but forwards, turned slightly towards her with his arms resting on his knees. A completely different body language, physically close but new, strange. Marian had a dizzying sense of unreality – had the whole world really changed, in a minute? This was the same sofa where they'd snogged, had sex, rowed, discussed money and parenthood, where she'd fed Ros and nattered to friends – and now, she thought, they were about to separate on it. Dennis's eyes were fixed on her with an expression that was both troubled and sympathetic. She wanted him further away, less in her face, but didn't want to say so and instead she shrank back into her corner, holding a cushion on her lap like a shield.

'You're right,' he said again. 'You and I deserve more.'

'Do we?' she asked. 'What would that be?'

He ignored her sarcasm. 'The trouble is not that we're unsorted, but that we're too sorted. We could go on indefinitely – but not like this. You said it, Marian.'

She had. Now she realized that she'd half hoped he would deny it, brush her remark aside, save the day, restore normality. She'd have accepted that, the anxiety and emptiness would have become only her problem, not theirs.

He'd put his arms round her and said: 'You know what I think?'

'What?' she'd muttered, stiffly, into his shoulder.

'We need to let it go.'

Marian remembered thinking that those words made it sound as if they were releasing something into the wild, which in a way they had been.

That was five years ago. Dennis had certainly embraced the challenge. The worst thing had been telling their parents, and Ros, who had only just gone to the States and whose response over the phone had been a robust: 'No way!' Which, oddly, had served to make them more robust, too. They were the grown-ups; she was their child. They had to display confidence in their own decision, and to give good reasons for it – hard, when they were so clearly not enemies, and there was no-one else.

'Has Dad been fooling around?' Ros asked.

'No.'

'Not as far as you know.'

'No. And neither have I.'

'So, what are you saying? That it's never been right?'

'No,' said Marian, because this was neither the time nor the place to admit uncertainty. 'Just that it's not been right for a while and we both know it.'

So gradually the fabric had been stretched, the fibres picked apart and the last firm, final pull administered in the court with neither of them present.

Once she'd got over the sadness of a chapter ended, Marian had not just adjusted but had been perfectly happy. Odd, she thought now, that one said 'perfectly happy' as meaning less than perfect happiness. She had good friends (among whom she still numbered Dennis) and a job she enjoyed, and had not pined for married life, especially as she and Dennis saw each other regularly. Ros had forgiven them and they had gone to the States together to attend her sunny, informal garden barbecue wedding to Jay. They had considered themselves lucky; Jay's nice father was not long widowed, and the day had been an ordeal for him. Marian was so content she even found herself asking whether she had ever been suited to marriage. The attractions of being answerable to no-one (not that Dennis had been a demanding husband, quite the opposite), with one's own place, and plans, were considerable. That was one of the reasons she so hotly resented her brother's pompous, well-meaning interference.

But now this.

Juanita bobbed up in front of her.

'He's here!' she exclaimed excitedly. 'Sir Anthony Chance is here!'

Nine

Once she'd handed Uncle Tony over to the organizers, Madeleine submerged herself in the chattering anonymity of the Tithe Barn. There was no problem locating a single space and once she'd laid her hands on a glass of white she claimed a seat at a table in the centre of the room. Some people were still milling about with drinks, others had already sat down. The decibel level was rising, the excitement tangible. Madeleine began to realize that her relationship with the speaker was going to be her trump card, if one were needed.

An MC in hunting pink appeared at the end of the top table and applied three measured strokes of the gavel.

'Ladies and gentlemen!' Madeleine glanced round. Oh yes, there were quite a few men, two of them at her table. 'Pray be upstanding for your top table and honoured guests!'

Rhythmic handclapping accompanied the procession. A couple of the women she'd seen at the door, the mayor and lady mayoress, Uncle Tony and four others. Standing behind his chair waiting for grace, Uncle Tony bathed the room in his charming, perspicacious, curious smile, for all the world as if this was the most remarkable, intriguing, delightful occasion he had ever had the pleasure of attending.

The MC besought silence for the lady chairman of the Marie Crompton Luncheon Club, who would say grace. The Lord was duly thanked in advance for 'the blessing of friends, the privilege of fellowship and the pleasure of good food' and they all sat down to a first course of crayfish tails in Marie Rose sauce on frisee lettuce.

At the top table, as his glass was filled, Sir Anthony turned first to the lady chairman, and began to talk animatedly. Programmed for social politeness, Madeleine too turned to the person sitting next to her, and said: 'I've been admiring that beautiful top you're wearing. Where did you find it?'

'I had it made,' said Rhada.

'The colour is absolutely glorious. Such a clever way to wear a black suit.'

'Thank you.'

'Who did it for you? I shall quite understand if you want to keep it a secret.'

Rhada was used to receiving compliments about her clothes, especially when they had an Indian twist. She smiled, and opened one side of her jacket to reveal the bright, toning lining.

'Oh my God!' cried her neighbour. 'How brilliant is that!'

'Now you see why I'm not going to tell you who she is.'

'I so do! You keep it to yourself – I would. But anyway, I can tell you who I am – Madeleine Kingshott.' She tapped her fingers to her chest. 'Maddie.'

'Hello Maddie.' Rhada extended a formal hand. 'Rhada Vashkar.'

They shook a little awkwardly, wrists bent, because they were close together. 'Tell me, Rhada, have you been to these lunches before?'

'I have. Most of them, actually. Although today of course is special.'

'Mm . . .' Maddie picked up her fork. 'This looks tempting, in fact really nice – oh, you haven't got anything.'

'It's coming,' said Rhada. 'I'm Hindu.'

Maddie put the fork down again. 'Let's hope the vegetarian is as nice. Here it comes.'

A tomato and couscous salad was placed in front of Rhada. Maddie peered at it.

'On a scale of one to ten – how dull, do you think?'

Rhada had to smile. 'I'm sure it will be delicious.'

'You're so polite,' said Maddie, loading her fork. 'It's funny, veggies rule the world these days, *except* at catered functions where they draw the short straw every time.'

Rhada popped in a small mouthful. 'Very good, actually.' She turned to the person on her left, one of the few men present. 'I wonder, could I ask you to pass the salt and pepper?'

'Of course.' He set them in front of her. 'How do you do, I'm Geoffrey Leach.'

'Rhada Vashkar.'

'Rhada . . .' A smile dawned on his pleasant, round face. 'Do you know I thought it might be . . . not *the* Rhada?'

'I've no idea,' she said cautiously, forking through the couscous. 'I suppose I might be.'

'Do you know someone called Colin Goodyear?'

'Colin – of course,' said Rhada smoothly with a hint of amusement; worldly wise and worldly warm. 'You know him too?'

'Just a bit! Since school.' He made a gesture towards the other side of the table. 'My wife, Rosemary, by the way.'

Rosemary was deep in conversation, but must have heard her name, because she flashed a quick smile in their direction.

Rhada said, 'Congratulations. Not many people manage to nurture friends from schooldays, especially men.'

Geoffrey shook his head. 'We haven't been in touch continuously, don't run away with that idea. It just so happened that we came down to this part of the world five years ago, I saw the name on a van in Bishop's Few, and thought, you never know . . . So I rang the number and we picked up where we left off.'

'Good for you,' she said, moulding her couscous into a neat pile, flattening at the top. 'Well . . .'

'Still remarkably unchanged,' went on Geoffrey. 'I'd have recognized him instantly, anywhere.' He chuckled. 'But then he's not been subjected to the wear and tear of family life.'

'No?' Rhada glanced covertly at Maddie, but she was turned in the other direction and unavailable. She altered her tone to one of fresh, bright enquiry. 'Tell me, do you . . .?'

'He speaks warmly of you.' It wasn't so much that he interrupted but that he was unaffectedly delighted with this particular coincidence and couldn't let it go. 'I'd go so far as to call it a crush.'

'Good heavens.'

He pulled a mock-apologetic face. 'I hope I haven't put my foot in it.'

'Not at all, I'm flattered.'

'Rosemary'd tear me off a major strip for that one.'

She waved a hand. 'Forget it.'

He did, at once, and bounced back. 'Anyway, how did you two meet?'

If Rhada had not minded the first remark, she did not care

for this question with its implied significance, and replied crisply: 'I do the accounts for Goodyear's.'

'Rhada! You have single-handedly rehabilitated the image of accountants, in this man's eyes at least.'

That old chestnut. She said nothing; her smile was as small as she could make it without appearing rude.

'So,' she said firmly, 'where were you before you came down here, and what brought you to this part of the world?'

He began to tell her in his affable, rambling way and, prompted by Rhada's practised conversational nudges, the Leaches' story kept them going well into the noisettes of lamb.

Della was bowled over. She had expected Sir Anthony to be interesting, and to have nice manners (probably – politeness was by no means a given with public figures), but not that he would be so charming, and in a different way from how he appeared on television. He was easy, amusing, self-deprecating, even slightly – it was the only word for it – boyish. He made her feel as though with her he was able to let the professional mask slip, or discard it altogether. He did indeed, as she'd hoped, exclaim in wonder at the Tithe Barn and the elegance of Della's *mise en scène*, and even lowered his voice to ask, as they sat down after grace: 'So many people, Della. What on earth did you say to them?'

She opened one hand in a simple gesture. 'We told them you'd be coming.'

'How wonderful – astonishing. You have done extraordinarily well. I'm deeply flattered.'

'But surely . . .' She folded and speared a piece of lettuce with her fork. 'You must be very used to all this.'

'Mmm.' He mused. 'It's true I'm lucky enough to get about a good deal, but this is such a treat for me. Such a beautiful part of England.'

'It is. And full of history. This house is in Pevsner.'

'And in the Domesday Book. Or at least the old house and the family who lived in it.'

'I didn't know that.'

She may have sounded a little crestfallen, because he said at once, 'Neither did I until I mugged up on it on the train.'

She laughed – he was so nice! – and said, 'The present owner is married to an American – she's done wonders for the place, without spoiling it at all. The costs of running a historic old house like this must be frightening; they have to do something, but it's hard to get the balance right, and I think they have.'

Sir Anthony glanced around. 'Are they here?'

'No, but Belle's slipping in later to hear you speak.'

'You must introduce me.'

'I will, of course.'

'How delightful this all is,' he said again. 'And what a good hostess you are.'

Della blushed like a rose.

Tony had spotted Maddie amid the throng, sitting next to an attractive young Asian woman. They made a striking pair – Maddie fresh, fair, open-faced, the model of English country breeding; the other dark, cool and impeccably elegant, a little haughty, perhaps? But though they were now turned away from each other he had seen them chatting agreeably, so the hauteur was purely a question of looks.

The main course of herb-encrusted lamb arrived, with gently wilted spinach and new potatoes gleaming with butter and freckled with snipped parsley and chives. Oh, and fresh mint sauce served in small, individual white china jugs. Tempting; he could almost taste how good it was going to be. When the soignée chairwoman encouraged him to start, he needed no second bidding. As he did so, and she began to expatiate on the day's good cause he realized, almost to his own surprise, that he felt every bit as glad to be here as he professed himself to be. This occasion felt less like a duty or a task and more like a jaunt – a spree! He had come here against the advice of others, he was taking the weekend, staying with the closest thing he had to family. *I'm bunking off*, he thought, *that's what I'm doing, and I'm going to enjoy myself.* And before him were spread, like a field of flowers an audience, mostly ladies, from whom the warmth and good humour rose in waves like the scent of honeysuckle. Every so often when he scanned the room he caught someone's eye, and there was a split second's shiny flirtatiousness. But nothing overt or trying; these were nice people with nice manners.

This was, he anticipated, going to give him great pleasure.

★   ★   ★

Juanita glanced across at Murray. She was pleased that he was one of the few men present, and proud of him for coming. His attendance went some way towards rectifying the balance regarding the Figes and their dancing: Brian Figes was not here. Also – and she often thought this when she watched Murray at a distance, with other people – her husband was handsome. He was every inch a real man, broad shoulders, curly hair, a winning smile, pretty much the same waistline he'd had on their wedding day, thanks to rugby and cricket. Harmony had come back from school one day and told her that Leanne's mum had said Murray was 'cute' and that Juanita had 'done all right there'. She knew it was true, and also knew that much of the time she took him for granted. Now he felt her looking at him and grinned. She sent a little frown back, not a serious one, but one that told him to pay attention to his neighbour.

Juanita liked to be busy. Her liveliness and energy were what had first attracted Murray, he'd told her so. These days he mentioned it with pride to other people; for instance when some new project or enterprise was mooted, he'd say: 'For God's sake don't tell Jan about it, she'll be running the damn thing and I'll need an appointment to see her!'

He was the only one who called her Jan. It was a sort of term of endearment.

'I knew this place needed a kick up the backside,' he'd say. 'That's why I brought her along.'

People always laughed and she'd join in, taking it as the compliment she understood it to be. But just occasionally she thought (or more likely imagined) that she detected a trace of something that wasn't pride, even teasing pride – the hint of a tone that invited mockery rather than admiration. She knew she stood in danger of becoming that cliché, the Madly Busy Woman, running everything, joining in, never still, seeking approbation everywhere but at home. Except that Murray encouraged her and was proud of her, most of the time . . .

At the moment Juanita was slightly light-headed with the early start, the adrenalin and two glasses of wine. She was the filling in a sort of conversational sandwich as the women on either side of her discussed Bus or Bust. The casual observer would have said that she was paying close attention, involved if not vocal, nodding and watching, gazing thoughtfully at her plate as if weighing up the arguments. But actually she was on autopilot, her mind drifting off on its own currents.

Meals were the thing. Food – its purchase, preparation and consumption – had always been the Wades' marital barometer. The cooking and sharing of nice suppers, with or without Harmony, who had become a picky eater, was what told them that all was well. Looking at each other across the table, something tasty in front of them, wine glasses in their hands, they reminded themselves of who they were in relation to each other. Murray told her about his work and the various (often difficult) people he had to deal with; she told him about the comings and goings at the health centre, when she'd been there, or about her various local causes, organizations and activities. The great thing was that being a busy person gave you something to talk about. She firmly believed it was essential for married people to have full and fulfilling lives independent of each other. That was what kept the spark alive. She glanced again at Murray who was refreshing his glass from the communal Semillon. A pity about the dancing, but you couldn't have everything . . .

'Still got your bicycle?' asked the woman on her right.

'I have,' said Juanita, 'and I can still get round the village loop!'

'What about your husband?' asked the other woman. 'Do you get him into Lycra?'

'Not as often as I'd like,' replied Juanita, and was rewarded with an appreciative chuckle.

The pudding was peaches filled with ratafias and baked with brown sugar and Amaretto, with a delicate swirl of whipped cream. Light, pretty and refreshing, Della had said to the committee in urging them to go this route – there had been one or two in favour of something more showy and substantial, but she had won them round.

'Do you know,' said Sir Anthony, savouring his with his eyes as it was placed before him, 'I don't usually do puddings but this is so attractive I shall sit here and admire it, and who knows?'

'Actually,' said Della, 'I make this at home from time to time, so I can vouch for it.'

'In that case . . .' He lifted his spoon.

'Do you like to cook?' she asked. 'When you get the time?'

'Mm . . .' He shook his head as he finished the mouthful. 'I don't know – I mean I don't know if I'd like it because I never do it. A pretty dreadful admission in this day and age and one I'm not proud to make. Living in London and on your own you become the most frightful eater-out. Which is lazy, and not good for the waistline.'

'Oh for heaven's sake.' Della slid an appreciative glance at his trim midriff. 'So what sort of cuisine do you like? What would be your desert island dish?'

'Peking duck,' replied Sir Anthony without hesitation. 'Very crisp, plenty of Hoisin sauce. But this,' he added, 'is the opposite of a desert island.'

When the comfort break was called, Murray made a trip to the Gents, for a change of scene as much as anything. He had come to support his tireless wife, and (if he was honest this was the real reason) because he was curious about the speaker. Whatever his own reservations he acknowledged that Juanita had done well to net Chance, who was one of the big media beasts and had drawn a correspondingly large crowd. They were going to do well out of this little do.

There were very few men present so, unlike the Ladies (he would imagine), the Gents presented an oasis of space and tranquillity. The drawback was that when, as Murray was washing his hands, Chance himself came in, Murray felt rather exposed and obliged to say: 'Hi there.'

'How do you do.'

'Thanks for coming; I'm looking forward to your talk.'

'I am too. Let's hope it does the trick.'

This struck Murray as an odd thing to say in the circumstances. 'Is there a trick?'

'I mean I'm honestly not sure what I'm going to say. I have ideas, but . . .' Chance made a twirling gesture in the air by his head. 'Who knows?'

'You're very cool.'

Chance gave a rueful laugh. 'If that's the impression it's a false one.'

'Good luck. Murray Wade, by the way.'

They shook hands. 'That sounds familiar – you're not connected to the lady with the Spanish name who first wrote to me?'

'That's my wife. Juanita.'

'Juanita. Is she in fact Spanish?'

'No, but her mother liked flamenco.'

'Do you know . . .' Chance leaned back on the wash basin with his arms folded. 'I have the greatest admiration for the people who organize these events. The energy and commitment, the fantastic attention to detail. It never fails to impress me. Move me, if I'm truthful.'

'Really?' Murray was gobsmacked and a little embarrassed but tried not to show it. 'They do work hard.'

'You must be proud of your Juanita.'

'Well yes – I am.'

'Lucky man.'

Chance kept his eyes on Murray throughout this exchange, with a gentle smile as if encouraging Murray to unburden himself. And for a moment there was a distinct possibility that Murray would do so – though unburden himself of what, he wasn't quite sure. Anything, really. He and Chance could have stood there and exchanged confidences like a couple of girls in the room next door. But then another chap came in and Chance raised a hand and said, 'Nice to meet you, Murray. I expect I shall see you later.'

Murray returned to his table and sat down. Coffee had been poured in his absence, and his was as he liked it, with the merest dash of milk. Two chocolates in gold paper cups sat on his side plate – that would be his and Juanita's, as she foreswore chocolate in the interest of her hips.

He looked across at her. He didn't know what she worried about, he liked her hips. He liked her bust, too, and all her sturdy, exuberant curves – the whole package. She was a gorgeous woman sitting over there, wearing the bright colour he liked, that showed off her dark hair. There was too much black about.

Sir Anthony Chance was sitting with his chair pushed back a bit, one arm hooked over the back, affable and relaxed, waiting for his cue. Della Figes, of whom Juanita was slightly in awe, was adjusting her notes, glasses on the end of her nose. The big moment was at hand.

Murray popped in a chocolate, and stirred his coffee. There would be no big moment if it weren't for Juanita. His wife, the do-er. The life and soul. She did so much and so willingly it would be too easy for him to fall into the role of licensed slacker. And he wasn't a slacker, licensed or otherwise.

Della Figes rose to her feet, and the sharp rap of the gavel cut across an audible wave of excited anticipation, as chairs were adjusted and faces turned, like sunflowers to the sun.

Ten

It was four o'clock when Gwen finished reading Paddy's novel. She closed it, slowly and carefully, laid it on her lap and sat there with her hands folded on top of it like a Victorian schoolgirl with a prayer book.

Damn.

There was no escaping the fact that it was rather good. She had been not just curious but gripped. She glanced at her watch – four hours had slipped by, and she had missed the Golden Anniversary Lunch. Even allowing for her stated ambivalence about the event and the speaker, that wasn't good. She had always intended to show up, but Paddy's writing had kept her where she was. The committee could not be expected to understand that, but what greater compliment could there be for a novelist?

Damn. Damn.

She remained motionless, trying to unpick her reactions. The raging jealousy had subsided, to be replaced by something more complicated. She was not so daft, nor so mean, that she wanted to deny Paddy's talent. There was no doubt that he had re-invented himself, and become not just a proper, professional writer, but a really original voice. Gone was the one-hit wonder who she had reassured and nurtured and taken into herself as if she were the fount of all inspiration. In its place on her lap was a sharp, self-confident, compelling writer in control of his very considerable powers and perfectly attuned to the zeitgeist. What she had just read was high-quality commercial fiction.

Oh, damn.

All this thinking about Paddy made Gwen shift restlessly in her seat. The sex had been incredible! But now she asked herself: How much had that had to do with the peculiar imbalance of their relationship at the time? She wondered whether he had changed, if his looks or behaviour had been tainted by success. Had her angry, troubled, passionate boy been replaced with a swaggering publisher's favourite? It was too awful to contemplate.

Whatever the case, she had now to decide what, if anything, she was going to say. It was flattering to be asked for her endorsement, and she had certainly not been prepared for the flare of lust – that was the only word for it – occasioned by his scribbled note.

She was still sitting there when the phone rang, and she let it ring out.

Della escorted Sir Anthony to the door of the main house. They were accompanied by Belle Martleby, the American chatelaine of Polsworth, about whom Della had to stifle an unworthy surge of resentment. Belle was groomed, glamorous and the mistress of the house, but she had done nothing towards the day's proceedings except bank the cheque for the Tithe Barn. Della had introduced her to Sir Anthony as promised but now she had a sense of being finessed aside, and her rightful position usurped.

Still, nothing – *nothing* – could tarnish the shiny perfection of the day. It had been a success beyond their wildest dreams, and in a way that neither Della nor any of the committee could have foreseen. Sir Anthony had torn up his cue cards right there in front of everyone, and had *confided* in them. They were enchanted; you could have heard a pin drop. And when he finished there had been that moment of silence before the great crashing wave of applause.

'There she is,' he said now, 'my lovely chauffeuse.'

'Oh, but it's Maddie!' cried Belle, advancing across the gravel. 'Hey, sweetie, I didn't know you were here . . .'

Della and Sir Anthony stood in the doorway.

He sighed, and turned to her regretfully. 'I suppose,' he said, 'that we must say good-bye. Though I really don't want to.'

'Oh, Sir Anthony . . .' Alarmingly, Della's eyes prickled with tears. 'I can't thank you enough. It's been quite wonderful. Memorable. We are so, so grateful.'

Belle and Madeleine were walking back towards them.

'I am summoned,' said Sir Anthony mournfully.

'Looks like it.'

'*Au revoir* then, Della.' He held her shoulders gently and kissed her, lightly but quite tenderly, on either cheek. 'I wish you well in all that you do.'

She stood there, incandescent, as he put one arm round his

goddaughter and shook Belle's hand briskly, with some appreciative words. Then it was into the Range Rover and off, his smiling
face at the open window sweeping past as the car turned and
was away, disappearing down the long drive. Groups of exhilarated
guests, lingering in the afterglow, also waved, as if bidding farewell
to a friend. They all felt that they knew him, Della realized, and
that it was their special privilege to do so.

'Well!' said Belle. 'What an utterly charming man!'

'Isn't he?'

'And his talk – was there a single dry eye?'

'Probably not.'

They went back into the hall. Before leaving (she had a meeting
of the parole board) Belle said, 'That thing of tearing up the notes
– could that be a trick? I wonder if he does it every time.'

At that moment Della hated her. She was glad they both had
to dash off in opposite directions. In the Tithe Barn the clearing-
up operation was well under way, but Rhada and Marian were
sitting at the end of the top table with a last cup of coffee and
she went to join them.

'Hail the conquering hero!' said Marian, pouring her a cup.

'Juanita and Murray just left, and Penny went ages ago,' explained
Rhada. 'And before you ask, Juanita called Gwen, and it appears
she got tied up at the hostel.'

'No surprises there, then,' said Marian. 'But anyway, what a
triumph. Don't take this the wrong way, Della, but he was so
much more impressive than I expected. We were all blown away.'

'Good,' said Della, who felt suddenly drained.

'I sat next to his goddaughter,' said Rhada, 'and even she was
surprised.'

'In a good way, I hope?'

'Very much so! She said she'd seen a whole side of Uncle
Tony, as she called him, which she didn't know existed.'

Della didn't drink her coffee. More caffeine on top of this
empty feeling would stir up her stomach. Her mobile phone
bleeped and it was a text from Brian – she used the opportunity to move away, and the others took the hint and allowed their
cups to be cleared.

The text said: *How did it go? Been thinking of you. Hope AC did
his stuff and you made a packet. C u later. xB.*

She pressed Reply, but found that she couldn't find the right words. Perhaps this evening when they were sitting down together she'd be able to convey to Brian quite how special it had been, but for now she could only manage: *Excellent, grt success. xxD*

She put the phone back in her bag. On the table next to where she was standing was a collection of rubbish, waiting to be scraped into a bin bag as the waitress bundled up the table-cloths: chocolate papers, menus, name cards – and Sir Anthony's notes, neatly torn into fours. Della checked that no-one was looking, picked up a handful of the torn notes and popped them into her handbag.

The moment she got in, Penny went upstairs and changed into her cotton drawstring trousers, a big shirt and flip-flops. The shirt was an old one of Graham's, but fresh out of the wash; wearing it felt subversive rather than sad. A thump of music from Nathan's room indicated that he was in there; the other two appeared to be out. She tapped on the door.

'Nathan! Nathan?' She knocked more heavily. 'Nathan!'

The thumping was turned down. 'Yeah?'

'I'm back!'

'Hi.'

'Want a brew?'

'No thanks, got one.'

'Do you know where the others are?'

'Sorry.'

'Okay.'

Downstairs she picked up the phone and dialled Graham's mobile.

This is the mobile of Graham Proctor. Please leave a message after the bleep and I'll get back to you.

'Graham, this is me,' she said. 'There's no need to call back. I want us to have that talk as soon as possible.'

The moment she put the phone down she burst into tears, mopping her eyes with his shirt, on which she could now, she thought, detect a trace of his scent, in spite of the washing. When the squall subsided she picked up the phone again and dialled Sam's number.

'Hello?'

'Sam, it's Penny.'

'Oh, hello.'

Penny suddenly, terribly, wished she hadn't rung, but it was too late now. 'I was calling about the tickets.' There was silence on the other end. 'Going to that show you mentioned?'

'Got it.'

'Well – just that I'd be up for that. Pretty much any Friday or Saturday. If you want to go ahead and book.'

'Wow,' said Sam. 'I don't know . . . The trouble is, you didn't seem too keen, and I've been kind of overtaken by events . . . I'm completely snowed under.'

'Never mind,' said Penny.

'No, I'm really sorry, I just . . .'

'It's okay. There's always a next time.'

'Let's speak again soon.'

'Of course. Bye Sam. '

'Byee.'

Penny was still sitting there, thinking the unthinkable, as Nathan came flopping down the stairs. His jeans were slung so low he was walking on the hems, and what should have been the waist-band revealed the elastic of his faux Tommy Hilfiger boxers.

'Changed my mind,' he said. 'Think I'll have that brew.' He looked at her as he filled the kettle. 'Thought you'd been out somewhere.'

'I did.'

'Good time?'

'It was all right.'

'Cool.' Nathan cast around. 'Got any of that cake left?'

Penny watched numbly as he raided the tin, showered crumbs, and splashed water into the kettle. He shot her a glance.

'You okay?'

'I'm fine.'

'You look knackered,' he said cheerfully. 'Any chance of a lift later?'

Geoffrey caught up with Rhada in the car park.

'What a smashing car.'

'Thank you.'

'I've noticed it's the women who have the sporty cars these days. Must be what they mean by girl power.'

Rhada smiled. 'It was nice meeting you.'

'A real pleasure. I can't wait to tell Colin. He's away at the moment.'

Rhada didn't reply, and Geoffrey continued: 'I couldn't stand to go on holiday on my own, but it doesn't bother him. He likes it. He's so self-sufficient. As a matter of fact I admire that.'

He seemed to be waiting for her endorsement, but she didn't give it. 'Good-bye Geoffrey.'

'Bye then, it was really nice meeting you.'

It was only when she was behind the wheel that Rhada realized how tense her jaw was – she had actually been speaking through gritted teeth, something you saw described in novels but which she hadn't thought possible till now. She didn't relax completely until she saw Geoffrey, whose movements she tracked in the driver's mirror, drive off in his Volvo.

The day, and specifically Sir Anthony's speech, had given her a lot to think about. The passage that rung in her ears was that concerning the solitary state: loneliness, isolation, solitude, and the differences between them. (Self-sufficiency had been in there too, but in the light of her recent exchange with Geoffrey she was temporarily editing that out). She was surprised at how frank the speaker had been about his past – his own loneliness, both as a child and even, from time to time, now. He had made the point – admittedly not a new one, but freshly expressed – that loneliness was an emotion experienced when contrasting oneself to other people who, in their turn, were not, or did not appear to be, lonely. Whereas isolation might or might not be lonely, and solitude was positively desirable if you were so inclined. He said that he had known all three, and that he now lived alone because he recognized that it was what he preferred. Some, he mused aloud, might say that he was missing something, that he had closed the door on certain fundamental human experiences, but while he understood their point of view he did not share it. His was not an incomplete life, but a fully complete, distinct one, peculiar to him. He realized that a great many – the majority, probably – of today's audience led what might generally be considered fuller lives with partners, children and communities in which they were actively involved, and he admired but did not envy them. He was glad they were there, as he put it, 'doing

it for him'. He had several godchildren, he told them – one of
them was here today – and he regarded the role of godfather as
a privilege and, as he put it, 'a treat'. (At this point Rhada had
sent a sidelong glance at Maddie, but she was maintaining an
expression of smiling neutrality.)

Sir Anthony had gone on to speak of diversity. Not just the
cultural and ethnic diversity of which we heard so much, but the
extraordinary diversity of any group of so-called ordinary people.
Take us, here, today, he said, looking around, and they'd all felt
bonded, part of the group and yet, as he said, extraordinary. Even
Rhada had felt that. She prided herself on a degree of detachment,
an ability to remain objective; she was not easily manipulated. But
there had undoubtedly been something about him that was not
simply the 'charisma' (overused word) of the famous or the professional sheen of the public figure. She had been struck by what could
only be called his humility. It had not seemed to be an affectation.
She remembered a show-business expression from somewhere: 'If
you can do sincerity you can do anything'. Had he simply been
'doing sincerity'? Of course she couldn't be completely sure, but
she thought not.

She tipped down the visor and looked at herself in the mirror.
She looked slightly different, in a way that was hard to pinpoint,
as if her face were a jigsaw that had been taken apart and reassem-
bled correctly but not quite firmly enough – it was looser, it
allowed for possibilities . . .

Smartly she flipped up the visor, and started the engine.

At home, Maddie made mugs of tea and brought it out on to
the sheltered terrace by the kitchen door for the two of them.
They sat on frayed wicker chairs with faded cushions; the table
was an old card table covered with a floral-printed oilcloth. She
put the tea down and fetched an open packet of chocolate Bath
Olivers, which she offered to Tony.

'Sorry about the packet. The boys have been at it.'

He took one. 'I don't blame them.'

She sat down and said admiringly, 'You must be knackered.'

'Eating lunch in pleasant company? It takes more than that,
I'm happy to say.'

'Talking for an hour without notes.'

'We all do it, all the time.'

'You know what I mean. Not to over a hundred paying customers.'

'I enjoyed it.'

'That must be why you're so good.'

'How sweet of you.'

Whatever he might say, she thought he did suddenly look a little tired. There was a slight film of introspection about his eyes, and his hands, she noticed, looked older, more tentative.

'Have a bath if you want,' she said. 'There's plenty of hot water.'

'Do you know,' he said, 'I might.'

He had a long, hot bath in the guest bathroom, which, although not en-suite, was right next to his room in one of those funny little truncated corridors that you found in old houses that had not been too radically modernized. Afterwards he put on his dressing gown and sat down in the chair by his bedroom window with a book; not the memoir of a distinguished journalist that he had been sent for review, but a novel taken from the spare room selection thoughtfully provided by Maddie. Somewhat surprisingly it was from the canon of new and vibrant lesbian literature that was currently storming the Booker barricades and of which he thoroughly approved, but his eye kept sliding over the opening paragraph again and again without his brain registering a thing. This was no reflection on the writer. It was quite simply impossible to plunge straight from his own imagination into another's. The *Daily Telegraph* crossword was what he needed, an activity just demanding enough to keep his brain occupied; a perfect way to unwind. He knew it would be in the house somewhere – he'd seen the paper in the drawing room last night – but he did not want to go back downstairs just yet. He put the book on the window sill and gazed out at the smooth green hill beyond the garden.

He had mentioned it in his speech – *'that inward eye that is the bliss of solitude'* – but in his case there were no dancing daffodils to call on. He felt strangely agitated and a little frail. For some reason he couldn't explain, today had taken it out of him. Perhaps it was because, after the trick with the cue cards, which he quite often used, he had gone out on a limb, abandoned the name-dropping anecdotes and talked about deeply personal things. He could not remember the last time he had wept – as a child, perhaps? – but he could very easily have wept now. To counteract this disobliging possibility he forced himself to think of his house in London, and what might be going on there. Clemency would have gone home of course; Lionel would doubtless be out with the dog. His study would be exactly as he left it; he didn't like things moved. There would be messages winking on the telephone, lying dormant in the computer, a few letters from the morning post – the weeks and months ahead being gradually nibbled away. Most of the time he took pleasure in having a full diary for a year ahead, sometimes longer. As well as stimulation there was security in the continuing influx of invitations, requests and commissions. At this moment he could happily have thrown the damn diary away (having shredded it first, of course; Clemency was strict about the need to shred). What he wasn't sure about, and indeed had never till now worried about, was what he would do when the diary was no longer full. He was already past the age when men with a day job retired, and nothing lasted for ever. Diana had the cottage in Henley to which she was already threatening to retreat in the autumn, and her various charitable and artistic committees; the pattern of her life could continue undisturbed well into old age. His own depended on a level of energy that he could not maintain indefinitely. For the first time he felt trepidation about the future.

From somewhere below his window and near the front of the house he heard the crackle of tyres on gravel, the slam of a car door, voices . . . A shout and a burst of laughter . . . Footsteps thundering up the stairs . . . The comings and goings of his god-daughter's busy family life. From where he sat tranquilly in his room with the sunlight on the hill beyond the window, the sounds were soothing. By the standards of his own definitions this afternoon, they provided a framework in which to be pleasingly alone.

Not long after that he fell asleep (something he never did during the day) and was astonished to be woken by a tap on the door – Maddie wondering how he was, and whether he'd be wanting supper.

*   *   *

When she got home, Della went straight to the freezer, took out a tub of her homemade fiorentina sauce and popped it in the microwave to defrost. She never wanted Brian to be on baked beans just because she'd been out for lunch. Then she went upstairs to change, hung up her smart clothes and put her hat in its box. Only when she was sitting at the refectory table with her cup of tea did she open her handbag and take out the torn fragments of Sir Anthony's cue cards.

She spread them on the table and turned them over, one by one, with increasing astonishment, for all of them were blank.

Eleven

When Juanita and Murray got back they found Harmony watching television in the living room. She was wearing threadbare joggers, a Simpsons T-shirt and slipper-socks. The programme was one of those human bear-pits where the desperately disadvantaged aired their grievances for the entertainment of the easily pleased under the calculating eye of a 'concerned' presenter.

'Hi there,' she said when Juanita looked in. 'How did it go?'

'Fabulous,' said Juanita. 'Absolutely brilliant.'

'What was it again?' asked Harmony.

'The luncheon club anniversary.'

Harmony made no comment on this but said, as she swung her legs off the sofa and got up, 'Actually I'm going out.'

'Turn that off, then,' said Juanita. 'Where are you going?'

'Round Maeve's?' There was a question mark, but it wasn't a question.

'Will you be in for dinner?'

'I'll get something at hers.'

Harmony headed for the front door, passing her father on the way.

'Have fun,' he said, and caught Juanita's eye as the door closed. 'Doesn't give much away, does she?'

'No.' Juanita absent-mindedly flicked and plumped the sofa cushions. She sensed a certain change in the air.

'So . . .' Murray perched on the arm of a chair. 'Looks like we're on our own.'

'That's right,' said Juanita. She heeled her shoes off one at a time. 'Ah . . .'

'You must be tired,' said Murray.

'Not really. New shoes, my fault.'

'Then you need a lie-down,' he said lasciviously. 'You did really well, Jan.'

'Thanks.'

'He was a lot better than I expected, too. I don't mind telling you he surprised me.'

'All of us,' she agreed, sitting on the sofa and massaging a foot.

'What's more,' said Murray, 'you've got great legs.'

Juanita laughed. 'Don't be daft. I've got fat legs.'

'No.' He came over and crouched down on the floor, cupping her calf appreciatively. 'Shapely.'

'If you say so . . .'

'I do.'

He lifted her leg and kissed it. 'Mm . . . Good enough to eat.'

His other hand slid up behind Juanita's knee and beneath her skirt.

She touched his head, his curly greying hair that was crisp as a dog's coat. 'Murray . . .'

'What?' He didn't wait for an answer, but scooped up both her legs. 'Why don't you just get comfortable right here on the sofa?'

She did, and he peeled her clothes off with the salivating relish of a man attacking a dozen oysters. It was a double-aspect living room and they hadn't even drawn the curtains. Just before losing the ability to speak, Juanita mentioned this, but Murray simply growled, 'Sod it, who cares . . . Let's make them jealous . . .'

Next morning Tony went for a walk. Accustomed as he was to walking in London, where even in the parks and on the heath there were plenty of people, it felt strange to be marching through the empty countryside, trudging up empty, open hillsides and through rustling woods, and never seeing a soul apart from the odd rabbit. People were coming for dinner this evening, he'd been told, and they were going to a drinks party tomorrow before lunch, so it seemed that a show of independence would be a help to his hosts, and Edmund had outlined this route for him, and given him a small freehand sketch map to help him on his way.

It took him the best part of an hour to get to the top of the hill – there were dips and declivities that you couldn't see from the bottom, which made it a lot further – and when he got there he could tell from his view of the house that this was the very ridge he could see from his bedroom window. He imagined himself sitting in his chair in the window, and seeing his own silhouette against the skyline, and raised an arm in salute – then lowered it again, feeling rather foolish. An enormous bird was wheeling overhead, describing stately circles on the thermals. Townie that he was he couldn't help feeling that it was keeping an eye on him – but of course the bird's eyesight was such that it would be looking for minute prey – voles, shrews and field mice.

He was rather puffed out, and about a hundred yards away there was one of those stone plinths with a kind of engraved compass on top. He got as far as that and sat down on one of the rough stones surrounding it, which might or might not have been provided for the purpose. In the act of sitting he felt the weight of something in his pocket and was reminded that he was actually carrying his mobile – Maddie had sensibly suggested it, in case he got lost or wanted a lift home; she was very solicitous. The mobile was switched off, he didn't care for it, but now he turned it on and carefully, prodding with one long finger, entered Diana's London number, and then 'Call'.

To his astonishment (he had no faith in these things), it rang.

And rang. Followed by her recorded voice, very quiet and collected.

He didn't leave a message. He was mortified. How could she not be there at – he looked at his watch – eleven forty-five on a Saturday morning? But then he reminded himself of the myriad things Diana might be doing: shopping, swimming, galleries, lunching with friends, walking like him, even (why hadn't he thought of it before?) relaxing in her riverside cottage. For which, bugger it, he didn't have the number.

He switched off the phone and put it back in his pocket. He sat there for quite a while, gazing down at the house, until the stone beneath his bottom began to bite shrewdly. Then he got up rather stiffly – he could hear the clicking of his knees in the silence – and set off on the return journey.

It wasn't long before he appreciated the truth of the observation that going downhill was much harder on the joints than going up. His thighs and knees complained bitterly, and even his neck and shoulders tightened with the effort of keeping his balance.

It was a relief when he reached the band of woodland and could lean up against a tree for a breather.

When he got back to the house it was to the east-wind atmosphere of a family contretemps. The empty kitchen showed signs of activity but there was no-one there, and there were raised voices at the front of the house. Maddie, an apron over her jeans, was in the hall with her hand on the banister, and Edmund and one of the boys were in the drawing room. As Tony arrived, the younger boy, Jack, came storming out and bounded up the stairs, ignoring his mother's tentative attempts to detain him.

'Let him stew,' said Edmund from the drawing room. Maddie gave a wan smile.

'Hello, Uncle Tony, nice walk?'

'Yes – though I may have overshot myself.'

'God, I'm sorry, did we send you too far?'

'It was entirely my responsibility.'

'You do look a bit bushed . . .' She peered at him, and then grabbed him by the wrist and towed him – there was no other word for it – into the drawing room where Edmund was standing by the window, puffing irritably on a cigarette.

'Ed – Uncle Tony's back.'

'Hello. Sorry you had to be confronted with my son's teenage tantrum.'

Tony shrugged. 'Please . . .'

'Sorry about this too.' Edmund held up the cigarette before stubbing it out. 'It takes a lot these days, but I was driven to it.'

'Ed . . .' Maddie was still holding Tony's wrist and now she gave it a shake, as if it were a rattle to attract her husband's attention. 'Why don't you guys escape, and go for a pint and a pie at the pub?'

'Not a bad idea, actually.'

Tony's heart plummeted. He had been so looking forward to a sit-down with an aperitif (sherry would have been his preference but it was not a drink the younger generation kept), a simple rustic lunch and a snooze. And here was Edmund jumping at the suggestion, though not all that graciously.

'You up for that, Tony?'

'It sounds splendid.'

'You need to do anything first?'

'No.' Too late Tony realized he was being asked if he wanted to use the lavatory. The minute they stepped out of the front door Edmund asked, 'You don't mind five minutes more walking, do you? Then I can have a proper drink.' Just then Tony experienced a pressing need to empty his bladder.

'How far is it?'

'Nothing – few hundred yards?'

'Fine.'

'Sure that's all right?' Edmund was already setting a brisk pace.

'I shall tell you if it's not.'

Edmund laughed heartily at this.

The Hare and Hounds was at least the very model of a country pub, and Tony sank gratefully on to a worn wooden settle near the window while Edmund got the drinks in. There was even, to his astonishment, a respectable amontillado.

'Got you a schooner,' said Edmund. 'Thought you could probably do with it.'

'I can't pretend it's not most welcome – thank you.'

'Did you have a good walk? Not too strenuous?'

'I walk miles in London.'

'Yes, but not so hilly perhaps. And more opportunities for R and R en route.'

Tony couldn't deny this. 'The view rewarded the effort.'

'Fabulous, isn't it?' There was no mistaking Edmund's proprietary delight in the compliment. 'God's little acre, we're very lucky.'

There was a pause while they drank, Edmund taking a long draught of Brockett's and Tony a couple of sips of sherry. Its warming strength coursed through his tired limbs and a sense of well-being began to steal over him. However, Edmund's face, as he wiped the line of foam from his top lip, was once more sombre.

'I only wish my sons thought so.'

'Different strokes for different folks,' murmured Tony.

'At least William's got his driver's licence now, and the prospect of a gap year ahead of him. Jack's just plain bloody mutinous. Well, you saw.'

'I understand that it goes with the territory.'

'Not in my family,' said Edmund rather pompously. 'It wasn't allowed.' He gestured with his glass in Tony's direction. 'Certainly not in yours, I bet.'

'I was too wrapped up in my books to be any trouble. A dreadful little swat. Even though I was a teenager of the so-called swinging sixties.'

Edmund considered this. 'Everything's "bor-ing". And William's no help; he doesn't want his style cramped by having a younger brother in tow. He has other fish to fry.'

Tony nodded sympathetically. 'That's very understandable. How much longer does Jack have at school?'

'Well . . .' Edmund drained his glass. 'Want the other half?'

'Just a small one.'

'I'll be right back.'

The sun striking through the pub window warmed Tony's back. There were one or two men at the bar and he watched Edmund greet them and chat, perhaps mention his name, because they glanced his way, that discreet look he recognized that was both wildly curious but unwilling to intrude or appear too interested. To avoid meeting their eye he brushed assiduously at the knee of his trousers.

Edmund returned. 'In answer to your question, he takes his GCSEs in a couple of months, God help us, but that's where the plan ends.'

'A Levels, University?'

'Dream on. Not at the moment.'

'What would he like to do?' asked Tony, discovering that he was genuinely interested in the answer.

'Something in —' Edmund made inverted commas with his fingers — 'the Meeja. Like they all do.'

'Nothing wrong in that.'

'Of course! Did that sound unforgivably rude?'

'That's quite all right,' said Tony mildly.

'Honestly, I do apologize.'

'Please. That was mischievous of me. I take your point entirely.'

'Do you?' Edmund scowled in anxious disbelief. 'They think they can just go out there and become a TV presenter or the girl-band correspondent of *Heat* magazine or something. They don't want to graft. They want some cushy one-year course followed by an equally cushy and highly paid job.'

'You say "they" – is that what Jack says?'

'Not in so many words.'

Tony suddenly experienced a flashback, an emotional memory, which he recognized as not just true, but relevant.

'Perhaps,' he said, 'he doesn't have the words to say what he wants.'

Edmund grumbled something about there being plenty of words for what Jack didn't like, but Tony didn't allow himself to be deflected.

'He's – what – going on sixteen? He has dreams. He should have dreams, at his age. But they're unformed.'

'It's very hard,' said Edmund petulantly, 'to be hated by one's son.'

'He doesn't hate you.'

'We never had this with William.'

'Perhaps he's a more straightforward kind of boy. Some people are fortunate in knowing exactly what they want to do. Either that, or not minding much. Easygoing, happy to go with the flow.'

'That's true.'

'You may find,' said Tony gently, 'and this is in no way to disparage William, that Jack is the more interesting boy.'

Edmund gave a sceptical grimace. 'Oh, *interesting*? That's not in doubt.'

Tony didn't smile. 'I mean more complex. He may surprise you, and go far.'

'It would be nice to think so.'

There was a pause during which each of them regrouped and allowed the other to do the same. Then Tony said, so tentatively that he almost seemed to be talking to himself, 'I wonder if there's something I could do to help?'

It was a very long time since Tony had reflected on his childhood. And that night, unable to sleep after the Kingshotts' exuberantly bibulous dinner party, was the first time in many years that he had done so in a spirit of dispassionate enquiry.

The first thing, the thing that underpinned everything else like dusty lino, was the boredom. The exquisite, trance-like boredom of life before boarding school, in the small seaside town where the Chance family had lived.

His parents – both of them now dead – had been hard-working, respectable, lower middle class people, devoted to their only child, Anthony, and to their community. Tony's father, Gordon, was the proprietor of Chance's Stationers in the high street. Leslie helped keep the books, and ran the house at 3 Marine Parade. Tony remembered the house as being taste-free rather than tasteless. There was no vulgarity, nothing to make a sensitive person cringe; more a kind of timid shrinking from the exercise of taste for fear of making a hideous mistake. Walls were white or cream, floors were beige or brown, pictures were small and symmetrically positioned, furniture was neat and plump, curtains (when drawn) caught back by bands of matching material, and ornaments were few and inoffensive. The bathroom and lavatories had matching towels, bath- and pedestal-mats in pristine pale colours. In the bedrooms Leslie allowed herself a little leeway – after all, no-one outside the family was likely to see those – and the beds had padded headboards, flower-printed coverlets and crisply flounced valances. In fact, Tony recalled, his mother had been something of a genius with beds. He had never since, either at home, in five-star hotels, or the homes of the rich and famous, come across beds of such utter fragrant smoothness, resilience and comfort. Beds intended for a good night's sleep, of course, not for sex. Nor for reading – the bedside lamps were squat and chastely shaded, quite unsuitable for deciphering print. As a boy, rather than leave the overhead light on and have to get out of bed to switch it off, Tony augmented the dim glow with a torch. Everything in 3 Marine Parade was astonishingly, delightfully clean, and he had liked that. Still did. He did not exactly regard cleanliness and order as next to godliness, but he did regard it as important – not something to be derided. At a young age he had appreciated his mother's constant, tireless efforts to keep a spruce, shining house for him and his father, and also the fact that she made no fuss about it. If a mess was inadvertently made – muddy shoes, food or drink spilt, childhood sickness – she cleared up and carried on with the greatest cheerfulness. Looking back now, from a time when few women of his acquaintance did their own housework and if they did, only imperfectly – 'better things to do' – he considered this his mother's towering achievement. Combined with the fact that Leslie, no beauty, was always neat as a new pin, and fresh as a daisy herself. How had she done it? He himself could not possibly have managed the Hampstead house without the assistance of Lionel and Lucia, the Andalusian cleaning lady.

Where Leslie was bustling and compact, Tony's father had been tall and lanky. Their wedding photo − discreetly displayed on a corner table in the living room − showed a handsome young couple, he in army uniform and she in a short, square-necked dress with a potty hat and peep-toe shoes. In their middle years, a tendency to staidness had turned them into an ill-assorted pair, with Gordon ever more gangly and Leslie chunkier. Gordon had grown a moustache. Leslie had a tight perm. For work in the shop Gordon wore a loose brown linen jacket. Tony was ashamed to admit that he had not admired or appreciated his father's labours as he had done his mother's. He had found the shop, with its till, its Basildon Bond and biros and its pocket-money toys, not to mention his father's brown jacket, undignified and embarrassing. Gordon employed local lads to deliver newspapers, but Tony never did deliveries, and was never asked. On the face of it he was idle, and solitary, his nose in a book or his ear to the wireless. But inside, in his head, all was turmoil and longing. His mind's eye strained to see something just out of reach.

Anthony was their adored son. He had never for a moment doubted that. He was secure in his parents' love, but increasingly they were baffled by him. He was very clever, and they had no wish to hold him back. It was a great day when he got the scholarship to a top private school, and a few months later they'd waved him off at the station with beaming smiles, though he now realized they must have been full of foreboding at the prospect of him departing for another world − leaving them behind.

The school, two hundred miles away in Berkshire, was noted for its academic excellence, and he felt immediately at home there. Within weeks he was put up a year, and there was no unkindness. The food had been the worst trial, but sheer hunger had helped get him over that, and like many a public schoolboy before and since it had turned him into an unfussy but appreciative eater. His trunk and its contents were perfect, prompting a favourable comment from Matron. Other new boys had clothes that were too big, or improperly marked, or insufficient – his were spotless, present and correct, the Cash's name tapes attached with invisibly tiny stitches, the packing exemplary. Such small things helped to ease his path.

And the lessons! Suddenly a door was opened before him and everything on the other side was new, and enthralling, and spread out like shining fields to a limitless horizon. Books, music, drama, the science lab, the art studio . . . For the first time his mind and imagination stretched, and breathed, and flew like the wind.

The one exception to this was the sports field, but it was accepted that such an exceptionally bright intellectual spark was unlikely to shine on the rugger pitch (in fact it would have been almost unfair to do so). He did discover an ability to tweak the cricket ball and made the third eleven as a bowler of unorthodox leg breaks.

He made only one real friend, an exhibitioner named Arthur Bright who was a talented actor. (Where was he now? Tony hadn't heard of him since.) But the great shift in his life was Mr Townsend.

Geoff (you soon got to know the masters' Christian names) Townsend taught senior Latin and Drama. Unlike the majority of the masters he didn't live in during term-time, but, glamorously, in London, from where he travelled down twice a week in a forest-green Morgan. These were not the only ways in which he was unlike a schoolmaster. He seemed not to notice that the people he dealt with were boys, and treated them as adults and equals. Discipline was therefore not an issue; the assumption was that people had come together with a common purpose and therefore had no reason to disrupt, disturb or subvert what was going on. This assumption pervaded the air and created, even in the most excitable and enthralling periods of school drama productions, a collegiate, democratic atmosphere.

Mr Townsend acknowledged by his behaviour that certain boys, Tony Chance among them, were his equals in intellect, if not in experience, and would openly consult them on matters of direction and interpretation. In Latin tutorials, with only eight boys present, their shared reading of Virgin, Ovid, Pliny and Cicero was enthralling – Mr Townsend was as enthralled as the rest of them.

This was Tony's first encounter with a genuine enthusiast –

someone with the ability to rediscover his subject afresh over and over again, and to communicate his excitement to others. Even Townsend's appearance – rangy and wiry, with snapping dark eyes and a shock of awkward curly hair – gave the impression of ferocious, barely contained energy and enthusiasm. Where the other masters wore their gowns like wings, flapping busily as they marched from room to room or across the quad, or neatly at their sides in class, Mr Townsend's looked as if it had been blown down the street by a high wind and had somehow or other landed on him without his noticing. It was generally lopsided, and he would end up discarding it, without comment, as though that was quite enough of that.

He also, and most importantly, talked about Life. Not in a lecturing way; he didn't have what was now known as 'an agenda' about moral precepts, principles or behaviour. He simply imbued his lessons with a sense of their context, so that Tony felt – no, *knew* – that all this good stuff was not just an academic exercise but an enrichment of everything that was to come.

And he was, of course, in love with Geoff Townsend. Not in a physical way; that side of things had never played a great part in his make-up. No, it was everything – the 'whole package' in modern parlance – that had bewitched and fired him. He had wanted to *be* Geoff Townsend, with his mysteriously exciting life in London, his mobility and dash, his unashamed passion for his subjects, his absolute originality. Even then, something told him that there were certain elements in Townsend's life which were hopelessly inaccessible to a gawky teenager (an inscrutably smiling blonde in a headscarf and dark glasses had occasionally been spotted in the Morgan), but the knowledge only intensified his passion.

The last play of Tony's school career was *St Joan*, which he himself directed. Arthur Bright was a poignant Dauphin, Joan herself was played not by a boy on this occasion but by one of the assistant music mistresses, Miss Dunlop. The latter was a small plain young woman (Tony could now see she'd been no more than a girl, in her mid-twenties) with thin hair and an overbite, but possessed of a white flame of intensity which came out when she played the piano or acted on stage. Geoff Townsend oversaw and produced, taking care of the administrative details and letting them get on with it. For the whole six weeks of the rehearsal period Tony had been in a sort of ecstasy of excitement. His vision of the play was so vivid and intense that he did not dare take his eye off it for a moment, lest he fail to bring it to life. His parents, he knew, would in their straightforward way be more taken up with the performances than his 'backstage' role; that was fine, for it was Townsend's approval he craved. For the first time in his life he felt the pain and bile of jealousy when after the third and final performance Townsend took Nina Dunlop in his arms, lifting her off her feet, and told her she'd been 'stupendous'.

Then, just as he was helping to dismantle the set through a glitter of tears he felt a tap on his shoulder.

'Tony.'

There was no surname-only nonsense with Townsend.

'Hello sir.'

'Congratulations.' Townsend held out a hand, and they shook.

'Thanks, sir. Was it all right?'

'No false modesty please. You know it was much more than that.'

'Really?'

'On some not-too distant occasion when you have more time, I want you to sit down with me and tell me how that was done.'

'Okay,' said Tony.

'I shall hold you to it.'

'Fine.'

A light touch on the upper arm. 'Bye for now, though.'

'Bye, sir.'

He wasn't sure what made him watch as Townsend left, congratulating other boys in passing. Perhaps he'd had some subliminal premonition, because that was the last time he saw Geoff Townsend. The invitation to explain how it was done never came, and six years later during a visit to his parents his father had pointed to a notice in the *Telegraph*.

'Name rings a bell – Tony, wasn't he one of your teachers?'

In the midst of life. Beloved son of Moira and Ian, and brother of Alasdair. Private funeral. Kind donations to the Maudsley Hospital.

He had sent a donation, and cried that night in bed. But the next morning, in spite of the sadness (his mother made him a cooked breakfast), he knew that he had been given something, even without the promised invitation. He was the inheritor of the Townsend mantle. That life cut short, he didn't know how (the Maudsley? he didn't care to speculate) was now his to live. And he would.

When they returned from the sedate drinks party next day, the Kingshott boys were up and about, if slightly rumpled. In contrast to William's rugby shirt and cords, Jack was top-to-toe in black, the t-shirt embellished on the front with a serpent's head, the fangs dripping poison, and on the back the words *Blood Fury* in silver Gothic script. His feet were bare and there was a silver ring, in the shape of another snake, on his left big toe. Maddie retired to the kitchen to bring the lunch up to speed ('joy of Aga'). Both boys helped their mother dish up.

'*Oh* yes,' said Edmund in response to his appreciative comment. 'Sunday lunch is a three-line whip around here. They want feeding, they turn up.'

'Would you like me to mention our little plan?'

'Yes, would you?' Edmund's relief was audible. 'Maddie's all for it, as you know.'

'I shall choose my moment,' Tony assured him.

Lunch was delicious: roast chicken with a hint of garlic and tarragon, followed by home-made lemon meringue pie. The boys wolfed theirs, speaking when they were spoken to. The adults, warmed by hospitality, were relaxed. At the end of the meal Edmund went to make coffee and William asked to be excused – things to do. Jack began stacking the pudding dishes. Feeling Maddie's eyes upon him, Tony took this as his cue.

'Jack – do you have a moment? There's something I want to ask you.'

'Sure . . .' Jack paused, dishes in hand.

'Sit down, then,' said Maddie.

Tony continued to smile benignly. Jack lowered his backside on to a chair, still holding the dishes, a hostage to fortune.

'I wondered,' said Tony, 'whether you'd like to come up to London for a while in the summer.'

'London?'

'Yes. You could stay at my house, and get some work experience at the BBC, or backstage at the Playhouse – any number of places actually; they're always after gofers in August.'

'Paid work?'

'Jack!' Maddie grimaced reprovingly.

'No, no, that's all right; it's a sensible question – I think your expenses would be covered, but not much more. I just thought that perhaps it might make a change.'

Jack's fingers tightened on the pile of dishes. His eyes flicked briefly to his mother and a pulse in his neck began to beat.

'What do you think?' mused Tony.

'Yeah!' replied Jack. A single syllable which even Tony, unfamiliar as he was with the argot of the young, recognized as utter and wholehearted endorsement.

'Good,' he said, smiling as Edmund returned with the coffee. 'It shall be done.'

Twelve

Take me to a park all covered with trees / Tell me on a Sunday, please . . .

Penny had always liked that song. But it was for her own sake as much as for Graham's that she chose to say her piece out in the garden. A great many people would have taken the view that there was no particular reason why she should consider him at all, but none of them was her, and for her his feelings did come into it.

The garden was a shared project. The house had been brand-new when they moved in, they were the first occupants, and they'd been happy out here, creating a garden from a wired-off square of unforgiving clay and builders' rubble. They'd rotavated and sowed, and laid tiles and turf, and grown plants from seed, and created a rockery and a water feature and a sunken patio, while the boys mucked about, enjoying the mess. It was exhausting work, but strenuous physical activity always made Graham randy, and they'd had some of their best sex during that spring and summer, the season of mud.

By sitting him down out here she hoped to remind him of all that, for no other reason than to remind him what he would be giving up. Also, she was taking the initiative, being proactive. He wanted 'a talk'? She would do the talking, and choosing the place put her in control.

She had tried to prepare herself for the slight shock of his return. She told herself she must expect to be momentarily thrown by the fact that he was still the same man, whatever was going on. But the mental preparation only worked up to a point. When she heard his car, and his key, and his voice – 'Pen? You there?' – it was all so precious and familiar that she went into the bathroom to compose herself, and waited a full minute before flushing the loo and emerging.

She had arranged for the boys to be out. (Had gone to considerable lengths, actually, because they were now all past the age when they could be packed off to a friend's for no particular reason.) She pretty much ordered Graham to take a shower, and when he came down she poured him a drink (scotch and Canada dry, long, with ice) and brought him up to the little deck outside the summer house. In high summer this was the spot that caught the evening sun; at this time of year it was still in shade, but there was something pleasing about looking back across the spring garden at their house, the home they'd made together. Look, and weep, she thought.

'So,' she said, 'you want to be somewhere else.'

'I didn't say that.'

'You didn't need to.'

'Pen . . .'

'You can go. I shan't stop you. You have a free choice.'

He gave her a puzzled frown. Her cuddly bear of a husband. 'Don't say it like that.'

'I'm not saying it like anything. It's true. You can go, or you can stay. And if you stay, you can stay for the boys. Not me, do you understand? For them.'

'I think we're taking this a bit too fast, don't you?'

'No,' she said. 'I want to be quick about it. Quick and clear.'

'If I did go,' he said slowly, and then more emphatically, as if preventing her from interrupting, '*If* I did, the boys would get over it, you know.'

'Probably, but why should they have to?'

'They're old enough to understand that these things happen. I'd still see them, after all. I bet half – more than half – of their friends' parents are divorced, or separated, or not married in the first place.'

'I don't care about that,' said Penny. 'I care about them.'

There was a pause, during which she felt the atmosphere change. For the whole of their married life she had never knowingly or deliberately challenged Graham. She was the world's most non-confrontational wife, and proud of it, even when other people had tried to make her feel guilty. In her book, support and under-standing were what marriage was all about.

'So, hang on,' said Graham, and she heard the edge of hard-ness creep into his voice. 'You're saying we should stay together for the sake of the children?'

'Yes.' He thought he had tricked her, but she knew what she was doing. 'Yes, I am.'

'And that – excuse me – that's a good thing?'

'I think so.'

He blew out his cheeks. 'They're hardly children any more.'

'They're *our* children.'

'I'm sorry, no, I'm sorry,' Graham said, meaning the opposite. He put his glass down on the deck and fidgeted convulsively. 'How can it possibly be good for ch— for offspring to live in a house where the adults are, what's the word? *Conflicted.*' He put a sarcastic emphasis on the word as if it were one he himself would never normally use, but which might appeal to her.

'But I'm not conflicted,' she said. 'Not at all.'

He thrust his face towards her, and it was an ugly face, one she didn't recognize. 'Penny!' he snapped impatiently. 'Must I spell it out? There is someone else.'

'I know, but I don't want to hear about her.'

'I'd have thought she was pretty crucial to this discussion.'

'Not for me.'

He sat back. 'I don't get it.'

'It's easy,' she said. 'You stay, and go on being a good father, because you always have been a good father. They love you, Graham.'

'I certainly hope so,' he said, picking up his glass and looking away as he took a mouthful. Now it was Penny's turn to lean forward, to abandon the cool persona she'd adopted and speak more urgently.

'You go on being that father, and we keep a happy home for them, just as we promised to do when we got married. As we *wanted* to do,' she reminded him. He muttered something that she didn't quite catch. 'I'm sorry?'

'I said, but what about us?'

'We shall be all right.'

'Do you mind me asking how?'

'Because . . .' She took a mental deep breath. 'You can keep your lady friend—'

'She's a bit more than that, Pen.'

'Whatever she is, you can keep her. I don't want to know a

thing about her, and I shan't ask. She's all yours, Graham. But you're mine, mine and the boys'.'

'Excuse me,' he said. 'Choice of words? Nobody owns anybody.'

'No, but some people belong together.'

There was another silence, this time a long one, which Graham broke by saying with a kind of shaky irritation, 'I can't think about this now.'

Just as he said it Jamie appeared at the French windows.

'Dad!'

Graham cleared his throat. 'Hi, son.'

'Can I go on the computer?'

'Sure – no downloading.'

'Yeah, yeah . . .' Jamie disappeared.

'"Nice to see you, Dad, how are you, how was the trip, missed you . . ."' grumbled Graham.

'That's the thing, you see,' said Penny. 'That's what you'll lose. Being taken for granted.'

Brian shuffled the torn pieces of card.

'And your point is?'

'There's nothing on them,' said Della. 'Not a word.'

'I don't suppose he needs notes at his age.'

'No, but he wanted us to think he did. He tore them up in front of us.'

Brian shrugged, put the pieces down on the coffee table and picked up his glass. 'So he's a performer. I think we kind of knew that.'

'I suppose . . .'

Brian gave her cheek a quick stroke with his crooked finger. 'Not disappointed, are you, babes? From everything you said it went down a storm.'

'It's not that . . .'

'What then?'

'I suppose – well, we all thought he genuinely was departing from what he'd prepared, that we were getting something special and unplanned. And now it looks as if that was all a kind of trick.'

'You think he says that to all the girls.'

'Yes – if you want to put it that way.'

'Hm.' Brian tapped his glass against his chin, considering. He couldn't think why he was sticking up for Chance, who as far as he could see was an old-school smoothie well able to look after himself, but he wanted to cheer up his wife. 'I tell you what I think – who cares whether he's genuinely off-piste or not, as long as it works and the punters are happy?'

'I do,' said Della. And then, before Brian could take it any further, smiled at him and said, 'But you're absolutely right. Come on, let's eat.'

Gwen knew that the general perception of the Horn was a scruffy, even seedy area. She preferred 'villagey'. She was at home in its maze of scuttling one-way Victorian streets in the shadow of the intercity railway, and in its High Street flanked by idiosyncratic small businesses and shops that reflected the area's ethnic diversity. For the last reason in particular Gwen was astonished on Sunday afternoon to see Rhada, immaculate in jeans and an olive leather jacket, on the opposite side of the road, studying the window of the Polish deli. Rhada didn't approve of what she called 'ghetto-ization', and thought of herself as a fully assimilated member of the English professional class. With this in mind Gwen would normally have respected her privacy and let her get on with it, but today something mischievous made her call out.

'Rhada!'

Startled, Rhada looked round with a hunted expression that softened only slightly when she saw Gwen.

'Hang on . . .' Gwen darted across the road, raising a hand in insincere apology to the traffic. 'Hi, what brings you over this way? Slumming?'

'I quite often come,' said Rhada stiffly. 'We just haven't bumped into one another before.'

'Now that we have, fancy a coffee? My patch, my shout,' added Gwen, as if the price of a latte might be the cause of Rhada's minute hesitation.

'A tisane would be nice.'

'We can get one on the corner here.'

In the café Rhada, at Gwen's insistence, sat down at a table while Gwen bought the drinks and a slice of date and walnut loaf.

'No obligation – we can share it.'

Rhada broke off a small piece with immaculately manicured fingers and popped it in her mouth.

'It's delicious actually.'

'I know.' Gwen looked at her over her coffee. What a caution. 'I was sorry I missed the lunch. Della emailed; she said it went well.'

'He was excellent,' conceded Rhada, 'I must say.'

'It wasn't deliberate,' said Gwen. 'I got tied up.'

'No, no – we guessed. At the shelter?'

'Yes.' Gwen justified the lie on the grounds that the alternative was simply too complicated in the time available. 'It's that sort of place, I'm afraid.'

Rhada brushed her palms together and delicately removed the herbal tea bag from her cup. 'I can't imagine it . . . Some time or other I'm going to have to see this famous shelter for myself.'

It was that 'famous' with its hint of patronage that prompted Gwen to say, 'How about now?'

'I'm sorry?' Rhada raised her eyebrows and took a sip.

'When you've finished your tea – it's only round the corner.'

'Oh – no!' Rhada laughed. 'I don't think so!'

It had not been nearly as grim or as squalid as Rhada had feared. Sitting on her balcony with a glass of Pinot and a background of cool jazz courtesy of Classic FM, she reflected that in fact it had been neither. Admittedly it had been empty – the doors opened between six and nine in the evening to let people in, and between the same hours in the morning to let them out again. The nice man Sean, Gwen's boss she supposed you could call him, had explained that they were not a full-time hostel, but a last resort for the desperate.

'A sanctuary,' she'd suggested.

'Good word,' said Sean. 'I hadn't thought of it like that, but you're absolutely right.'

At that moment Rhada had caught Gwen looking at her, a look that darted right across their differences. A little secret shaft of – not gratitude exactly – but appreciation might be the word.

She thought about this as she prepared her supper of goat's

cheese, rocket, toasted pine nuts and cherry tomatoes. She took
trouble over the simplest food, she liked colours and textures on
the plate, nourishment for the eye as well as the palate. But she
wasn't a big eater, in fact when the food was ready she left the
white plate on the green glass table by the vase of peonies, just
because it was all so pretty and nice; a treat in store. This was the
sort of thing – especially after the events of the afternoon – which
filled her with a simple pleasure in her lot.

Out on the balcony again she reminded herself not to be smug.
The visit to the shelter had been a humbling experience. She was
certainly seeing Gwen in a new light. Rhada had always been
wary of Gwen – the clothes, the attitude, the slightly patronizing
air with which she approached the Marie Crompton committee.
And she was pretty sure Gwen saw her as prissy and stuck-up.
There had been something of a stand-off between them. That was
one reason why she'd been so surprised when Gwen had hailed
her in the High Street (the other being her own embarrassment
at being seen there at all). She'd felt trapped, teased – caught out.

But the shelter, and Gwen's pride in it, had been real. The
trouble was the place had taken on a semi-mythical status in the
life of the committee. 'Oh, Gwen's held up at the shelter again.'
Or, 'Got to dash, it's my shift at the shelter'. But now Rhada
could see that these were real imperatives. And the cleanliness
and order of the place had impressed her. Standards were imposed
and maintained. Proper food was cooked. The lounge contained
books, papers and board games as well as a large television. Of
course, she hadn't met any of the patrons . . .

Her balcony overlooked the canal-side walk and she could see
two men sitting on the parapet sharing a drink from a can,
conspicuous among the strolling couples, bustling buggies and
swooping rollerbladers. They wore jeans and trainers and could
have been any age between twenty-five and fifty. Both had ruddy
complexions – not the fresh colour of rude health but the suffused
dull red of booze and bad diet. Though she fully believed them
to be harmless, Rhada was rather afraid of such people. She didn't
care to dwell on the lives they must lead, the desperate measures
to which they resorted – and of course the long nights, spent on
the street or in places like the shelter. Gwen and Sean had told
her there was no drink allowed there, so how did men like these

manage? She pictured violence, bed-wetting (in fact every kind of bodily excretion), vile language and behaviour, and disgusting smells. But – she had seen it for herself – there was a basic sense of decency in the place.

As she watched, the two men got up and began walking away. One had a tightly buttoned denim jacket and a curious hopping gait as if he were walking on hot coals, the other moved with something between a lope and a shuffle. He threw the can into the canal.

Rhada found that she was actually craning, bending her neck and shoulders to follow their progress through the bars of the balcony. Straightening up, she realized she'd slopped some wine on herself. Fetching a cloth from the kitchen she wondered if she would be able to cope with such people. The dirt, the unpredictability, the general unpleasantness? The answer was probably not. But Gwen did, all the time, and that must surely affect how she saw the rest of them.

Rebuking herself, Rhada mopped up, replaced the cloth, and took her glass to the table. All the pleasures she enjoyed – her blessed solitude, the stylish comfort of her flat, the array of choices that lay before her every day – she was in the habit of regarding as hard-won prizes, the fruits of her own industry and hard-won independence. Now, for the first time in years, she thought of her parents and all they had done to launch their beloved daughters into the world.

She put down her fork, with an untouched mouthful on it. She could not have swallowed the food, her throat was constricted. Her watch told her it was seven p.m., the wrong time to ring Chennai. She covered her eyes, but that didn't stop her mind's eye gazing down mournfully at this Indian Bridget Jones, hedged about with carefully chosen possessions, alone on a sunny evening when teenagers, families, lovers and – yes – tramps were out there enjoying one another's company.

She gave a little sob, and choked it back, dashing at her tears with an Egyptian cotton napkin. Crying was not the answer. Self-pity was a waste of energy, as her beloved father had often said. Pity the less fortunate, appreciate your good fortune and make the most of your advantages. It was never too late.

Putting down her napkin, she went to the phone.

Thirteen

'I'm coming over,' said Ros. She sounded as if she might add something, but then simply repeated: 'I'm coming over.'

'How lovely,' said Marian, who was taken aback but pleased, too. 'All of you?'

'Yes, I thought I wouldn't leave any limbs behind this time.'

'You know what I mean.'

'It'll be just me. What would be great is if we could fix it to fly back together.'

'Good idea,' said Marian. 'Let's try.'

There was the tiniest pause before Ros said, 'Mum . . . I'm coming over for the wedding.'

'Good.' Marian didn't want her daughter's caution and tact; she wanted swiftly to move on.

'I want to be there, for Dad, but there was no need for all of us to schlep over. Jay's not fussed, and I'm quite sure they're not fussed about him.'

'Darling, I'm sure—'

'You know what I mean. And it's a long flight with a baby. Besides, we've been looking forward to *you* coming to see *us*.'

'Yes,' said Marian. 'Me too. You don't know how much.'

'There you are then.'

Marian was in the garden clearing bindweed and goose grass, a hugely satisfying exercise – great wheels and loops and tangles of it woven in among the perennials, you just grabbed an end and pulled, and out it came like bunting from a conjuror's hat. She sat back on her heels and wiped her face with the back of her gardening glove.

'Mum?'

'Yes?'

'What are you doing?'

'I'm outside, weeding.'

'That explains it – you sounded funny. Be honest, you don't mind about the wedding, do you? You're okay with this arrangement?'

'For goodness' sake!' Even to her own ears Marian was rather too emphatic. 'You're father's wedding? You should be there.'

She meant it, but when Ros immediately said, 'Yes, that's what I think,' she experienced a bolt of pure misery.

To stifle the pain she asked brightly, 'So what date's that?'

'July the fourteenth. I'll be over on the twelfth. I was thinking maybe I could come to you on the fifteenth, and we could fly back on the Wednesday.'

'Have you already booked?'

'Well yes, actually I have.'

'So it's Hobson's Choice.'

'Mum . . . Come on.'

That had been more than two months ago, since when Marian had apologized for her grumpiness (Ros said that under the circs she was entitled to be grumpy), and booked her ticket on the same flight as Ros. But she was jealous, there was no getting away from it, and her jealousy made her ashamed. She had not the slightest expectation of attending her former husband's wedding, nor the remotest chance of being invited, but Ros's attendance brought home to her the reality of it all, and that did hurt. This was not the same as Dennis's visits to Ros in the States, the perfectly natural and appropriate contact between loving father and daughter. This was the signal that from now on there was to be another home for Ros – and another woman in it. Would Ros see Ruth as her stepmother? Surely not, she was too old for that, but even the thought of Ruth saying 'Just call me Ruth' was irritating and upsetting.

Also, would Ros like her? Obviously it would be a good thing if she did – good for Ros, good for Ruth, and for Dennis, and for Lucy-Anne who would now be getting a second grand-mother. But please God, prayed Marian, let her not like her too much!

It was now Sunday afternoon, the day after the wedding, and Marian was expecting her daughter at any moment. The Saturday had been a pretty, flighty, summer's day of sunshine and feathery high cloud; today was dingy, warm and wet, with a scudding wind and spattering showers. The wind had brought down some green leaves and they gave the garden an autumnal look. In the smaller of the two spare bedrooms Marian's clothes for the trip were already laid out on the bed with her case next to them, shoes and books installed at the bottom. She hated packing, and hated it even more when there was a rush. She wanted the three days before departure, three days when she would have Ros to herself, to be tranquil, not rattled by her suitcase blues. She had laid in a supply of fresh, simple food and some nice white wine, including a couple of bottles of Prosecco, which Ros loved.

She was a little nervous, and the waiting didn't help. It was a relief when Ros's hire car, a red Corsa, pulled up outside. Marian saw it through the bedroom window and watched for a moment, taking advantage of being, for a few seconds, the unseen onlooker. From this angle she couldn't see Ros's face, but she could see her hands, removing sunglasses, tipping down the visor to check her look, retrieving her handbag from the passenger seat . . . By the time Marian was downstairs and had opened the front door Ros was already leading her case, like a robot dog, towards the house.

'Mum! Oh, Mum, hi – it's good to see you!'

They hugged and Marian wondered why she had ever felt nervous. Whatever else had changed, Ros hadn't. She was still as smart as ever, still dependable and savvy, and *sane*. The sort of young woman you'd want with you, as Dennis often said, if you were up the Orinoco when the boat sprang a leak.

Once she'd taken her case up to the bedroom Marian still thought of as hers anyway, Ros made a lightning tour of the house, to see if anything needed doing. She had always been intensely practical – and needed to be, considering the man she'd married – and kept saying things like, 'If you've got a decent drill you know I could do that for you while I'm here . . .' But Marian wouldn't hear of it.

'Stop! You make me feel so inadequate.'

'DIY just isn't your thing, Mum, but I kind of enjoy it.'

'No, Ros, no – you're on holiday. And I have my little men.'

'They cost.'

'Not a lot, and every penny well spent. Come and sit down.'

'Okay, okay!' Ros lifted her hands in surrender. They parked themselves in the garden, Marian in the sun, Ros in the shade of the apple tree. 'Anyway, it's all looking great. And you look great, you really do.'

'Why thank you.'

'I like what you've done with your hair.'

Marian touched it self-consciously. 'They're called lowlights.'

'They suit you.'

Ros looked much the same, but that was good. Marian still didn't quite know how she'd given birth to a person with an innate sense of style, but somehow, against the genetic tide, it had happened. She looked American: if Ros hadn't existed, Gap would have had to invent her. She had the trim, coltish figure that looked good in sporty clothes and hair that, when cut short, fell into feathery sun-bleached fronds around the sort of face that appeared always lightly tanned and to need no make-up. Since going to live in the States she'd had some orthodontic work done and her lovely, even smile completed the picture.

Marian bit the bullet. 'So come on, how was the wedding?'

'Actually, it was really neat,' said Ros, and Marian recognized the American expression as a useful portmanteau word conveying suitability, a degree of charm, nothing too overwhelming. 'You want me to tell you about it?'

'Just a quick run-down.'

There had been only about twenty people there, apparently, and the civil ceremony was held in one of the college gardens, followed by lunch in a 'glorious' panelled room. Marian asked about the food as being a safe subject and one on which she was prepared (permitted, even) to voice an opinion.

'Superb,' was Ros's verdict. 'Champagne and hors d'oeuvres, filet mignon with these really, really, tiny, delicate vegetable chips, and béarnaise sauce, green salad – and then panacotta with summer berries. Excellent wines, champagne for the toast . . . Very chic and very delicious.'

'That does all sound lovely,' said Marian, continuing in the same casual tone, 'And Dad, he was a happy bridegroom?'

'He did look happy,' said Ros, as if allowing, for her mother's sake, that appearances could lie. 'She seems nice. And right for him, as he is now, if you know what I mean.'

'I think so.'

Ros gave her a sidelong look. 'You want "he wore, she wore"?'

'Why not?'

'Okay. He wore a light grey suit with a blue button-down shirt and a dark blue tie. She wore a floral dress, kind of retro, with platform sandals.'

'Flowers?'

'No. If you don't count a rose in her hair.'

Marian didn't venture a comment, because for some reason the single rose had robbed her of the power of speech.

'I could show you some pictures; I got a few on my cell.'

Marian shook her head.

'How about some of your granddaughter?'

'Now you're talking.'

The next day though, at breakfast, she said, 'Perhaps I will take a quick look at some photos. Just to get the idea.'

'Sure.' Ros produced her mobile. 'They start here. Press the arrow to move on.'

Marian managed half a dozen, and that was more than enough. Ruth's forties-style dress showed off a curvy figure and the rose in her stylishly disarranged hair added a wanton note. Dennis was a smile on legs and unnaturally smart; that must have been the most he'd spent on clothes in years. He had a new haircut – shorter but unstructured, without even a hint of a parting. Perhaps he was trying to look like George Clooney. Ruth was shorter than her; even in the platforms, the top of her head was only up to his shoulder.

She was surprised to see a couple of old friends in the group photograph.

'Isn't that the Kitsons? Anna and George?'

'Yes – from London?'

'That's right.'

'They were nice. They sent their love.'

Marian handed back the mobile. 'I didn't know Dennis was still in touch with them.'

'From what I gather they see quite a bit of each other.'

Another pang. Marian hadn't seen the Kitsons for ages. Things were separating out.

Over the course of the next two days she felt herself moving from one mode – the wedding, looking after Ros – to the next, which was leaving for her holiday in the States. She realized how hard Ros must have worked to have everything in place before she left.

'You know me,' said Ros. 'Ms Organization. And I'm lucky, Jay's great with Lucy-Anne, they'll be having a ball.'

'I can't wait to see her.'

'It's mutual. She's been "Gann-ing" away for weeks. She's used to having grandads, because Wilf's often round and Dad's been over a couple of times, but you're a big excitement.'

Marian had difficulty falling asleep the night before they left, and when she did drop off it seemed like seconds later that she woke at four a.m., her brain motoring. Even the little packing that remained got her into a flap, and she thanked heaven for Ros who went around briskly putting plants in the sink, emptying the fridge and checking window locks. At the very last moment, as they were taking their bags to the car, she found herself inexplicably close to tears.

'O-K,' said Ros. 'Wagons roll! Mum?'

'I'm sorry. I'm so sorry, darling, I don't know why . . . Damn.'

'Don't worry.' Ros put an arm round her shoulders. 'I understand.'

When they got going, Marian felt better. It was good to be in Ros's capable hands; driven smoothly, no parking to worry about, speedy advance check-in done online, timing taken care of. But whatever her darling daughter said, she could not possibly understand. Not completely. This departure, though it was one she'd looked forward to for ages, represented a seismic shift in her life. Dennis had moved on and whatever *he* said, the old friendship could never be quite the same, nor should it be. She had seen the pictures; his magnetic north was elsewhere now. And she was flying off not just for a holiday but into a new life in which she would be truly a singleton, a modern grandmother with resources, options and time. She no longer had an ally who knew her almost as well as she knew herself. Her decisions from now on would be hers, and hers alone. Even Ros's awesome competence carried a premonitory force, a reminder of future dependency.

By the time the plane lurched into the air and Heathrow

dwindled into the chequered commuter-land countryside, she'd
begun to feel calmer.

'Don't know about you,' said Ros, 'but when that trolley comes
round I'm having a vodka tonic.'

'Me too,' said Marian, clenching her fist as she added, 'The
holiday starts here.'

'I'm sorry,' said Juanita, 'I've already done my thinking. It's someone
else's turn.'

'You make it sound like a fairground ride,' said Della. She
looked around and smiled ruefully. 'I see no queue.'

'Anyone use the word "roller-coaster" and I go too,' said Gwen.

'We must never take anyone for granted,' Della reminded them.
'We all have lives to live, and other commitments.'

'We don't take her for granted,' said Penny, 'we just can't do
without her.'

'No-one's indispensable.'

'Least of all me,' said Juanita. 'I'm the one who forgot to ask
Sir Anthony about his fee, remember?'

They laughed, rather too heartily.

Rhada said: 'I think we should minute the most tremendous
thanks to Juanita for all she's done for the Club, notably for
providing us with the biggest draw we've ever had.'

They all said 'hear-hear' and Penny gave Juanita a kiss on the
cheek.

'This may seem precipitate,' continued Rhada, 'and Juanita will
be a hard act to follow, but I think I know someone who might
be worth asking . . .' She paused, rolling her Parker between her
forefingers and thumbs.

'Go on then,' said Gwen. 'Don't toy with us.'

'Who do you have in mind?' asked Della.

'Madeleine Kingshott. I sat next to her at the Golden Lunch
– it turned out she's Sir Anthony's god-daughter, and very well
connected.'

'That's true,' agreed Della. 'She seems good friends with Belle
Martleby and all that crowd. She's a lovely person, but won't it
seem a bit pushy?'

'I'm not suggesting we ask her to be speaker-finder just like
that,' explained Rhada patiently. 'One of us – I don't mind doing

it since it's my suggestion – should write and invite her to be on the committee. To give us the benefit of her advice and contacts and so on. The next two meetings are taken care of and I'm sure between us we can keep things going into next year, by which time she'll be assimilated, and hopefully have got the idea.'

'Well,' said Della, 'what can I say? I think it's a brilliant idea. What does everyone else think? . . . Nem con! Can we leave it with you, Rhada?'

'You can,' said Rhada. 'Absolutely.'

Juanita collected Harmony from band practice on the way home. While Harmony made her farewell to the other members of Black Notes in the shed to the rear of the house, Juanita chatted to the host mother, Olwyn.

'You're very brave to do this, week after week.'

'That or mad. But frankly I'd rather know where they are.'

'They can come to us every other week if you like.' Juanita had the idea pretty much at the same time as she mentioned it.

'Oh! Can they?' Olwyn looked gobsmacked. 'How come? I thought you were too tied up?'

'Not as much as I was.'

'That would be amazing – have you got somewhere they can go?'

'The loft's converted. Murray used to have a model railway up there but he's outgrown it and he keeps saying he's going to sell it on eBay.'

'In that case, if you're sure . . .'

'Quite sure.'

Harmony entered the hall from the back, carrying her guitar. Olwyn said, 'Your mum's just offered to have band practice at yours every other week.'

'Has she?' Harmony looked doubtfully at Juanita. 'Have you?'

'I have. You'll need to watch out for your father though.' Juanita exchanged a mischievous look with Olwyn. 'He'll want to join in.'

'Get *off*.'

'Bye! Bye!' cried the mothers, having stolen a march for once.

* * *

'Hold on,' said Murray. 'Just a cotton-picking second – you did what?'

'Said they could practise here every other week.'

'Babes, are you out of your tiny mind?'

'It'll make her feel we're in the loop, that we're interested. And I have felt a bit guilty about Olwyn.'

Murray rubbed his brow fiercely. 'Where will we put them for a start?'

'In the loft, I thought.'

'I get it. This is an underhand way to force me to sell my train set.'

'Not underhand.'

'Have you been up there recently?'

'Harmony will help,' said Juanita.

'From the safe distance of the leisure park . . .'

'Well, if she doesn't,' said Juanita, 'it won't happen, will it?'

Maddie, while seeing that it was really kind of Uncle Tony to invite Jack up to London for 'a taster session' as he put it, had her reservations. To put it mildly.

She confided her fears to Belle when they were out for a hack. It was a hot day so they were taking it fairly easy, letting the horses walk at a gentle, nodding pace between the trees on the brow of the hill. When they reached the compass-stone – the same one Tony had rested on back in the spring – they paused to admire the view, though Maddie could take little pleasure in it today. Her head was full of a hectic kaleidoscope of imagined scenes, none of them encouraging, involving Jack as her godfather's guest for a day in town. The day was scheduled to begin with coffee (she had never known Jack to drink coffee) at Tony's mansion in Hampstead, followed by a visit to Broadcasting House, lunch at the Ivy and a brisk 'whizz round Tate Modern'. Everything about this programme, starting with the coffee and ending with modern art, sounded impossibly far outside Jack's comfort zone.

'A pox on his comfort zone!' cried Belle. 'The whole idea is to prise him out of it. And anyway, you underestimate him. It's an adventure.'

Maddie was glum. 'I so hope nothing happens to make either of them go off the idea of next month.'

'Why should it? How could it?'

'Belle,' said Maddie, 'this is Jack we're talking about. Our household is riven with rows every time he's home.'

'Yes,' said Belle, 'but that's with Ed, surely, who – forgive me – has no idea how to handle him. This will be different. Jack will raise his game when he's away from the two of you. Especially with someone famous.'

Maddie sighed. 'And then there's his appearance. I tried to get him to look more – you know . . .'

'I'll bet that was the biggest waste of time.'

'At least he was clean.'

'Result!' Belle leaned between the horses and laid her hand on Maddie's shoulder. 'Relax, honey. He'll have a ball.'

Maddie sort of knew Belle was right, but she would still have been happier to pack Jack off in a couple of weeks with no opportunity to change his mind. Whatever Belle said, Jack was *not* adventurous, not in the way she meant. Not like William, who skied and played rugby, and had his Duke of Edinburgh gold award. William couldn't wait for his gap year to start in September, to get to New Zealand and participate in all those lunatic adrenalin sports: jet-boating and wall-walking and bungee jumping and lord knows what else. Jack's ambitions, if he had them, were more secret and a lot less well-defined. She, if not Edmund, knew that. She lived with the twin fears that while William might break his neck skydiving in a foreign land, Jack might go seriously off the rails right here on their doorstep. Hard to say which was worse. Both were too dreadful to contemplate.

Forty minutes later, at the bottom of the hill, they parted company, with Belle dropping her reins and raising her clasped hands above her head.

'Courage!'

Jack had a window seat. As the train began to move, Tony – Jack had been urged to call him that – lifted his rolled-up paper and touched it to his forehead in farewell salute. Jack half-raised his own arm to return it, but was overcome with self-consciousness and turned the gesture into a more conservative, rather girlie wave. It wasn't till Tony had slid from view that he breathed out completely for what seemed like the first time that day.

Oh. Fucking. Wow!

Wicked!

The preceding eight hours had made him realize how long it was since he'd been happy. Not that he was miserable the whole time. Rationally, he knew that he had nothing serious to complain about. His parents were basically pretty much okay, they lived in a nice house even if it was stuck in the back end of nowhere, and most of the teachers at school were at least trying. The reason he felt misunderstood was because, crucially, he hadn't understood himself. But today, not every second, but most of it, he'd been in his element, where he could move and breathe and – yes! – be himself.

Tony was a top bloke. You could tell just from his house, which was so cool, so *loose*. A house where all the dull stuff was taken care of, so other stuff could happen. Loads of books and music (not all of it classical), several of the thinnest, meanest, wildest HD TVs Jack had ever seen, a sound system that ran into every room, a kitchen with weird Japanese units disguised so you couldn't see the join, or the knobs, a 'film library' with DVDs of every film known to man . . . And then there were the other people: a glamorous secretary who looked like a breakfast-TV presenter, and some sort of right-hand man who was the gayest thing Jack had ever encountered, right down to the green suede loafers.

After Tony's original visit Jack and William had speculated on his sexual orientation. Was he or wasn't he? William's view was predictably robust.

'Of course he bloody is! You can see it a mile off.'

'You say. Doesn't mean he screws around.'

'They're all promiscuous, it's a known fact. Watch your back, bro!'

'Fuck off. You're just jealous.'

William's response to this had been to smirk as if to say Jack could think what he liked, but he was deluding himself. In private, Jack had not been able to dismiss the possibility of Tony's being gay. His parents had never mentioned or implied such a thing, and he was super-sensitive to the vibes. But now, as the train gathered speed on its way out of London he realized that whatever Tony's preferences, they were so not an issue. His was a world where such things simply didn't matter. There was no pressure, no agenda, and yet his was a life lived purely for pleasure. And profit – he must be coining it in. Oh, and there was a great dog. The dogs at home were mostly outdoor dogs, and the two that weren't were psychos that Jack went out of his way to avoid. But Marlon was a full-on pet, all over you and allowed to be. Everyone there – Tony and the other two – had agreed that Marlon had taken to Jack immediately, and that Tony had better shape up. Marlon was given titbits, and allowed on beds and furniture, and wore a kerchief round his neck – actually, that *was* pretty gay . . .

But Jack was in heaven. In two weeks he'd be coming back. He'd be part of that household, part of that world. And he knew he could do it, that it would suit him, that he could become part of the team. No-one would want to make him be something other than what he was. He would fly!

Maddie tried to gauge, from her son's demeanour as he got off the train, how it had gone. But the truth was he looked exactly the same as when he'd got on the train early that morning.

'Hi,' she said.

'Hi.'

'All right?'

'Yes.' He gave the monosyllable an emphatic, upward inflection as if wondering why she needed to ask.

When they were in the car she gave it another try.

'So it all went well?'

'Yeah.'

'How was the Beeb?'

'The what?'

'Didn't you go to Broadcasting House?'

'Oh. Yeah – pretty much what I expected.'

Back at the house she asked, as Jack galumphed up the stairs, 'All in all – a success?'

He stopped and glanced down over his shoulder. 'Don't worry. We're still on for August.'

Fourteen

Whatever doubts Gwen entertained about the authenticity of Paddy's success, his launch party dispelled them. The invitation had trumpeted 'a champagne celebration' in the atrium of the Coverley Collection, Gant Street, Marylebone, a venue that initially meant nothing to her. The website showed a large, handsome but unremarkable Victorian house, and several interiors of great magnificence, including the atrium, displaying the accumulated treasure of its late owner, Sir Samuel Coverley. He had been a world traveller, and ahead of his time; the collection ranged from African tribal masks to the beginnings of Art Nouveau. There was some especially lovely jewellery and glass, if the website's featured items were anything to go by. There was a number and email address for replies, but Gwen didn't respond until the morning of the party when, finding herself with nothing better to do, she accepted.

On arrival the first thing she noticed was the sheer number of people present. How did – how *could* – the tortured and reclusive Paddy know so many? She gave her name to the trio of size-six greeters and plunged into the maelstrom. She was not, she considered, an unconfident person; she prided herself on her ability to hold her own in most company, and at the very least to suffer no loss of self-esteem if she failed. But this . . . Where to start? The high ceiling of the atrium captured the parrot-like din of the massed drinkers and sent it ricocheting deafeningly around. The main priority, she decided, was to find Paddy, but first she needed to collect herself.

She crossed the atrium to the far side and stood with her back to the throng, staring at a cabinet of French porcelain. Handily, the glass of the cabinet reflected a partial view of the room. And of her. She was struck, not altogether pleasantly, by how fierce she appeared. The planes and lines of her face were uncompromising, and her hair stuck up like the erect hackles of a suspicious terrier. She was wearing her best jeans and a purple silky T-shirt, but now she saw that the T-shirt made her biceps look muscly.

A grey-haired woman in an embroidered tunic came and stood next to her.

'Nice to have something to look at, isn't it?'

Gwen agreed that it was.

'I think we all find these occasions a bit of a trial. Whoever I'm speaking to I'm not the person they're after and they're always seeking an exit strategy. And vice versa, as often as not.'

Gwen made a non-committal sound. They both peered at the glass.

'What are those nymphs up to?' murmured the woman.

'I was wondering that.'

The woman turned from the cabinet and held out her hand. 'Camilla Bowes, by the way.'

'Gwen Paget.'

'Hello Gwen. What's your connection with publishing's man of the moment?'

'I knew him back in the day.'

'Hang on . . .' Camilla folded her arms and placed a forefinger against her lips. 'Gwen, you say.'

'That's right.'

'From the famous writers' circle?'

Gwen demurred. 'I don't know about famous.'

'No, no, you are,' said Camilla excitedly. 'He wasn't sure if you were coming. He is going to be so thrilled and delighted! Believe me – I'm his agent.'

'Good job,' said Gwen.

'Not a hard one, but look.' Camilla grabbed Gwen by the upper arm. 'Have you spoken to him yet?'

'Not yet, I've only just arrived.'

'You must! Come with me, we'll find him.'

'There's no rush.' Gwen extricated herself gently but firmly. 'I'll catch up with him in due course.'

'Promise?' Camilla peered into Gwen's face. 'You make sure you do. He'd be mortified if he missed you. Oh! Victor . . .' A bearded man in a Nehru jacket put his arm round Camilla and her moment's distraction gave Gwen the opportunity to escape.

She made a circuit of the perimeter. On either side of the room were displays of Paddy's novel: the cover – a noir-ish study of two figures by water, with an industrial skyline in the background; a giant photo of the author; and two boards, one displaying commendations (including, she was surprised to see, her own), and the other the publisher's promotional plans and deals already done on the book (extracts to be published in the *Sunday Times* and the sale of American rights were prominent among these). To one side of each display was a table, manned by a Size 6, with shiny piles of the book. Gwen took another glass of champagne and positioned herself so she could keep an eye on the room while studying Paddy's photograph.

He looked the same, but subtly emphasized and enhanced. The sallow, dark-chinned, undernourished appearance had been carefully maintained, though his hair was a little shorter and artfully ruffled, probably with the aid of product. The photo had been shot at an angle so that he looked down, unsmiling, at Gwen over his right shoulder. The effect was quizzical and sexy. He wore a shirt with a loosened tie – nice touch that, she thought; wearing a tie only under duress.

And then suddenly there he was, talking to a group right in front of her. She even recognized the jacket, a well-worn olive-green cord with mismatched buttons. When he glanced over and saw her she almost wished she hadn't shed Camilla quite so abruptly; it would have been nice to be seen talking to someone else instead of standing on her own staring at him over her glass. She lip-read his 'excuse me' and then he was right next to her. Change number one: he smelled nice.

'Hey,' he said. 'I was wondering if you'd make it. Really good to see you.'

'And you.' She sent a glance round the room. 'Haven't you done well?'

She meant it as a compliment, but it sounded rather sarcastic.

'We'll have to see,' was his comment. 'I wish I was as confident as them.'

'*Sunday Times*, American rights, what's not to be confident about?'

'The critics?'

'Anyway,' she said. 'Many congratulations.'

'Thanks for sending that quote, by the way. More than generous.'

'I meant it. Thank you for putting it on the board. Makes me feel like a player.'

Why had she said that? It made her sound needy and neurotic, as though she needed the exposure. And yes – he was looking at her keenly.

'You all right, Gwennie?'

'I'm fine.' She gave a dry little laugh. 'A bit jealous, maybe.'

'Oh God . . .' He frowned in a kind, regretful way. 'Don't be. I got lucky. And I owe you a hell of a lot.'

'You don't owe me anything,' she said (liar!). 'You wrote the book.'

'I did. I put in the graft, but you provided the necessary push.'

'Push?' She might as well have said *Ha!* 'You jumped!'

'Sorry about that, but you know damn well I'd never have gone otherwise. I was too comfortable.'

Gwen knew then that she was about to say something she'd really regret – something personal and bitter and damaging. Like the guests Camilla had described, she needed an exit strategy.

'Go on,' she said. 'You've got people to speak to, a room to work.'

'You're right, I do, but Gwennie – stay, will you? Don't go without saying.'

The opportunity to point out the blindingly obvious was right there, but she disdained it.

'Okay.'

'It's great that you're here.' He took a step backwards. 'And do me a favour, yeah?'

She tilted her head.

'Write, will you?' She stared back at him. 'It's what you do. You owe it to yourself at least. Just fucking write!'

She didn't speak, didn't even nod, and then he was back in the thick of it. Gwen saw Camilla's face, now hectic with excitement and champagne, peering past him at her, probably asking pertinent – no *im*pertinent – questions. Gwen reflected that in the few minutes they'd talked he hadn't once touched her. They hadn't touched, when touch had once been the chief currency of their relationship. Clearly touching was no longer on the agenda, not tonight, not for Paddy, anyway.

Victor, the man in the Nehru jacket, was moving towards her. Before he realized she'd seen him she walked away, leaving her half-full glass on the table by the piles of books. She didn't care if she was being rude – she needed air, and anonymity. Out in the street she walked for ten minutes fast, without stopping, before realizing she didn't know where she was, and had to ask a passer-by for the nearest tube station.

On the underground her humiliation turned to fury. Paddy had been a washed-up nearly man when they'd been lovers. Who the hell was he to order her to write?

'No,' said Sean at the shelter, in response to Rhada's enquiry. 'She's swapped her shift tonight. Gone up to London, I believe.'

'I wondered,' said Rhada, glancing down at her carrier bag, 'whether you, or anyone, would like some samosas?'

'Would we ever?' Sean took the bag from her, parted the handles and inhaled deeply. 'Yum-yum. You make them?'

'I make a batch quite regularly,' said Rhada, who had slaved over the stove the whole of the previous evening.

'Just on the off-chance?' Sean was teasing her.

'They're always very popular.'

'I must say it's really nice of you to think of us. These'll go down a storm. My problem's going to be getting this lot past the rest of the team.' He stood aside. 'Want to come in?'

'Oh, I don't know about that . . .' She glanced round him into the hall to where a man was sitting hunched up over a folded newspaper. 'I don't want to get under your feet.'

'Don't worry, you'll get kicked if you do. Come in and have a cuppa.' He took her arm and drew her in. 'Let them thank you themselves.'

The door closed behind her. The man in the hall looked up and Sean waved the bag under his nose.

'Home-made Indian grub, Phil – tell the others. First come first served.' He gestured grandly towards Rhada. 'Made by this lady.'

'That smells bloody lovely,' said Phil. 'Thanks, Miss.'

Rhada was pleasantly surprised by his politeness. But it turned out to be the norm – nearly everyone that evening addressed her as 'Miss' or 'Ma'am' or 'Lady'; it reminded her of the Indian community in which she'd been brought up, the friendly formality of it.

Sean heated up the samosas in the oven (she prevented him using the microwave, which made them soggy), and because this took a little longer quite a queue built up outside the kitchen. Encouraged, she suggested they lay them out on the table in the dining room so she could explain what they were and what she'd put in them. The difficulties she had with people's appearance – bad teeth, unwashed hair, dirty hands and clothes and so on – were still present, but diminished slightly with exposure. A lot of them did smell bad, but the aroma of the samosas helped with that, and the appreciation was sweet indeed.

Having been the first to meet her Phil plainly saw himself as chief spokesman.

'You're an excellent cook, Miss.'

'I'm glad you like them. I got this recipe from my mother, and she got it from hers. That's how it goes in Indian families.'

'Best way,' he agreed. 'I used to make curry in the army.'

'You should try again,' she said, and then added, 'You could make one here.'

'Oooh, I don't think so . . .' Phil glanced at Sean, who was leaning on the end of the table. 'Not allowed.'

'I don't see why,' said Sean. 'In fact, why not?'

Rhada found herself saying, 'I could help you make a curry.' Sean smiled placidly at her. 'But if you cook with me, it's clean hands.'

'That's right,' said Phil, looking round at the others. 'You got to be clean in the kitchen.'

It took no more than ten minutes for the samosas to disappear. As Rhada put the empty Tupperware boxes back in her carrier, Sean said: 'You'll be held to that, you know.'

'I hope so.'

'He'll ask when you're coming back.'

She looked at him as he opened the door. 'This time next week?'

'You're on.'

I'm sending a good old-fashioned letter, Tony had written to Maddie and Edmund, *because of the privacy it affords. Email is swift and convenient but computers tend to be communal. And a phone call isn't a matter of record. I simply wanted to say that insofar as I'm a judge of these things Jack's day in London was a great success. I certainly enjoyed it and Jack is delightful company – a very witty, observant, refreshing boy with an original mind, he does you credit. Everyone liked him, so you need have no fears for the planned longer stay next month. It's going to do both of us good . . .*

'He's like a man from another age, isn't he?' said Edmund. 'Charming letter, but is he talking about the same boy?'

'Don't let's quibble,' said Maddie. 'Everyone's happy, that's it.'

Edmund put his arm round her and nuzzled the side of her face. 'Shows we did something right . . . By the way, you had a call. Someone called Rhada. Don't know what she wants.'

'I'll come straight to the point,' said Rhada, 'and ask whether you'd be prepared to join us on the Marie Crompton committee.'

Maddie was glad the conversation was taking place on the phone so Rhada couldn't see the face she pulled.

'Gosh, this is unexpected. I don't know . . .'

'Someone's departed recently and when I mentioned you the others jumped at the idea.'

'How flattering! To be honest, Rhada, I'm not a committee person.'

There was a cool little laugh at the other end. 'Who is? I'm not sure there's any of us that would describe ourselves that way.'

Maddie realized she was being politely rebuked.

'I didn't quite mean that. I'm happy to help out with projects—'

'Brilliant!'

'Yes, but I do prefer to avoid the commitment of regular meetings.'

'There are only six a year,' said Rhada. 'It's not arduous, I promise. Do say yes.'

'I'm sorry,' said Maddie firmly, 'I really can't.'

She quite enjoyed her first meeting. Well, perhaps 'enjoyed' was an overstatement, but it wasn't nearly as bad as she'd feared. It was held in the just-this-side-of-twee converted farmhouse of the chairwoman, and there was wine, coffee and nibbles. Everyone was effusive in their thanks and welcomed her aboard with open arms.

'We perfectly understand,' said the chairwoman, Della, 'that you were press-ganged.' Here she shot a look at Rhada, who made a muscle-flexing gesture and got a laugh. 'Never mind, we're delighted to have a new face at the table, and I assure you we won't take advantage!'

It was almost embarrassing, and Maddie found herself saying, 'But since I'm here I must make myself useful.'

There was more laughter, over which Della assured her that she mustn't worry on that score, they were going to make use of her!

It had turned out that this was just a 'loose ends' meeting before the summer break; there was no lunch in August, and September was taken care of. A good chunk of time was taken up with discussion of the Golden Anniversary, which Maddie found a bit surprising, but maybe it was meant as a sort of compliment to her.

'What an incredible day,' said the secretary, Penny, a nice woman with a harassed, run-down air. 'I think it changed lives.'

'It certainly got us the bus,' agreed Della.

Rhada said to Maddie, 'He's an extraordinary man, your godfather.'

Maddie confessed that she was beginning to see that. 'You have to remember he's been part of my life for ever, he and my mother were friends at Cambridge, so I've always sort of taken him for granted.'

They all agreed that a prophet was without honour, and so on. A woman with spiky hair spoke up from the end of the table.

'So what do you think of him now?'

Maddie looked at the questioner. She sensed a tension round the table — a soft intake of breath, a twiddling of pencils, a little bridling, a sense that the question was if not rude, at least inappropriate. But she hadn't much cared for the collective feather-bedding, and rather liked the question's directness.

'I'm very fond of him; he's been a brilliant godfather — never a birthday or a Christmas without a crisp bank note.' Chuckles here. 'And of course he often pops up on telly. But since I heard him give the talk down here I admire him more than I did. He did seem to say some jolly sensible things.' Fearing that this sounded like faint praise, she went on: 'He was brilliant, I thought, but then he is a professional speaker, so I suppose . . . But he seemed very spontaneous.' She petered out, all eyes upon her.

'Of course you weren't there, Gwen,' said Della. 'You missed a treat.'

Gwen addressed Maddie. 'I'm beginning to see that.'

Maddie found herself liking this Gwen. She was a bit of an

oddity, not like the others, but she was certainly the Tabasco in this particular mix.

'Maybe,' she said, 'you'd like to come to me for a meeting in the autumn. If you don't mind trekking out of town – we've got the space.'

There was a warm chorus of approval for this idea. *Oh well,* thought Maddie, *I was bound to become a do-gooder one of these days and it might as well be now.* She caught Gwen's eye and they exchanged a smile.

Gwen had great respect for the complicated psychology of writing. God knows she'd advised enough other writers, including Paddy, on how to deal with it, but now she was tussling with it herself and the experience wasn't proving a happy one.

What had he said? *Just fucking write. You owe it to yourself.* Once she'd got over feeling mortified and hopping mad she'd considered these words very seriously. Was it just an exit line to get her off his back? Was he being a patronizing git? Or was it a sign of the de-infantilizing of their relationship, a spot of writer-to-writer straight talking? His manner had suggested the latter, but that was almost more grown-up-ness than she could currently handle.

It was the July meeting of the Marie Crompton committee that coincided with (or might even have been the cause of) her change of attitude. Not long before that, Sean had told her of Rhada's visit to the shelter, 'the Night of the Samosas', and then Gwen had encountered her there the following week when Rhada was teaching Phil, Rosa and a couple of others how to make vegetable curry. A small pang of jealousy was superseded by admiration for Rhada, who she knew would have had to overcome anxiety and fastidiousness, but who was doing a good job. Gwen herself wasn't sure she'd want to eat a vegetable curry cooked by that lot, but fair play to them.

'Well done,' she said, as she was making tea for them all in the kitchen and Rhada was stashing her box of herbs and spices in the food cupboard. 'It's sort of strange seeing you here.'

'I've had fun,' said Rhada, taking off her apron.

'Smells good, too.'

'It needs to simmer for a while yet.'

'They'll eat anything, any time. Think you'll do it again?'

'Of course she will,' piped up Sean. 'Won't you, Rhada?'

When Rhada had gone, he said to Gwen, 'That's a very nice lady. How do you know her?' When she'd explained, he added, 'She fits a lot in with the day job, doesn't she? And stays looking like that? Is she single?'

'Sean.'

'What?'

'Have you been hitting on her?'

He grinned. 'Not yet.'

'Jeez!' Gwen had to laugh. 'You are *so* not her type!'

'We'll have to see,' said Sean. 'Worth a try.'

This exchange had hummed like a vibrating wire in the back of Gwen's brain for days afterwards. The trouble was she had got so used to seeing herself as different. She could even see that her continued involvement with the Marie Crompton was because the other women confirmed her sense of her own difference. Marian sometimes referred to her as the 'radical conscience' of the committee, and though it was meant as a joke she felt flattered by it. But now here was Rhada chopping sweet potatoes and coriander alongside gap-toothed Phil and stinky Rosa at the shelter, without turning a hair – not visibly, at least. In that context Rhada was still the same – immaculate, well-presented, a little prissy. Completely her usual self, take it or leave it. And they weren't just taking it, they were lapping it up. Especially Sean, who was plainly smitten.

The corollary of this was that she, Gwen, was clearly *not* so very different from anyone else. You didn't need to wear combats to be radical. Anyone, given the necessary good will and resolve, could work at the shelter. And though not quite everyone could write a novel, she was beginning to appreciate that the skills could be learned, and the right mindset achieved, and that if she wished to call herself a writer she'd better get her arse in gear and start doing some writing.

A damn sight easier said than done, as she was finding out. In the sequestered untidiness of home she paced about looking for things that had to be done before she could begin. Her pride protested furiously against simply taking Paddy's advice (she chose to ignore the fact that he had successfully taken hers), and besides, she was blocked. She wasn't even sure that the novel she'd begun was the right one. Like some marriages, it seemed to thrive on separation. When she was engaged in some other activity – reading, Googling, feeding next door's cat – she felt quite warmly towards it, was able to kindle a small spark of enthusiasm. But the moment she was at the keyboard and had it, so to speak, under her fingers, it turned cold and intractable like dried-up Plasticine. The paralysis wasn't helped by the knowledge that she ought to have been able to unlock it by an effort of will, as she advised others to do.

The meeting at Della's was the first she'd been to since Paddy's book launch. In between there had been ten days of mind-numbing avoidance and inertia. But there had been a change in the air on the committee: Juanita had gone; Marian had sent apologies, she was in the States; Penny was pale and harassed; Rhada she now saw in a completely different light; only Della was the same. And then there was the new member, a posh, pretty girl (the sort you called 'girl' well into their sixties) evincing all the aw-shucks reluctance of the co-opted member, but clearly ready to pull her weight. It turned out she was some relation of Anthony Chance, but she didn't play on that. Gwen had rather taken to her. Very probably, *she* thought she was different. Gwen was coming to realize that the Marie Crompton was a far more disparate group of individuals than she had given them credit for till now.

When she got back – it wasn't a shelter night – she dug out a notebook and biro, put on a Philip Glass CD, rolled some dope and sat down to write. It didn't matter what, she told herself, the object of the exercise was to go with the flow and cover the page.

Two hours later she had covered not one page but six with her spidery writing in which not just the letters but the words were joined together with long, hammocky lines. And when she re-read what she'd written she discovered that she had drawn on ideas which were part of the embryonic novel languishing on her hard disk, so all was not wasted.

She didn't feel pleased, or congratulate herself – to do so would have been to tempt fate. Instead she laid the pen and pad aside, swapped Philip Glass for Annie Lennox, and embarked on a little clearing up to the accompaniment of 'Sisters are Doing it for Themselves'.

Fifteen

Penny conceded that the boating holiday had been a good idea of Graham's. Granted he had probably suggested it because with Dom and his friend along, the two of them would have very little time – and no space – to themselves. They would be running a kind of floating mini-holiday camp – separate berths; closeness without intimacy; and the boys to feed, occupy and generally provide a distraction.

They were cruising down the Kennet and Avon canal. Dom and Ivan were pleasantly bored a good deal of the time, but they had iPods and Xboxes with them. The highlights of the day were the locks. They'd brought bikes, and now and again the boys would take to dry land and ride on to some pre-arranged stopping place. Penny would be in the minute galley, or sitting on the stern of *Calagogo* with a book watching the water slide gently away behind them while Graham drove. It was good that he had something to do. She could tell that he was reasonably content; he'd always been a sucker for systems and gadgets and the narrow boat tickled that particular nerve. Also, they were away from home but had a homelike array of small activities to earth them, and they were on the move – a moving target, making it harder for their preoccupations to get a purchase.

The weather had not been great, but it was all right till now. There had been periods of soft drizzle, but plenty of moody, tepid days that suited their sluggish passage through the folds of Somerset. Today however there was more persistent rain, and Graham and the boys had embarked on a complicated outing to go to the cinema, involving first the bikes, then a bus to an out-of-town leisure park. Penny could have gone, but the film they wanted to see was boy-stuff and besides she was attracted by the idea of an afternoon on her own. Dom, bless him, had suggested they bring back fish and chips 'to cheer her up' (what did he know?) but she'd declined. The thought of the oily packages making the long journey by bus and bike wasn't appetizing.

She told them to go ahead and eat at the diner on the leisure park.

'Sure you'll be okay?' Graham had asked before setting off.

'I'm looking forward to it,' she said. 'I like being on my own.' She knew it was impossible, not to mention dangerous, to be truthful all the time, but she wanted to be straightforward, to lead by example. And it worked – Graham brightened visibly.

'I bet you are. Nice bit of P and Q.'

He gave Penny a kiss on the cheek, one that lingered for a nanosecond longer than was usual of late, and then joined the boys waiting impatiently for him on the bank. She watched as they wobbled away along the towpath, Graham bringing up the rear, and had to batten down the emotional hatches a bit (she was falling into a nautical way of thinking).

An hour after they left the rain stopped, and the sky lifted. She moved her nest of deck cushions to the prow of the boat and made herself comfortable with a mug of coffee and a book. She opened the book, but didn't read; it was so nice watching the ducks and moorhens, the gentle river traffic, the walkers, dogs and joggers on the towpath. There was another narrow boat, the *Raggedy Ann*, moored alongside theirs, and the woman was pottering about, shaking out rugs and watering plants. She gave Penny a wave and called out.

'This is more like it, eh?'

'It's lovely.'

'Got rid of them for a while? I saw them pedalling away.'

'They've gone to the pictures.'

'Good God!' The woman laughed. 'I hope they've taken rations; that's quite a trek from here.'

Penny only hoped they wouldn't abandon the enterprise and reappear, perhaps waving the fish and chips to cheer her up. But they didn't, and she knew they'd done well when at five o'clock Dom texted: 'In the Q!'.

She appreciated the rare, precious peace, though she was conscious that she would not relish it so much when it was no longer rare and precious. She liked the bustle and domestic imperatives of family life, and feared she was one of those women who would suffer acutely from empty-nest syndrome. Especially now when everything was an unknown quantity. More and more she found herself remembering those early days in the house when they'd been so busy (but never too tired for sex), and everything – house, garden, kids, holidays – was communal and shared. There was a simplicity to those days; the fresh air and exercise had their emotional equivalent.

Now she had negotiated this fragile and, if she continued to be honest, uneasy peace. Their togetherness was freighted with complications. But she didn't regret it. She had no idea whether Graham was seeing Sam (she was sure it was her old friend Sam, who had gone strangely quiet of late), and she was never going to ask; that was her side of the bargain, to feign a lack of interest. But she was only human, and couldn't help wondering. If he had been seeing her in recent weeks it couldn't have been very often or for very long, a fact that even the boys had noticed.

'Has Dad changed his job?' Dom had asked.

'Not as far as I know.'

'Only he's not away so much.'

'Well, he wants to see more of you.'

'Cool.'

Nathan, though, was not so easily fooled. His question had sent shivers up her spine.

'You and Dad okay?'

'Of course we are! How do you mean?' She shouldn't have added the second bit; it told him exactly what he wanted to know.

'What's with all the happy-families stuff?'

She laughed. 'That's good, isn't it?'

Nathan was at the kitchen table picking a candle to bits; little knobs and flakes of wax were littered over the surface.

'Not over-compensation, then.'

'Over-compensation? For what?' She was like a guilty politician, always answering questions with questions.

'You tell me, Mum.'

'Sorry,' she said, shrugging, smiling, trapped. 'Can't help.'

Nathan gathered the bits of wax together with the side of one hand and scraped them off into the cupped palm of the other. Then he tipped the bits into the sink – no change there then – and left the room without saying anything else. Penny was used to her sons' elliptical speech, and expert in its interpretation, but this leaving her holding the conversational baby was a new one.

She tried not to look ahead to the empty-nest moment. The boys were the basis of the contract she'd made with Graham, and when they were all gone, the contract would be fulfilled. He'd be entitled to say, 'Job done, I'm off.' But that was still about five years away. Minimum. A lot could change in five years. In the meantime, she'd made her bed and was quite prepared to lie in it.

The bed bit they were managing. They were bed-mates in the strictly non-sexual, non-progenitive sense. When they were wakeful they read, and listened to the radio, but avoided talking about anything except practicalities. This official sexlessness was rather more comfortable than the unhappy second-guessing and repression that had preceded it. She had never exactly lusted after Graham, never *desired* him as he had once desired her, and if he no longer desired her because he wanted someone else, then there wasn't so much difference, she rationalized, between then and now.

They were still in a trial period – she'd had to agree to that, it was only fair – but she'd stipulated that it be no less than a year. They had to go through all the usual annual things – Christmas and birthdays and anniversaries and school events and holidays, like this – to see if it could be done. The truth was that while Graham was managing, so was she. She supposed that this was what the life-coaches and agony aunts meant when they spoke of 'taking control' and being 'proactive'. She had devised and proposed a plan and it had been adopted. She was sure that Juanita, not to mention Gwen, would consider that she was letting Graham have his cake and eat it, but all she could say was that wasn't how it felt.

Later on she took a glass of wine to her place on deck, and then her supper, an omelette with tomato salad. It was beginning to be dusk around eight now, but because it was warm she stayed there, watching the stars come out, and the rise of a softly freckled half moon. The towpath grew shadowy and quiet and she could hear the secretive gloops and rustles of animals and birds, some bedding down for the night, others presumably setting out on nocturnal adventures. In the middle distance beyond the water meadows she could make out the moving lights of cars on the main road. The windows of the *Raggedy Ann* glowed cosily; she could hear the couple talking over the clink of plates and glasses, soft jazz in the background: a whole small, other world. The woman was often chatty, a glass or a cigarette in her hand; she was older than Penny, a child of the sixties, attractive but marked by a rackety life and unprotected sunbathing. He looked older because his hair was grey (as hers probably was if she let the copper tint grow out) and he was quieter, but he had a twinkle in his eye. Penny enjoyed having these temporary neighbours, and the fact that the other couple saw, in them, only a happy family holiday with a dad who took the boys off on bikes.

She went downstairs, 'below decks' for a while, washed up her supper things, read for a bit and then put on a sweater and went back up, in time to see the cycle lights bobbing along the path.

'Ahoy there!' called Graham.

Dom said, 'Mum, you should have come!'

'No you shouldn't,' said Graham, padlocking his bike to the capstan on the bank. 'I enjoyed going but it was a right load of rubbish.'

'Go on, you were bricking yourself, Dad,' said Dom.

'Yeah,' agreed Ivan, and added politely, 'But it was pretty scary.'

They emerged from the darkness and came over the little gang-plank on to the *Calagogo*. The boys went immediately down the ladder to their computer games. Graham stood by her and stretched. A year ago he'd been getting a paunch but, she noticed, that had gone.

'How've you been?' he asked. 'Did you stay here all the time?'

'Yes. I was outside for most of the afternoon, it was nice.'

'Not cold?' He placed the back of his hand to her cheek, and she shivered.

'No.'

'Fancy a snifter?'

'Do we have one?'

'We've got some of that rum. Coke if you want it.'

'Yo-ho-ho,' she said. 'Why not?'

Marian had been with Ros for a week and all that time the weather had been almost unbearably hot and humid. 'Almost' because the house had air-conditioning, and they had a pool, too – nothing grand but one you could do half a dozen strong strokes in, and Jay and his father had erected a summer house from a kit, with a deck big enough to put up a folding garden table for four. She was warming to Jay; on his own turf he was more communicative and she could see that in his gentle, unassuming way he was a support to Ros, and a useful counterbalance to her manic energy.

Marian couldn't get over the house – the size, the number of rooms, the state-of-the-art gadgetry, especially in the kitchen where there seemed to be an electronic tool for everything from slicing pineapple to warming plates. Jay and Ros's bedroom was palatial, with an en-suite that included a Jacuzzi bath, a walk-in shower and Jack-and-Jill basins, an eminently sensible idea. But when she oohed and aahed they laughed at her.

'It's all pretty standard,' said Jay. 'This is just an estate house. We were stretched to get it but if we're lucky we'll stay here a long time.'

Outside, as well as the pool, there was a big garden, laid mostly to grass, and because the development had been carved out of woodland, some fine big trees in which grey squirrels scampered and leapt. They didn't have any flower beds; they just liked the space for Lucy-Anne to play in as she got older, and for them to sit out with friends. Jay had a mower like something built by the Marines, and had fun making patterns on the grass when he cut it.

Marian still wondered how they managed on the salary of a freelance website designer, but Ros planned to go back to work in eighteen months so that would help. They seemed to be prospering, but in this land of plenty it was hard to say.

Jay's studio, on the mezzanine floor to one side of the gallery, remained a private, unexplored zone. She knew he must be benefitting from the Internet boom, but there was something else, work he did in the evenings with music on, that she was curious about.

No doubts about Lucy-Anne, though. She was a joy. And so bright! She remembered things, like where Marian had left her sunglasses, and that she liked yoghurt with her granola. She watched Marian as though she were a member of some rare species – a white tiger, perhaps, or a unicorn – with a mixture of admiration and curiosity. There was a hymn from Marian's school days, in which the saints cast down their crowns, 'lost in wonder'. That was Lucy-Anne, and it was delightful to be the cause of it. She took advantage by asking about Jay.

'What does Daddy do?'

'He draws.' Lucy-Anne, drawing herself as it happened, didn't look up.

'What does he draw?'

'Pictures,' said Lucy-Anne, in a what-else? tone.

'Yes, of course, but pictures of what?'

A scribbling silence. 'Everything.' She sat back. 'Look Gan – car.'

It took Wilf to draw back the veil on that one. He turned up unannounced one morning when Lucy-Anne was taking a nap and Ros had taken Jay to collect his car from the garage. Marian was loading the dishwasher when a man appeared at the patio door; a not-quite strange man, but nonetheless disconcerting.

'Ah! Oh – is it . . .?'

'Wilf, yeah. Hi, Marian, sorry I startled you.'

She recognized him now from his brief appearance at the wedding. But then he had been a sad-faced, self-contained figure on the sidelines, still getting over the death of his wife, finding the occasion hard. Marian was not at all prepared for this genial, loose-limbed, grizzled charmer in faded jeans, nor for the tsunami of sex-appeal that accompanied him into the room.

He grinned at her. 'See they got you working.'

'About time,' she said. 'I've been waited on hand and foot for the past week. But they're both out so I thought I'd steal a march . . .'

'You carry on.' He opened a cupboard. 'I'll make us some coffee.'

He was completely at home in the kitchen and by the time she closed the machine the cafetière was full and the mugs ready.

'Cream, sugar?'

'Neither thanks.'

He poured, raised an amused eyebrow. 'Poolside?'

They went out and sat at the table on the deck.

'Here we are then,' he said. 'Darby and Joan.'

'I suppose.' She laughed. She felt a little out of her depth, but not uncomfortably so.

'But hey,' he said, 'it's your lucky day – I'm the pool boy.'

'Really?'

'I do their pool maintenance. In and out like a ghost when no-one's looking. It's my specialty.' He looked at her. 'You been in?'

'Lots of times. With Lucy-Anne.'

'What a doll.' He jerked his thumb at the water. 'Luxury, huh?'

'For a Brit, it is.'

'Not so bad here, either. They're doing okay, these kids of ours.'

Emboldened by his friendly informality, Marian said, 'Now tell me – I'm dying to know – what sort of work does Jay do? Other than the web design? I mean I know he's an artist.'

'Darn right. You seen any of his stuff?'

'No, that's why—'

'Time you did. When you've finished I'll show you.'

'He won't mind?'

'Why should he mind a little fatherly pride?' He gazed at her as though she were much the most interesting thing on his mind. 'You don't look like your daughter.'

'No.' She smoothed the back of her hair to protect her face from his scrutiny. 'Unfortunately.'

'How's that?'

'Oh, I don't know, she's a sort of golden girl, she didn't get that from me.'

'Your husband neither.'

'Ex-husband. No.'

'You're right though, Rosamund would pass for a Californian. You're the English rose.'

'You call her Rosamund?'

'It's her name.'

'To her face?' Marian was astonished.

'Sure.'

'Only if Dennis or I did it she used to think we were angry with her.'

He shook his head. 'Rosamund's an amazing name, not a pissed-off one.'

'Then I'm pleased you use it,' she said. 'Too late for me, I'm afraid.'

'It's never too late.' He put down his mug. 'We should go out one night.'

She was sure she'd misunderstood. 'We were planning a dinner at IHOP with Lucy-Anne.'

'No, I mean the two of us.' He pointed at her, then himself. 'You and me.' He didn't wait for her reply, but stood up. 'You ready to look at some pictures?'

They went up to the gallery and into Jay's studio. It was small, and untidy without being messy – a nice room. The pictures were cartoons and they were everywhere. Brilliant cartoons of social and family life, full of observation and detail, laugh-out-loud funny. Marian was entranced.

'Have you heard of Posy Simmons?' she asked.

Wilf was perched on the edge of the desk. 'Tell me about her.'

'Just that she's a bit like this – a proper artist who does cartoons of families and professional affectations and middle-class mores. Everything, really.' As she said it she realized Lucy-Anne had been right.

'Sounds great. I'll check her out on the web.'

'Do . . . But these are *fab*,' she said earnestly, anxious not to diminish Jay with the comparison. 'I had no idea.'

'He keeps it to himself. The other stuff brings in the dough, but this is his real passion.'

As she moved round the walls, peering, she asked, 'Does he sell them?'

'Starting to. Probably why he hasn't mentioned it.'

'Tempting fate,' she agreed.

As they came out into the gallery they could hear Jay and Ros outside. Wilf said, 'Tomorrow suit you for dinner?'

'I'm not sure . . .'

'If I don't hear from you I'll pick you up at six-thirty.'

'Okay – thank you.'

He followed her down the stairs. 'And don't let them talk you out of it, huh?'

'Has he?' said Ros. She called to the pool where Jay was bouncing Lucy-Anne in her armbands. 'Jay, did you hear that?'

'What?'

'Wilf's taking Mum out tomorrow night!'

'Oh boy.' Jay shook his head. 'Incorrigible or what?'

The place was a converted station goods yard serving steaks and beer, with a small stage at one end on which a blues band was just setting up. Marian hadn't expected music: it somehow changed the tenor of the occasion. Wilf was in jeans and a check shirt; she felt wrongly dressed in her safe black trousers and red jacket.

'You should have warned me,' she said. 'I look like the typical uptight Brit.'

'And there was I thinking you looked terrific,' he said, handing her a cold bottle of beer. 'That okay? They could do you a wine but I don't recommend it.'

She'd have loved a glass of wine, but not wanting to seem any stuffier than she felt already, she said, 'No, this is perfect.' She took a long swig and felt better. 'What a great place.'

'I knew you'd like it,' he said, and for some reason she felt flattered as though he'd given her a compliment. 'Wait till you hear the band. Couple of these guys I used to play with.'

'I didn't know you were a musician,' she said, although she seemed to remember some jokey talk about Wilf and his 'ageing rockers'.

'Not any more. There's no high like it but I only ever had a dozen chords and I needed to get out before I became pathetic.'

'You . . .' She was going to say 'could never be pathetic' but changed it to, 'I realize I don't know what you do.'

'I'm kind of retired now, but I was a carpenter. Specialized in retro stuff – Irish pubs, farmhouses, panelling, all that. There isn't an O'Leary's for miles around that I didn't have a hand in.'

'So it was a successful business?'

'Yup.' He nodded. 'I made money and had a ball making it. Molly and I were high on the hog for quite a while. She'd been through tough times with me, so she deserved it.'

Marian felt she should acknowledge the redoubtable departed Molly.

'You must miss her terribly.'

'Not so terribly, not any more. We made each other happy; now she's gone that's what I remember.' He took a swig of beer and wiped his mouth, as if wiping away that subject before starting on the next. 'These days I take a few commissions from friends, and help out the youngsters.'

'They're so lucky to have you,' she said. 'I wish I lived closer so I could be of some use – in the same country, even!'

'What's to stop you?'

He asked so casually that she was caught off-guard.

'Nothing, I suppose.'

He smiled steadily at her and then looked away towards the stage. 'Want to grab some food before this kicks off?'

Marian was glad that when the band did begin to play, it was music for listening rather than dancing. A few diehards and exhibitionists took to the floor, but Wilf didn't suggest they join them. Because they were near the back it was possible to talk, though it meant putting their heads close together.

They left at ten, and came out into a close, starry night. The wide, low-rise street was like an Edward Hopper painting. A woman, leaving behind them, touched Marian's arm and said, 'I just love your jacket – what a colour!'

'How kind – thank you.'

'You're English.'

Marian laughed. 'How could you tell?'

'You look great, anyway, girl.'

'That was nice of her,' said Marian as they walked to the car.

'People speak as they find around here.' He clicked the key and the car winked at them. 'She liked your jacket; she was going to tell you. By the way, did I forget to mention? *I* like your jacket.'

'You said. And thanks, Wilf, for an absolutely lovely evening.'

'My pleasure, Marian.' He held the door for her, closed it, and walked round to the driver's side. 'Nothing I like better than cool blues with a hot lady.' He didn't look at her as he said this, and that made the compliment somehow more resonant; it hung in the air between them, like a scent.

When they pulled up outside the house it was dark except for a glow in the hall.

'They left a light on for you,' he said. 'Stay right there.'

He jumped out and ran round to her side, then walked her, like a queen, to the front door. She was suddenly uncertain of the protocol, what to do, how to behave – it had been a long time.

She held out her hand. There was safety in formality. 'Thank you again, Wilf. I'm glad to have got to know my fellow in-law better. It makes me feel I know Jay better, too.'

He held her hand for a second before releasing it. 'How long are you over for?'

'Another two weeks.'

'We'll see plenty of each other, then,' he said. 'I come and go.'

'Hope Dad gave you a good time,' said Jay next morning at breakfast.

'A very good time, it was great fun.'

'Where'd he take you?'

'Oh, what was the name? Part of an old train station – there was a band.'

Jay and Ros exchanged a look and whooped. 'Casey's!' said Ros. 'That's his favourite.'

'Not every day he takes someone there,' said Jay. 'Consider yourself a smash hit.'

Sixteen

Rhada was a Friend of the Guildhall Theatre and as such benefited from a two-for-one deal on first nights. She didn't always take advantage of the offer, she quite liked going alone, but on this occasion she knew just the right person to ask.

'What a happy thought,' said Colin. 'I'd like that very much.'

Ayckbourn, Rhada considered, made very suitable entertainment for single people – his plays provided proof, if proof were needed, that marriage was no happy ending, and indeed that getting too closely tangled up with anyone was unlikely to prove a comfortable experience. This was what she'd always thought.

She met Colin in the foyer. He bought programmes, then they went up to the bar to order drinks for the interval, and they took their seats.

'Front stalls!' he exclaimed. 'This is a rare treat.'

'They are a bargain,' she pointed out. 'And anyway, my days of squinting and craning at the stage are over. Front stalls for a play, centre dress circle for a musical.'

'I so rarely do either. Not organized enough. Cinema's my thing – as you know.'

'How was your holiday, back in the spring?' she asked.

'Holiday . . .' Colin furrowed his brow. 'Ah, you must mean the long weekend in Montant.'

'Is that where you went?'

'It was delightful. Very relaxed but sophisticated. It would have suited you, actually. As it was I had to content myself with being that interesting single gentleman with a good book and a faraway expression. I ate too much though – you do on your own, even with Patrick O'Brian for company.'

This was Rhada's moment and she would have seized it if at that very moment the lights hadn't gone down, and the audience buzz subsided to an expectant rustle. Then at the interval the bar was so crowded and noisy she didn't get round to it then, either. It was only when they were installed in Viva Pizza! deciding, over an American Hot (Colin) and a Quatro Stagione (Rhada), that though the performances had been good it was all a bit predictable, that she said, 'To be honest I rather regretted not coming with you. In the spring.'

'Oh, did you?' She could hardly believe how much emotion there was in those three syllables. 'I understood, of course, but I was very sorry I couldn't persuade you. I thought of you a lot on my solitary wanderings.'

'I don't go away enough,' she said. 'But I'm remedying that. After Christmas I'm going to visit my family in India, in Chennai.'

'Are you indeed?' He looked delighted, full of admiration. 'I was under the impression you'd lost touch with your relations.'

'I had, but I had one of those moments. You see all those programmes on television about people rediscovering their roots . . .' She gave a little shrug. 'I thought, I have all that, and I'm ignoring it. I rang them up.'

'And were they absolutely flabbergasted?'

'They were, but so thrilled. To be honest I'm a little nervous about seeing them after all this time.'

'Don't suppose you're the only one!'

'No.' She took a breath. 'Colin, I did wonder whether you might like to link up with me somewhere, towards the end of my trip. Depending on your plans, of course. It doesn't have to be India; I could break the journey on the way back. We could have that weekend that we missed.' Unusually for her she was gabbling, and corrected herself. 'That I missed.'

'Splendid idea,' said Colin, lightly, relieving her of her anxiety. 'I'd be more than up for that.'

She took a sip of wine and looked him in the eye. 'May I say something?'

'Please.'

'We've been good friends all this time,' she went on. 'We get on so well, we like the same things, we do things at the same pace . . .'

'You see no reason to change all that.'

'I suppose – no.'

'Perfect,' he said. 'Friends it shall be.'

★   ★   ★

At home, there was a message from Sean on Rhada's answering machine. But her last thought as she curled up beneath her pristine duvet was:

'I've got a friend!'

Della and Brian usually reached the semi-finals of the tennis club mixed knock-out tournament. They were good players, who took the line that tennis should be fun, so they didn't stress over it; they played within themselves. This meant that they would generally beat the first four couples they encountered pretty easily, but with a degree of good humour and casualness that left the opposition spitting feathers. Confronted with serious opposition, usually in the semis, they tended to bow out gracefully, not in a complete white-wash, but with that same air of not trying too hard which was guaranteed to infuriate the opponents who were left wondering: Had they really won? Or simply been allowed to?

It was a bloody good trick if you could pull it off, other members agreed. But then the Figes were such a lovely couple, you had to hand it to them. Della was quite simply a sweetie, who would do anything for anyone, and Brian was such a character! When he wondered aloud in the bar how on earth she put up with him, most people thought the same thing. The answer (said the women) could only be love.

The Figes weren't daft – they knew what people thought and said. Della in particular knew exactly what she was good at (she still remembered, with pleasure, the compliment given to her by Sir Anthony), and she definitely wasn't one of those who thought it honourable to try, and fail.

The rumba was a case in point; she still smarted when she thought of it. She and Brian enjoyed their dancing, and she was proud of the fact that they attended classes as a couple and so could go through their paces when a social occasion required it. But the rumba had defeated them. They had been quite simply unable to summon the necessary stylized sensuality, the choreographed vertical sex, which was especially galling when most of the other combos – even stately-as-a-galleon all-female couples – managed to ham it up quite successfully. Worse still, they'd been unable to laugh it off. They'd got cross with themselves and each other, and in the end found reasons to be absent for two or three weeks until the rumba was done and dusted. This wasn't a plan they'd discussed; it was understood between them. Not nice, not dignified; mortifying.

Della had since given this small failure a lot of thought, and had reached the conclusion that their inability to rumba was due to something more fundamental than mere footwork. They'd been uncomfortable. The dance required something that was inaccessible to them. But why? She and Brian had a good sex life, in the sense that they still did it regularly. Della believed profoundly in not letting oneself go; personal maintenance was high on her agenda, not only for reasons of self-esteem but because she owed it to Brian. No-one was getting any younger but that didn't mean one should cave in under the pull of gravity . . .

But Della had a secret; she didn't enjoy sex. She didn't know if Brian knew, and if he did whether it made any difference. It was so much easier for a man – they conquered, they saw, they came (she had read it somewhere, very neatly put in her view) – but all the same she hoped he didn't notice; she loved him very much and would have hated to hurt his feelings. She'd nearly been rumbled by the rumba.

Tennis wasn't the rumba. The Figes were pretty comfortable with their game, but it was crucial to know your limitations, and not to try too hard, because the resulting humiliation would be messy and difficult, two words not in Della's lexicon. This year they had reached the semis as usual, and were up against the Lumms, a couple noted for their competitiveness, older than them but classic club players, crafty and consistent. Theirs was a brand of tennis against which it was nigh impossible to feign insouciance. The Lumms simply wouldn't notice, or care, what you were up to, but would get on with the job of returning the ball – every time.

Della prepared herself mentally for this tricky encounter, prepared to smile and smile and not to run too fast. What caused the change was a chance remark of Brian's on the day of the match, as he slung their racquets in the back of the car.

'Here we go again,' he said. 'Another triumph for the plodders over the naturally talented.'

'Yes,' she said automatically. And then, as they pulled out of the drive. 'Why?'

'Because that's what happens. What tends to happen.'

'What we let happen,' she said, quietly, because it had always been an unspoken understanding.

Brian hadn't heard, and continued cheerily, 'Who cares anyway? Not us, eh babes?'

'Maybe we should.'

'Let's go out there and play our game and if that means letting the Lumms trudge on their dreary way all the way to the rose bowl —' he waved a hand — '*che sera sera.*'

Della turned to him and said more firmly: 'We could have our names on that rose bowl.'

'You what?' Brian laughed heartily. 'Don't start thinking like that, or it won't be any fun.'

'No, honestly,' she said. 'I think we should try to win.'

'Okay . . .' This was more of an I-hear-you.

'Really try, Brian. Go for it.'

He glanced at her, frowning. 'Go for it?'

'Absolutely.'

'O-kay!' Brian gunned the accelerator. 'Let's do this thing!'

So they went for it. Della leaped and darted at the net like a thing possessed until she was running with sweat, and Brian pounded, grunting, back and forth behind her till he was purple in the face. She discovered surprising resources of stamina and concentration, but Brian nearly lost his temper several times, especially when he fell over at full stretch and cut his elbow, prompting the Lumms to rush to his aid, all concern, with their neat first-aid kit, and offering to postpone the remainder of the match to another day. Incensed by their patronage he opted to play on, the Figes with even greater ferocity, the Lumms pattering about the court, never seeming to hit top speed; their strokes lacked any style or panache, but lo! The face of the racquet met the ball fair and square every time and sent it firmly, gently, back. The match drew a little crowd, and hard-fought points won a round of appreciative applause. If some of the onlookers had come to see the cavalier Figes taken down a peg or two, they stayed out of respect for an exciting game, fiercely contested.

Della and Brian still lost convincingly, but Della had enjoyed it. She was on a high. This, she thought, must be what was meant by the endorphin-rush experienced by long-distance runners. And could this be her husband, Brian the funny man, this scarlet-faced, sweat-sodden bloodstained warrior? As they exchanged a sticky kiss before walking to the net at the end, Brian muttered: 'What a fucking humiliation, and we were in the zone, too!'

'Never mind,' said Della. 'Let them trudge all the way to the trophy.'

The Lumms were magnanimous in victory.

'Great game,' said Pete. 'We'll be lucky if the final's half as testing. You forced us to play defensively for three sets.'

'Maybe,' said Brian bitterly. 'But you didn't crack.'

The two women exchanged a look, and Della wished them luck. When they came off the court the young coach from the next town came over to congratulate the Lumms and then held out his hand first to Della, then Brian.

'Well played. That was a wicked game.'

'Thanks,' said Della because Brian couldn't bring himself to.

'There was some real juice out there.'

Brian scrubbed his brow with his wrist band. 'Unfortunately, we still lost.'

'A pleasure to watch, though.' The coach looked at Della with frank admiration. 'What got into you today? You were a different woman.'

'I found my inner scrapper,' said Della.

'Keep it up,' said the coach. 'You should go to the dark side more often.'

They stayed for a drink and Brian cheered up considerably in the genial atmosphere of the bar. Pete Lumm might have worn him down on court, but he couldn't hold a candle to Brian when it came to the colourful post-mortem. By the time they got back in the car his humour was largely restored.

'You were right,' he said, looking over his shoulder as he reversed. 'I feel better for that. Now it's over.'

'Me too.'

He paused before pulling away. 'What did he mean by "real juice"?'

'That we played well, I suppose,' said Della. But it wasn't that. Or not entirely. She could feel the sap rising as the sweat cooled.

When they got back, for the first time ever she took the initiative, and her husband, before he had even showered. And came, joyfully and unprettily.

'Bloody hell,' said Brian when he'd recovered. 'What are you on, girl? We must get slaughtered at tennis more often.'

Seventeen

Oh. Wow!

From the second-floor window of 10 Christchurch Grove, Hampstead, the newly arrived Jack saw his own home in a new light. People were always saying what a beautiful house it was, and what 'a lovely part of the world' it was in, and he could sort of see that. But it was in the back end of nowhere. And in a valley – no wonder he felt buried alive! His bedroom there looked over the garden at the side, the patch of lawn where they used to play games (not so often now), the orchard and a collection of utilitarian outbuildings. Beyond that, low hills. Nothing much on them. Nothing going on. Here – bloody hell! His room looked right out over the whole of bloody London! Skyscrapers, parks, towers, churches, giant cranes, the Eye, and that was just the surface. Underneath was all the . . . the *stuff*: the people, cool and hot, and the talk and the scams and the ideas and the wild and crazy partying . . . As a matter of fact Jack wasn't so bothered about that, but he liked to know it was out there.

Tony – Jack was getting used to thinking and saying that – had mentioned unpacking, but all Jack did was drop his rucksack and the painfully new case his mother had bought at John Lewis, on the floor, and go to the window to gaze. It was a casement window, part of a sort of tower that clung to the outside of the house, so standing there was how Jack imagined being in the prow of a ship. In the garden below he could see Marlon trotting around, sniffing and wagging busily. Next, Tony came out, and immediately looked up and waved to Jack. Jack waved back, something he'd never have done at home if that had been his father – way too gay. It was odd; he felt like a kid, younger than he was, but like a grown-up at the same time.

Tony made an open-up gesture and Jack pushed the window wide.

'Hi there.'

'Comfortable up there?' said Tony, holding his hand up to his eyes. 'Got everything you want?'

'Yes thanks.'

'Lunch down here in half an hour, that suit you?'

'Great – yeah.'

He stepped back from the window, trying to give the impression that he was busy, engaged in that mysterious process of 'making himself at home'. He hadn't quite managed it yet, but he was optimistic. Tony had indicated the stereo, TVs, computers, thousands of books, the DVD library – and told him to feel free. Would he ever!

Turning away from the window he surveyed the room. It was huge, with a shiny wooden floor, a big woven rug with an asymmetric pattern in blue, brown and black, and a couple of enormous painting – canvases, not framed or mounted. One of the paintings was of broad stripes of red, black and yellow like a melting tiger; the other was grey with a big soft ball of black (how did he *know* it was a ball?) in the middle of it, like a post-nuclear sun. Jack liked both the pictures a lot. His bed was double, the frame a sort of bleached ashy wood, with thick white sheets and a blue woven bedspread that looked as if it came from the same place as the rug. There were open shelves, one of which already held some books, and an open space with a rail and hangers. The two overhead lights were on pulleys, so you could bring them right down to read by. Near the window was a squashy sofa in caramel corduroy, so unstructured that you just sort of fell on to it and it shaped itself round you. Jack had never been in a room which was both so sparse and practical and yet somehow so luxurious.

He lay on the bed for a few minutes, experimenting with the light, and then did the same thing on the sofa, trying out different positions. Then it was nearly lunchtime, and he was starving, so he went downstairs. Not yet being quite sure of the geography of the house, he was standing in the hall like a prat when the gorgeous woman – Clementine? something like that – appeared and said, 'Hello, Jack, you look lost.'

'I am.'

'I'm Clemency, remember?' She smiled and his skin prickled. He hoped he wasn't blushing. 'Looking for lunch?'

'Yeah.'

'Look no further. Me too. Come.'

Jack followed, on fire. Result! First time out he'd thought Clemency was like a TV presenter. This time he thought she was more like a character from one of those rom–coms his mother liked so much, where the only good thing was the talent. He had never before actually seen a real–life woman wearing a straight, tight black skirt with a little slit at the back so that her calves winked at him as she walked, and a fitted white shirt tucked into the skirt with a big shiny black belt, and black stilettos . . . As she walked ahead of him everything went in and out, as though set to music.

They went through the enormous living room toward patio doors. She glanced over her shoulder.

'Hope you're hungry.'

Tony was out on the patio, where a table was laid beneath a parasol the size of a small planet. He half-rose at their approach.

'Greetings. You found each other.'

'We did,' said Clemency. 'Both suffering from hunger pangs in the hall.'

'Let the pangs be assuaged,' said Tony as they sat down. 'Lionel's prepared his famous cold collation.'

This scarcely did justice to the spread, which as well as a platter of cold meats included a veal and ham pie, three kinds of salad including potato, a huge floury loaf and a cheese board.

'Will this be all right?' asked Tony. 'We don't want you to starve.'

'It's brilliant,' said Jack.

'Come on then,' said Clemency. 'Tuck in.'

He did, and for a while they talked across him, not in a way that was rude or dismissive, more as if they were leaving him space to get on with it. Just as he was starting on a third phase, this time of bread and cheese with chutney, Lionel came out of the house with the dog on its extending lead. The moment Marlon saw them he shot forward, nearly yanking Lionel off his feet. Tony stopped this charge by throwing a lump of bread into his path. Marlon sniffed, pawed and swallowed, his eyes glazing over and his jaws snapping and rotating convulsively as the bread stuck to his soft palate.

'You'd think that dog was never fed,' said Clemency. She had pushed her chair back and was sitting with her legs crossed. Jack thought she might be wearing stockings, very sheer ones: her legs were pale, with a sheen. He shifted uncomfortably on his seat.

'After all that,' said Lionel, who had now shortened the lead. 'We'll be off.'

'Lunch is excellent by the way,' said Tony. 'We've done it justice, especially Jack.'

'Good.' Lionel glanced at Jack who nodded vigorously.

Marlon's tongue was lolling from the side of his mouth. Clemency said: 'Isn't it too hot to be walking him at this time of day?'

'It is, but we didn't get out this morning what with one thing and another.'

Jack sensed that there might be a bit of headway to be made in this area. He swallowed. 'Perhaps I could take him for a walk some time. We've got dogs at home.'

'They do,' said Tony with feeling. 'Good offer, eh?'

'You're very welcome if you'd like to,' said Lionel, adding doubtfully, 'He's a bit of a handful.'

'So are ours.'

'No reason why not then.'

Tony clicked his fingers and Marlon towed Lionel to his side. As he fondled the dog's ears, Tony said, 'He's not as other dogs are, Jack. Yours are active, disciplined country dogs – this one is an over-indulged townie with a lot of dismaying habits.'

'Yes,' said Clemency, 'Lionel told me about some of those.' She made a face at Jack. 'You don't want to know.'

'He does now,' said Lionel. 'Time we were gone.'

'Me too.' Clemency picked up her plate and glass and rose from the table. 'See you, Jack.'

'See you.'

He watched her go back into the house. He'd always wondered what was meant by 'sashaying' – now he knew.

Tony's voice recalled him gently. 'This afternoon, Jack, I have a small job for you.'

Small was right. It turned out not to be much of a job, not work at all really, but he wasn't complaining about that. Tony was sorting some of his own books, the ones he'd actually written, and Jack was set to separating hardbacks and paperbacks, putting them in date order, and then the foreign editions according to country and date, and so on. There were numbers of them, and he spun it out. Tony wasn't about (he discovered later that he was taking a nap, something he quite often liked to do).

Around three Clemency looked in.

'I'm going now. How are you getting on?'

'Okay.'

She came closer, surveying the boxes of books. Her scent was sweet and heady. It reminded him of his father's Elkie Brooks CD, *Lilac Wine*.

She touched his shoulder. 'Losing the will to live?'

'Not yet.'

That made her laugh. 'You're doing well. After that go and chill out — it really is liberty hall around here, you know.'

'Thanks.'

'By the way, there's something I've been meaning to ask you. Do you ever do babysitting?'

'Um . . .'

'Only my usual girl's on holiday, Mama's on the other side of town and I'm desperate for help with one or two evenings.'

'Er . . .' Jack's tongue was slow but his brain was racing. He had never in his life babysat, but he was old enough, and how hard could it be?'

'How does five pounds an hour sound?'

'Good.'

'Says he!' She laughed. 'Don't worry, it's not six-month old triplets or anything; Freddie's six. He sleeps like a top and can sit in front of more or less anything on the box without batting an eyelid.'

'No,' said Jack, 'that'd be fine.'

'Right, you're on. I shall take you up on that.'

'Cool.'

'Good luck with your labours. See you tomorrow.'

Her scent hung in the air after she'd gone, and for that reason Jack applied himself assiduously to the books for quite a while longer. The summer holiday stretched before him . . . Four weeks of unalloyed bliss.

★　　★　　★

At first it was hard to accept – to believe – that he had so much freedom. At home, though his parents weren't tyrants, they were on his case; it was part of the job description. They worried, and enquired and sometimes, especially in his father's case, seemed actively to provoke confrontation so they could convince themselves they were in charge. What they couldn't seem to grasp was that Jack wanted a quiet life. It was perversely flattering that they assumed he was hell-bent on drugs, binge-drinking and under-age sex, but they'd got it so wrong. All he wanted, on those occasions when he stamped out of the house, was to be left alone. Even then it wasn't as if he could get anywhere that the activities they worried about were on offer. Over the last year or so he'd spent literally hours sitting under a tree watching the comings and goings at the house and wondering what *they* thought he was doing, or if they were thinking about him at all.

When he didn't feel flattered, he felt insulted, because they were lumping him together with all those stereotypical sitcom teenagers who wanted to spend all night clubbing and all day in bed – well, actually, there was some truth in the latter, he could easily have slept from midnight until two p.m. every day, but never mind.

Here, though, they were interested in him, and what he said and did, and no-one assumed control over his actions. About two-thirds of his time was taken up with doing stuff for and with Tony: research of a simple kind, on the web or occasionally in libraries; a day a week at the Beeb, fetching coffees and running errands for the *Daily Review* production team, being 'a regular Ganymede' Tony said, whatever that meant; and odd jobs at home such as sorting the books and walking Marlon. In the evenings, if he wanted to, he went with Tony to plays, films, exhibition openings and book launches. Not once did anyone say he should look or dress differently, and the people he met on these occasions seemed genuinely interested in him and his opinions.

He was also free to go into town on his own, but he didn't take too much advantage of this. He wasn't yet confident of his way around, and began by exploring Hampstead and gradually working his way down through Kentish and Camden towns. He didn't have the money for greater adventurousness anyway.

His father had given him forty pounds a week pocket money and he spent it on tubes, buses, snacks and the occasional beer – he'd never looked much more than his age but it was easier here where people didn't know him and didn't much care. The curfew was ten, but he was seldom that late – the lure of the viewing room with its mega-telly drew him back long before then. On one occasion he went into a club but the girls were scarily pissed and up for it and he didn't like dancing, so he wasn't tempted to make a habit of it. Besides, the older people were far more interesting.

In the end he'd only babysat for Clemency in Muswell Hill once. She had a small terraced house, but nice. The little kid, Freddie, was quite cute; they watched *EastEnders* together and then he went to bed without any trouble. Clemency left for her date looking fantastic in tight jeans and a black shirt with silver jewellery.

'This is so nice of you, Jack,' she said. 'You are such a star.'

Not only that but she'd left a whole packet of kettle chips and a bag of funsize chocolates in the kitchen with instructions to eat as much as he wanted and take the rest home with him. It was practically heaven. When she returned, her taxi waited outside for Jack. She was a little bit pissed, laughing a lot.

'I can't tell you how grateful I am, Jack. If it's any consolation it was worth it. I had the most wonderful time!'

She gave him a kiss as he went out of the door. Even knowing that the kiss was, in a sense, the result of another man's attentions couldn't spoil Jack's euphoria.

Quite apart from Clemency, there was Tony's friend Diana, a creature of such fragrant beauty and sophistication that he had to remind himself she wasn't much younger than his own grand-mother. She was about to move out of town, Tony told him, so they were treating her to a farewell celebration, with a weird musical at the Donmar, and the Ivy for dinner afterwards.

'I envy you, Jack, experiencing London for the first time,' she said over dinner. 'What do you think of it?'

'It's brilliant,' he said. 'What I've seen of it. But it's so massive. I tell you what, home will never be the same.'

Two weeks ago he would never have embarked on such a lengthy and opinionated answer, but he was gaining in confidence.

Diana laughed – a musical laugh. 'But you'll appreciate it more! Home isn't where you want to be all the time, nor should it be at your age, but it's where you can always go back to.'

'Yes,' he agreed, 'I'm beginning to see that.'

From the depths of her reclining steamer chair Maddie murmured: 'Feels strange, doesn't it?'

'Strange but nice,' agreed Edmund.

Three days into their indulgent break at Isola Bella they had achieved a state of Zen-like indolence.

'I hope they're both all right.'

'We'd have heard if they weren't.'

'I know, but still.'

The holiday was courtesy of a record-producer's passion for trout fishing and the extremely advantageous deal struck by Edmund's solicitors. It was the first time in years the two of them had had this much time together, in unashamed luxury, without either of the boys. William was staying with a friend in Norfolk – the same friend with whom he'd be setting off to South America in October. Jack (it was almost too good to be true) was contentedly deployed in London. Just for once Edmund, not one of nature's holiday-makers, had come up with the idea of an escape.

The hotel was small and charming, and the owners had created this ochre and cobalt-coloured Moorish terrace on the roof, with plants, statues, and curving steps down to a beautiful pool. The son of the house looked after drinks and lunch, while his father got creative in the kitchen in the evenings. The town was ancient and mellow but not historic enough to be touristy, and the surrounding countryside tawny, studded with cypresses, heavy with wine.

Maddie had bought a novel at the airport. She never read as much as she thought she was going to on holiday – her brain slipped out of gear – but now she picked it up. Her eye was caught by one of the laudatory quotes on the back cover.

'*Astonishingly good . . . Dark, funny and perceptive . . . I hate him!*' The quote was attributed to 'Gwen Paget, author of *Green Shoots*.'

Maddie read it twice to make sure and then leaned across to nudge Edmund, who had dropped off with his Sudoku open on his chest.

'Ed!'

'What?'

'This book I picked up at the airport – one of the women from the luncheon club has written on the back!'

'Vandal.'

'You know what I mean. She's said nice things about it. They must have asked her to.'

'Hope she was well paid.'

'Ed. The point is she's an author herself, she wrote something called –' she checked – '*Green Shoots.*'

'Never heard of it.' The Sudoko slithered off Ed's chest and he grabbed it. 'Have you?'

'No, but that doesn't mean anything. She must be quite well-known if they asked her to do that; isn't that interesting?'

'It's quite interesting . . .'

Maddie thought it *very* interesting. Gwen – she'd liked her. Gwen had saved her from feeling like some standard–issue county lady. And now it turned out that she was a writer, a reputable one.

The moment she got back she was going to contact Gwen and ask her about it.

Eighteen

In early September the town of Bishop's Few and its surrounding villages began to stir again. After the stasis of the summer, newsletters began once more to appear, school gates bustled, invitations were sent out, posters for Harvest Fairs went up and people remarked happily that the weather often improved just as the kids went back.

The Marie Crompton committee had its first meeting of the year – they followed the academic pattern – at Madeleine Kingshott's house. Della, who was giving Penny a lift, commented that it felt quite strange going somewhere different.

'About time,' said Penny. 'You've been marvellous having us all at yours over the years. It's definitely someone else's turn.'

'I think you're right,' said Della. 'Perhaps the meeting should rotate from now on. Among those who have the space,' she added, in case that had sounded dictatorial.

'Apologies again from Marian, by the way,' said Penny.

'Again? Is everything all right?'

'Very much so, I think. She's staying on for a while with her daughter in the States.'

'Good for her,' said Della. 'Maybe she won't come back at all!'

'I think that's a real possibility. She's having the time of her life.'

Della glanced across. 'Are you thinking what I'm thinking?'

Penny looked out of the window. 'It was a very happy message.'

So happy, in fact, that Penny had cried, though of course she was pleased about Marian's 'wonderful guy'. She wouldn't have thought it was possible to cry so much; it seemed the flow of tears must cause dehydration.

Her experiment hadn't worked. The boating holiday had raised unrealistic expectations; Graham couldn't stick to his side of the bargain. Back at home his restless discontent was painful to witness. He came and went, he slept next to her, but poorly (she'd heard the word 'Sam' in his dreams), and at weekends they ate together but he wasn't with them. His mind was elsewhere. As for the boys, their father's distracted, unwilling presence couldn't possibly be doing them any good; this wasn't what she'd wanted at all.

Nathan knew it, as usual. 'He doesn't want to be here.'

'Oh, Nat, he loves you . . .'

'Don't give me that. What's the matter with him? It's like before; he doesn't want to be at home.'

And then, of course, she said it. Said the bad thing, the thing she'd wanted to protect them from, only because she didn't want them to think the fault was theirs.

'It's quite possible he doesn't want to be with *me.*'

'What?' Penny could see the mental tape fast-forwarding, the horrible thoughts piling up. 'You're joking.'

'I wish I was.'

They were in the kitchen, the place where nearly all her most intimate conversations with her sons took place. Nathan leaned back against the worktop, the heels of his hands pressed into his eyes.

'Shit.'

'Nat . . .' She stretched out her hand, not that he could see. 'It's not the end of the world.'

He kept his eyes covered, and asked, 'Is he – you know – is there . . . ?'

'I've no idea,' she lied. 'Not that I know of. These things happen.'

Now he lowered his hands to reveal his shockingly torn and wounded face. 'But you don't have to sit there and fucking well let them.'

She hadn't been able to tell him that she *hadn't.* That she had tried, and it hadn't worked. That in the straight fight between Sam and her sons, the boys had come off worst. That steadily, inexorably, their father was leaving them.

'Here we are!' said Della, hauling Penny back to the present. 'Isn't this gorgeous?'

Gwen had arrived first.

'Sorry if I'm early; I wasn't sure how long it would take on the scooter.'

'You've got a scooter!' cried Maddie. 'I always wanted one of those.'

'It's no Harley Davidson.'

'It must be fun, though.'

'You should get one.'

'You never know.' Maddie led the way into the dining room. 'Glass of wine?'

'Thanks.'

They sat down at the table, over which Maddie had placed a protective cloth. 'I didn't know you were a writer.'

'My dark secret.' Gwen laughed shortly. 'How did you find out?'

'I bought a book at the airport on the way to Italy – your name was on the back.'

'I know the one,' said Gwen dryly.

'To be honest I was thinking I might have made a mistake till I saw what you'd said on the back, and that made me get started.'

'And what did you think?'

'It was terrific, you were absolutely right. I'm going on Amazon to check out what else he's written. And you, too. That's much more exciting!'

'Everybody's travelling,' said Della, looking round at the assembled company. 'Marian in the States, Rhada off to India in the new year . . .'

'That makes two,' said Gwen. 'I'm not going anywhere.' She turned to Maddie. 'Are you going anywhere?'

'Good grief,' said Maddie, 'a week in Tuscany is my ration for the foreseeable!'

'Penny?'

'No.'

It looked ominously as though Penny was welling up, so Della swiftly stepped in.

'Anyway, I must begin by thanking Maddie for broadening our horizons and inviting us to meet here. It's very kind of you, a lovely change.'

'Minuted,' said Penny, glad of something to do. 'Hear hear.'

'My pleasure,' said Maddie. 'The house is unnaturally quiet when the boys are away.'

Della put a tick against 'Apologies and thanks' and was about to move on when her mobile rang.

'I'm so sorry, I should have turned it off, do you mind if I just . . .?' She took the call and turned a little away from the table. Rhada made some polite comment about the Persian rug, and they admired it. Della rang off.

'You'll never guess.'

'Let me try,' said Gwen. 'Juanita.'

Della looked astonished. 'How did you know?'

Gwen tapped her temple. 'Writer's intuition.'

'Of course. Anyway you're absolutely right, she couldn't stay away. She's outside my house at this moment, wondering where we all are. She misses us apparently.'

Even Penny looked more cheerful. 'She's probably regretting saying Harmony's band could practise at their house.'

'Who is Juanita?' asked Maddie.

'The one you replaced,' said Gwen, 'but don't get excited, it's too late to back out.'

Della said, 'You probably met her at the Golden Anniversary. Very bubbly, in pink.'

'I don't remember.'

'She's the one who got us your uncle,' explained Penny. 'Clever lady.'

'Godfather.'

'Sorry.'

'Anyway,' said Della, in case they were thinking of it, 'we mustn't mock.'

Mock? Penny was never going to mock anyone, ever again.

When the meeting ended, they were all rather slow to leave, and not only because Juanita had arrived, prompting a top-up of cups and glasses. It was pleasant to slip out of committee mode, especially this evening when they were somewhere different and so much seemed to be happening in everyone's lives.

For her part Maddie, having been parlayed on to the committee, was happy. They were an amusing bunch of women and made a nice change from Belle and the rest of the county set. At nine p.m. Edmund put his head round the door.

'Oops, sorry, ladies.'

'Please, this is your house,' said Della. 'It's we who should apologize.'

Edmund came in. 'Good meeting?'

'Yes,' they chorused, 'very good.'

As they left, Maddie and Edmund stood in the lighted doorway waving them off, a little vignette which Penny couldn't help noticing. She began to shake, and Della took her arm.

'Come along,' she said. 'Hop in. Tell me all about it on the way home.'

Penny had always been aware of Della's innate superiority – her elegance, her charm, her *in-controlness*, so it was doubly humiliating to be a weeping mess in the front seat of the Figes merc.

'I'm sorry,' was all she kept saying. 'I'm so sorry about this . . .'

'About what?' Della, on the outside of a glass and a half, drove slowly, eyes on the road. 'You have nothing to apologize for. But if you want to tell me, please do.'

In the end it all came out, and was only just ebbing away when they pulled up outside Penny's. Della glanced at the house.

'So who's in there at the moment?'

'The boys. I don't know about Graham . . . His car's not here, it might be in the garage, but I doubt it . . .'

'You know, Penny, I do admire you.'

'Admire?' Penny gave a croak, halfway between a sob and a hollow laugh. 'What on earth for? I've completely messed up, my husband's gone off with another woman, my sons think I'm a doormat . . .'

'They won't when they understand. And you did absolutely the right thing. You gave him a chance, on your terms. He couldn't keep his side of the bargain, but that's his problem. He'll lose you, he'll lose the boys—'

'Not them,' said Penny, 'he'll never lose them.'

'All right, but from what you say he'll have to win them back, your eldest anyway. And that's good.'

Penny blew her nose. 'You really think so?'

'I jolly well do. I realize nothing I can say will make you feel less sad at the moment, but you simply mustn't feel foolish or guilty. You've been a wonderful wife as long as you were allowed to be, and you've done all you can to keep your family together. In fact, thanks to you it will still be a family, just different.'

'Oh, I don't know.' Penny smiled wanly. 'But I do appreciate your kindness, Della.'

'I'm not being kind. I'm being truthful.'

Inside the house, with Graham not back, Penny felt distinctly shaky, but better. She could still scarcely believe that Della had said those things to her. Jamie was in the kitchen making a sandwich.

'Hi Mum.'

'Hello hon.'

'Fancy one of these?'

'What's in it?'

'Cheese and Marmite.'

She yawned, suddenly exhausted. 'Go on then.'

'Have this one.' He slapped it on a plate and handed it to her. 'Don't worry, I'll make another.'

Brian was at the computer, crunching numbers. He had recently been obliged to get glasses, but Della liked him in them; they made him look serious.

'That was a long one,' he said.

She put her arms round him and rested her face against his.

'Have I told you lately that I love you?'

'If memory serves, you have . . .' He pressed Quit and turned his mouth to hers. 'But I don't mind you doing it again.'

Gwen liked being back in her house. It hadn't always been thus, but now that she was more focused on her work her possessions seemed to have fallen comfortably into place around here. They, like her, were calmer.

She was amused that Maddie had been reading Paddy's book. He'd emailed her to say that sales had been okay, but perhaps not enough to justify the hype. They'd kept in email contact, comparing notes, and had agreed in a casual way to meet up – as friends and fellow-writers was the implication – when Gwen had finished her novel. Gwen was by no means sure she was ready for the 'friends' bit, but with the work going better she could at least hold her head up in his company, and who knows what might develop?

She turned the hall light off, and the landing light on, and went up to bed, leaving the Marie Crompton file on the chair at the foot of the stairs.

It was fortunate there was a good rental market in town, because Marian couldn't stay with Ros and Jay indefinitely. They said they would have been more than happy for her to do so, but she wouldn't have been comfortable. She didn't want to impose on their busy lives – and then there was Wilf . . .

The apartment she found was over a florist's called Blooming Miracles. Ros was appalled – 'Mum, you can't!' – but the owners were charming and delighted to have this well-spoken Englishwoman of a certain age living above the shop. The solicitors in Bishop's Few had been understanding, and agreed to keep her job open for three months. More problematic was how to keep her house in the UK looked after, but the neighbours had come up trumps and Dennis (motivated no doubt by his own newfound happiness) had offered to keep an eye on things as well.

She told herself it was no big deal, just an extended holiday, though she did help out part-time at the florist's. It was a small-town life she'd taken on.

But oh – she felt reborn.

Along with the invigorating air of the new world, she was breathing the oxygen of real freedom. She had only what she needed in the way of possessions, she was airy, light and un-cluttered, moving through her days with a spring in her step that hadn't been there in ages.

Wilf was certainly a big part of that. It was delightful to be sought-after once more, to spend time with someone who found her charming, amusing, good company – and sexy, he made that plain. They had not yet slept together and she was relishing the wonderful zero-gravity of the pre-sex period. Something told her that when it happened she wouldn't be disappointed. She liked everything about Wilf: his looks, his voice, his laid-back charm and dry sense of humour. They went together so well it was ridiculous. But there was just that tiny chance that sex might mark the beginning of the end, so she was in no hurry.

Ros, of course, was watching her like a hawk, but she had

nothing to worry about. Marian was simply sloughing her old skin and re-emerging, shiny bright.

The doorbell rang and she picked up the intercom.

'Hey.'

'Come on up.'

She replaced the intercom, opened the door and left it wide.

Nineteen

Carefully, Tony unwound the strip of sealing tape from the Gentleman's Relish pot and scrunched it up. Marlon sat by his chair, gazing up expectantly. Tony opened the pot and peeled off the tinfoil disc. He looked down at Marlon.

'Long way to go, old chap, I'm afraid.'

Marlon continued to gaze. Tony picked up the mail and riffled through it: three invitations, two bills, two handwritten letters (one from Diana), four junk. He picked up the one from Diana and opened it; she was the only person he knew who still wrote letters for their own sake, and they were always beautiful letters, her elegant hand in blue ink flowing over the grainy handmade paper. She really had very little to say, but she said it so nicely. She was loving her 'provincial lady' life in Henley, she said, and was rapidly turning into a pillar of the community; she really needed Tony to come down and give her a shot of metropolitan cynicism and sophistication . . . But joking apart, she did miss him. How was he? What was he doing? How was the book? Was there anything exciting in the pipeline? And what about that charming boy – would he be visiting again? Would Tony please tell her all these things by whatever means suited him best. Now she had to go to a meeting of the gardening club of which she was in grave danger of becoming chairman. But she was oh, so content, and sent her love as always.

Tony smiled to himself and left her letter open next to his plate. Diana always maintained that it was not what you said, nor how you said it, but how you made people feel that was important, and she was the embodiment of the precept. Her letter, just as her presence always did, lifted his mood.

The other letter was in black biro on a sheet of office A4. The handwriting was jagged and somehow unmistakably youthful.

'Dear Tony,' he read. 'Sorry this is a bit late, beginning of term's always pretty mad. Thank you very much for having me to stay this summer. I had a wicked time and it was a fantastic opportunity.' (He didn't say for what.) 'Being in London was pretty wild after

Bishop's Few but I really appreciated it. Also, being at the BBC and going to things gave me a lot more idea about what I might do in the future. Thanks again for everything. Give my regards to Clemency and Lionel, not forgetting Marlon! Yours, Jack.'

Tony re-read this letter a couple of times. It couldn't have been more different from Diana's, but it was equally sweet in its way, and its mixture of knobbly gaucheness and enthusiasm touched him deeply.

He ate one slice of toast and – since Lionel was not around – put a smear of Gent's Relish on the other one and gave it to Marlon. Then he popped Diana's letter in the breast pocket of his shirt and, carrying Jack's, went out into the hall and up the stairs. A second later Marlon galumphed after him and quickly overtook him. At the first landing Tony paused to catch his breath, before continuing to the second. Once there he went into Jack's room – no longer, he discovered, the 'spare bedroom'. He walked over to the case-ment window and opened it. A damp, heathy blast of air pushed him in the face, air with a hint of winter on its breath. Gazing down he seemed to see himself standing on the grass on Jack's first day, looking up at where he was now . . . Where Jack had been.

Lionel and the cleaning lady had tidied the room but it was somehow different, in that it still bore Jack's trace. The space had more presence, the paintings a different air because they had watched Jack, and he had looked at them. Marlon – a giveaway this – went straight to the Fredrikson sofa and jumped on it, turning round and round a few times before making himself comfortable. There were a couple of extra pictures up here, too, ones Jack had admired in other parts of the house (possibly out of politeness, who knew?) so they had moved them. They held their own pretty well with the two Ray Bareks, so the boy had taste. On the bedside table was an alarm clock, presumably Jack's, which ought to be sent back, except that Jack would certainly be coming again . . .

Tony sat down on the sofa by Marlon. He felt a little tired, and disposed to give in to it. He needed and wanted to slow down. Unusually he had no appointments. He could do as he wished. With one hand on the dog's head, he re-read the letter, and as he did so his face softened.

It had, indeed, been a fantastic opportunity.

★   ★   ★

Della liked to keep one step ahead of the game. The next meeting was some weeks away – they would have had the October lunch by then – but there was no harm in banging out the agendas. The template was the same, but there were always one or two topics that needed to be given a separate slot, and it was her job to make sure they were covered.

Brian had just got in with their takeaway from the Sampan. It was part of the new dispensation: once a week they ate out, or ordered in. She heard him rustling and clinking in the kitchen and then he put his head round the door.

'Dinner is served.'

'Wonderful, I'm coming.'

He advanced to behind her chair and looked down at the screen. 'All done?'

'Nearly.' She heard him chuckle. 'What?'

'"Matters Arising",' he said, making inverted commas in the air. 'Why does that always tickle me?'

'I've no idea,' said Della. 'Anyway. Done!'